P

A SMALL M̲͟.̲͟.̲͟.̲͟.̲͟.̲͟

"A story with a penchant for good criminal justice dealings and journalism."
— *Independent Book Review*

Praise for other
A Murder on Skis Mysteries

The Man Who Had 9 Lives
Finalist for American Fiction Award

"Addictively readable."
— *The Prairies Book Review*

"Fun to read and guaranteed
to keep you racing to the end."
— Jack Rightmyer, *Albany Times Union*

"Addictively readable."
— *The Prairies Book Review*

"Will Dazzle the Reader."
— *AuthorsReading.com*

Witch Window
"Distinguished Favorite"
— *Independent Press Awards*

"The Best Books We Read"
List — *Independent Book Review*

"Intellectual and valuable, while still maintaining the excitement of solving a crime."
— *Indies Today*

Back Dirt
Finalist for American Fiction Award

"Phil Bayly spins a captivating yarn."
— Reader's Favorite

"Chock Full of Exhilarating Twists and Turns."
— *Saratoga Living Magazine*

Loving Lucy
"Bayly draws on his experience covering real crimes. A chilling mystery."
— *Vail Daily*

"A must read, hang on to your chairlift!"
— *The Grateful Traveler*

Murder on Skis
"Readers in Montana who love murder mysteries… It's a thrilling new piece of fiction."
— *Valley Journal*, Montana

"*Murder on Skis* is a must read for all fans of a good murder mystery book."
— Reader's Favorite

Jim & Michele

2024

MERRY CHRISTMAS,

LOVE,
Phil &
CAROLYN

A SMALL MOUNTAIN MURDER
A *Murder on Skis* Mystery

Other **Murder on Skis** Mysteries
by Phil Bayly:

Murder on Skis

Loving Lucy

Back Dirt

Witch Window

The Man Who Had 9 Lives

A SMALL MOUNTAIN MURDER

A *Murder on Skis* Mystery

Phil Bayly

A SMALL MOUNTAIN MURDER
A *Murder on Skis* Mystery
©2024 by **Phil Bayly**

WWW.MURDERONSKIS.COM
ISBN: 978-1-60571-651-0

Cover Design: Carolyn Bayly,
Debbi Wraga, iStock 98379368
Cover Photo: Carolyn Bayly
Author Photo: Carolyn Bayly

Printed in the United States of America

To my brother, Skip. The leader of the pack. On our ski trips to Wisconsin, the cold and the ice and the terror had no bearing on his ability to laugh.

To all the small ski areas across the country, past and present. They taught us, day and night, and gave us a lifetime.

And to newspapers, big and small. The end of them will be the end of us.

"Great things are done when men and mountains meet."

—William Blake

"Let everything happen to you. Beauty and terror. Just keep going. No feeling is final."

—Ranier Maria Rilke

1

"I beg for your forgiveness," the state senator blubbered.

Tears streamed down the face of the man who had started his morning as one of the most powerful politicians in Wisconsin. But he got caught.

"I beg you to forgive me." The word "beg" was thundered, the way Senator Stansfield Miller used to thunder adherence to his unforgiving ideology. He built a political power base around traditional rules and conservative morality. Then he got caught.

"I have sinned," he sobbed. "I have fallen from my place on the mantle. But I am human. To err is human, to forgive is divine. Forgive me. Forgive me."

The senator cried in front of his audience outside the domed state capitol of Wisconsin. It was a cold day in December.

It was all calculated. The senator knew that in freezing temperatures and a brisk wind, there would not be endless questions from the bloodthirsty news media. Their fingers would grow numb. Their will would wither. They would give up and retreat to the warmth inside the capitol building.

The senator stood in front of an evergreen tree. It was decorated with Christmas lights.

"Let those bloodsuckers crucify my carcass while facing a reminder of the happiest holiday of the year," he had told staff members. It was all calculated.

Senator Miller asked his wife to forgive him and stand by his side. But she was having none of it. So, he stood alone. The unanimous feeling in the Miller camp was that he was better off standing alone than sharing the camera lens with an angry wife whose eyes could saw a log in half.

It was also a universal feeling in the senator's camp that his wife was the smarter and tougher member of the family. His political party learned too late that they had run the wrong Miller for office.

The senator considered holding a bible, but aides had talked him out of it. That had backfired before.

His speech couldn't look calculated, they told him, even though every act and scripted word of it *was*.

Already, the politician and his closest aides were planning his comeback. They speculated on how much time it would take for the voting public to forget—or, at least, look the other way. There was plenty of time before he had to run for re-election. Others had weathered worse. He'd recover, he thought. *If* he wasn't forced to resign.

An online news rag termed the act "bumping uglies," when it described exactly what Senator Miller had been caught doing with a Senate intern. And it wasn't just once. A newspaper reporter had exposed the year-long affair involving the senator and a political-science major at a local college. And two more interns had told the reporter that *they* had been targeted by the senator before that.

The setting chosen by the legislator to perform his mea culpa was ironic. Looking down on him from the top of the capitol dome was Lady Wisconsin. Or, rather, the Daniel Chester French sculpture posed for by a New York City model in 1913. Her name was Audrey Munson. She was a model and a silent-film actress who did one of the first nude scenes in the history of American cinema.

Senator Miller's faith in the voters' forgetfulness turned out to be a fantasy. His constituents held firm to his mantra of family values, even if he didn't. And shortly thereafter, his political allies acknowledged the voters' will.

Senator Stan Miller was forced to resign. He was finished.

The newspaper reporter who broke the story, Carol "Quip" Kelly, filled two glasses from an expensive bottle of wine and toasted his wife.

"No," his wife said. "I'm toasting you. You took another one down. You're going to get all the bad guys, one by one. I'm so proud of you."

The bottle had come to their table "compliments of the house." Quip Kelly was a star on the rise. They sat at their table at the Statehouse Restaurant and looked out on the waters of Lake Mendota. The lake would freeze after Christmas. Fishermen would drill holes in the ice and chase fish where sailboats chased the wind only a few months prior.

"Thank you, Shara," Kelly said. "You're brave to stick with me, to stick these things out."

Quip Kelly was a giant-killer, a newspaperman exposing the politicians who promised voters one thing while practicing quite another. His quarry fell in equal numbers on both sides of the aisle.

Kelly didn't care if they were Republicans or Democrats. Both parties had their share of hypocrites. And Quip had the patience, the means, and the contacts to tell the truth about a rotting core within the nation's political body.

It wasn't always about sex. Sometimes it was about money. Maybe a senator steered money to a charity and half that money bounced back to the senator.

But it was about sex a lot of the time. "Power is an aphrodisiac" was the saying at capitol buildings across the country.

Only two days prior, Senator Miller stood tall on the pedestal he sculpted for himself. He stood outside a small movie theatre in Madison. At the time, it was showing a film about an adulterous affair. And there was lots of skin.

"I am honored to sponsor this bill," Senator Miller had declared that day. "And when it becomes law, the threat to our families from this establishment will end."

The senator was seeking headlines by singling out the movie theatre that showed obscure, once-in-a-while-naughty, art films. He couldn't beat the First Amendment, but he could attack almost every other principle the little movie theatre stood on. It was Goliath crushing David.

"Isn't a movie house of this sort common in college towns, Senator?" Quip had asked at a news conference called by Senator Miller. "Is this about morality?"

"What kind of question is that?" the senator had snapped back with a self-assured grin. "Of course, it is. Without morality, this country doesn't have a leg to stand on. A husband and wife are duty-bound to be faithful to one another, to raise a family in a good moral environment!"

"You'll get no argument from me," Quip responded. "But how, then, do you explain your own behavior with a certain Senate intern whom you have been spending nights with at the Edgewater Hotel for a little over a year?"

"What the hell are you talking about?" the senator choked. He barely got the words out. His throat was suddenly dry, severing a more aggressive protest he wished he had at his disposal.

"Your wife was at home on those nights," Quip said. "I actually stopped by your home on one of those nights to check up on her. I didn't tell her about my discovery. I thought that was a discussion you should probably have with her."

Senator Miller had a blank look on his face as he was suddenly ushered into a waiting van by his aides. His face was red and his eyes were wet.

Other members of the news media had turned to Quip as the senator's vehicle sped away.

"Seriously?" one newspaper writer had asked, with a smile growing on his face.

"Holy shit," a television reporter had exclaimed.

"Do you really have this?" a colleague had asked Quip.

"Read about it in tomorrow morning's newspaper, my friends," Quip had told them with a smile. "Complete with pictures. Senator Miller couldn't keep his hands to himself. Once our paper hits the newsstands, we'll be happy to share it all with you."

"I feel bad for his wife," another reporter said as he was walking back toward the capitol building. "She was tough, but she was always nice to me."

Politics was becoming a smelly business. State employees, government watchdogs and politicians themselves were growing sick of the stench.

And they had become Quip's sources. They provided Kelly with evidence to unmask misconduct. If those sources said it publicly themselves, they might have to answer for it. They might lose their jobs.

But Quip Kelly was willing to say it for them. He answered only to the truth. He became the salvation for those who had seen enough uncivil behavior by so-called public servants. When it came to calling them out, Quip had no qualms. It was a crusade to clean up his country.

"I hate to tell you this. I'm going to have to leave soon," Quip Kelly told his wife as they celebrated at their table at the Statehouse Restaurant.

"For how long, this time?" Shara asked, deflated. She thought she had just gotten her husband back after his latest scoop. She grew lonely when he left town.

"Maybe only a couple of weeks," Quip told her. "Something has come up. I've found the girl."

"Amanda Taylor?" Shara asked. "The police haven't even found her."

"She's hiding down in Florida," Quip leaned in and quietly told her. "She's agreed to speak to me. This will corner my next target, Senator Swensen. It's all pretty ugly. It will finish him."

"I thought you were working on a story about the congressman. The liberal guy, Bat Bellows," Shara said. "I'll be able to write my story on Bellows while I'm in Florida," he told her. "And there's a new guy named Brown that I'm getting information on. But the Swensen story can't wait. If Swensen gets wind that I've found Amanda Taylor, he'll go on the attack. I have to strike first. I'm sorry, honey. I've got to go back underground."

Quip's wife, Shara Adams Kelly knew the drill, even if she didn't like it. When Quip was close to wrapping up an investigation, he chose to disappear from sight. At some point, Quip knew that if a powerful politician learned they were the target of Quip's next exposé, they would try anything to stop him.

What would a desperate politician do to stop Quip from writing that article? He didn't want to find out. So, he adopted a pattern of disappearing in the weeks leading up to a story's telling. Only a short list of people knew where to find him, an editor or two and, of course, Shara.

After dinner at the Statehouse Restaurant and a romantic weekend at the Edgewater Hotel in Madison, Quip was gone. Another crusade was underway.

2

Aspotless Stetson spun in the hand of Tillison Tucker as he entered the administration building of Snow Hat Ski Enterprises in Colorado.

"Good morning," he greeted his employee behind the reception desk as he whisked past, toward the staircase.

"Good morning, Mr. Tucker," she smiled. She was wearing a turtleneck under a ski sweater. In most business offices, her apparel might be reserved for "Casual Friday." But at this office, it was part of their everyday brand. It was a reflection of the product they sold to customers who came to the Snow Hat Ski Resort.

Tucker climbed the stairs at a trot. He avoided the elevator whenever possible. He did what he could to stay fit.

He might be the owner of close to two thousand ski runs and 350 chairlifts, but he rarely found time to get on skis himself.

He was tall and slender, six foot four and 220 pounds. In his early sixties, his hair was quickly turning from a soft brown to gray. These days, he also had to wear wire-rimmed glasses.

Close acquaintances called him "Tilly." He grew up in tiny Warner, New Hampshire. But he moved to Colorado after graduating from Dartmouth and had taken to dressing like a cowboy. He wore expensive boots, cowboy shirts, bolo ties and his Stetson. Even in a cowboy outfit, he looked a bit nerdy.

"Good morning, Tina," the towering man greeted his administrative assistant with a smile as he topped the stairs and walked by her desk. "Has Ronny called?"

"No, he has not," responded Tina Hernandez. "Would you like me to place a call?"

"Yes, put him through when you get him," responded Tucker. "Where the heck has Ronny disappeared to?"

Tucker closed the office door behind him and took a position behind his big mahogany desk. Snow Hat had been a busy job when it was the only ski resort he owned. But now he was the CEO of a national ski pass, acquiring ski resorts across the country.

His business had now become a conglomerate, earning hundreds of millions of dollars a year. He'd named his pass after his original ski resort, the Snow Hat Ski Pass.

He now ran twenty ski resorts from coast to coast. That meant he had twenty times the employees he used to have. He paid a fortune in salaries and benefits. Plans for an IPO sat on the desk in front of him.

For skiers and snowboarders, the arrival of national ski passes meant more accessibility at discount prices. For Tillison Tucker and his investors, it meant a mountain of earnings.

But there were also challenges. His new snow kingdom was big and somewhat unruly. Long lift lines sometimes resulted at his marquee resorts. And his new employees to the east didn't necessarily want to adhere to the new rules their new employer to the west laid down.

Many of the biggest ski areas in the Rocky Mountains were relative newcomers to skiing in the United States. They didn't even exist until the 1960s.

Tillison Tucker's newest acquisition, a small mountain in Wisconsin, had been around since 1938. And folks at that small mountain in Wisconsin felt they knew a thing or two about running a ski area.

Tucker tried to be patient. He answered to a board, but they gave him a blank check and a regular pat on the back. They respected him for his handling of money. He could think big without overlooking the small things.

As CEO of Snow Hat, he strived to save money on costs that he considered beyond the view of the customers. He bargained for better deals on fleet vehicles and constructing employee housing. He even lowered the cost of soap in bathrooms. He owned a lot of bathrooms.

"Mr. Tucker," said Tina Hernandez as she opened the office door and poked her head in. "Ronny Schwartz doesn't answer his phone. The desk at his hotel also says he isn't answering his room phone."

"Keep trying, will you, Tina?" Tucker asked.

Ronny Schwartz was Tucker's number-two man. He was smart and reliable, a go-to guy. Ronny was forty-one years old and divorced. He lived for his work. He was glad for the chance to take exactly two ski runs each morning. Then he was either at his desk or already in Tucker's office.

"How's the snow?" That was the first question out of Tucker's mouth each morning when they began their meeting.

Two weeks ago, Tucker had asked Ronny to travel to Wisconsin on his behalf. Ronny had been instrumental in singling out that busy little ski mountain for acquisition.

"People in the Midwest love to ski," Ronny had said. He was the right man for this job.

Ronny would help familiarize their new employees in Wisconsin with the way Snow Hat got things done. And he was also asked to carry out a secret mission or two. Tucker knew that Ronny was the right one for that job also.

One secret mission involved preparations to launch a new business. The other secret mission involved revenues. Tucker thought the revenue at their new mountain in Wisconsin was out of sync with business at the turnstile. He believed that they should be making more money.

"Do you think someone's cooking the books?" Ronny asked his boss.

"I don't know. And it's not something we can ascertain from here," Tucker told him, sitting behind his big desk. "I want you to take a trip to Wisconsin. You'll figure it out."

Ronny Schwartz grew up a little more than an hour from the small mountain that Snow Hat would one day acquire. Growing up, it was called Fox River Runs.

He was born and raised in the Chicago suburb of Evanston, Illinois. People from Chicago who skied, normally skied in Wisconsin. They had a half dozen small mountains to choose from near Lake Geneva.

Remaining in his hometown to go to college at Northwestern, Ronny earned spending money on weekends teaching at those small ski mountains around Lake Geneva.

Now, Tucker needed a man on the ground there. And Ronny knew the lay of the land.

Ronny Schwartz flew out of Colorado two weeks before he suddenly fell off the radar. He took a direct flight to Chicago and drove over the border into Wisconsin. He updated his boss by phone twice a day, once in the morning and once in the evening.

But Tucker hadn't received a call that morning. And he hadn't received one the previous evening.

Where, Tucker asked, had Ronny gotten off to? Had he gone to visit family? Had he mentioned his plans to anyone?

Tucker asked Tina if Ronny had told them that he was going to visit family. Maybe the CEO hadn't paid attention at that moment. Tucker and Tina both knew that he was sometimes guilty of tuning out small talk.

But the CEO did pay attention to details when they affected his business. He knew, for example, that Ronny had a weakness for alcohol after a long workday. Ronny also had a fondness for female companionship. Did he bring the wrong girl back to his hotel room?

Tucker opened his file on the new acquisition in Wisconsin. It began as a small ski area before World War Two. A farmer ran a rope tow over automobile wheels fastened to trees. The rope was pulled by an old Ford engine.

It initially was called Cob Hill, a suitable name considering corn cobs were found scattered across the property. The 200-foot peak was surrounded by cornfields.

Then, it was renamed Fox River Runs. The Fox River carved through farmland near the ski runs.

Years ago, the owner of the small ski area used bulldozers to push dirt to the top of the hill, making it taller. The peak was now 270 feet.

There were twenty-three trails and nine lifts. It was wider than it was tall. But it was taller than the flat land surrounding it. Some locals called it "The Big Bump."

When Tucker acquired Fox River Runs, he built a brand-new ski lodge. He had plans to expand a small hotel that already existed at the bottom of the ski trails. New snowmaking equipment was installed and brand-new PistenBully groomers were purchased, so skiers and snowboarders had fresh corduroy every morning.

Then came the new name.

Standing at the peak of his small mountain, Tucker thought that he could view more horizon than he'd ever seen. Southern Wisconsin was flat. His new ski hill was five miles from Illinois, and Illinois was the second-flattest state in the whole country.

Tucker decided to call his new ski area Big Horizon. He wanted to celebrate the "Prairie Pride" embraced by Wisconsin residents. And he wanted his ski resort to sound big and important, like Big Sky in Montana. He wanted skiers and snowboarders at his small mountain to know, from now on, they could expect big things.

3

The sound of the metal gate scraping against the asphalt didn't alarm him anymore. He no more heard it than he heard the water licking the shore. He had grown accustomed to everything going on around him.

It wasn't an easy adjustment. Quip Kelly needed a place to hide, where he could organize his next shocking newspaper story. He was working on three columns that would expose three politicians. Voters would learn that the men they voted for weren't who they said they were.

He would release the stories one at a time. He knew they were powerful. The resulting scandal would probably end their political careers.

The biggest bombshell of all was the one Quip planned to drop on Senator Raff Swensen. Because Quip was playing a dangerous game, he needed to take precautions. That's why he went into hiding. When the article came out, he would be safe. As an added precaution, he traveled with a 1911 A1 Colt .45. It was his grandfather's service weapon in World War Two. Quip hoped he'd never have to use it. He preferred to hide.

Quip's current sanctuary was a marina in a neighborhood no one envisioned when thinking of a marina. It was in a lower-middle-class coastal town in Florida. The neighborhood bordered a string of factories and the water smelled suspicious. It wasn't a place tourists saw unless they were lost.

The marina was separated from the dodgy neighborhood by tall, chain-link fences topped by razor wire. Homes and businesses there all had bars on the windows. Quip could hear police sirens at any time of the day or night.

A passcode was required for anyone to enter the marina. When the code was punched into a keyboard, the metal gate would scrape against the asphalt as it opened and closed.

But inside the razor wire, he felt safe and invisible. He rented a boat there for a month. He worked on his investigation every day and slept on board the boat every night.

The small cabin cruiser was named *Hilda*. It was moored to one of three piers at the marina. There was no steering wheel or control panel on the craft. He wasn't sure that there was still an engine down in the hull.

But she had what he needed. There was Wi-Fi, a twelve-by-eight-foot cabin with a hot plate and a small refrigerator. There was a small rear deck with a built-in table and seat, and a bow that he could climb upon with a chair and watch the sun set.

Hilda was in need of a scrubbing and a paint job. The aging mahogany varnish inside the cabin was sticky. The on-board toilet didn't work. He had to walk up the dock and use a bathroom behind the marina office. When the office was closed, he had to use a porta-potty.

When he had to buy groceries, there was a store just outside the tall fence with the razor wire. The store had a bright red roof and a sign with letters painted in random colors. It looked like a ride at an amusement park.

The grocery store had been robbed two weeks ago. A clerk was shot when he tried to resist. It was Quip's second night at the marina when he heard the gunshot while he was falling asleep. But after the initial shock, Quip and the other customers returned to the store without thinking about it.

Quip Kelly's real first name was Carol. It was a family name. He was a smart aleck as a child, quick with the comeback. Quip was a nickname that stuck.

It was a fitting name for the profession he had chosen. He signed the bottom of his news columns simply with a "Q."

Quip had a solid build with a strong chin that jutted out. He wore his brown hair in a businessman's cut, not too short, but tidy. He never missed his appointment with the barber. Not a hair stylist, but an old-fashioned barber.

After graduating high school in Milwaukee, he did a stint in the Marine Corps. He was still regimented about keeping things clean. *Hilda*'s state of perpetual grime disturbed the Marine in him. He tried to push those obsessions aside since leaving the Corps. But he still performed daily scrubbing on the boat.

Straight out of the Marines, he enrolled at the University of Wisconsin in the journalism school. He had seen some things and he wanted to get them off his chest.

Quip went to work for the newspaper in Madison; he was promoted to a beat at the state capitol. He covered issues of the day and the governor and senators and state representatives.

With time, he learned that most of those elected officials were sincere and worked in the best interests of their constituents. They did the best that they could.

However, there were some who found the spotlight irresistible. They'd perform attention-getting stunts to get in front of the cameras. They'd search the newspaper to see their name in print.

There were also legislators who grew exhausted by the debates, the confrontations, and the risks. Their priority shifted to winning re-election. Their greatest inspiration came from the perks of the job, the money and the favors and the best seats at the best restaurants.

Until Quip, the worst of the lot at the state capitol used fear to keep their wretched secrets safe. But Quip wasn't afraid of politicians. And readers were drawn to his bravery.

Quip's first few scoops prompted an interview with a national television news program.

"You are doing something remarkable," the interviewer said. "At a time when community newspapers across the country are closing at a rate of two per week, your newspaper's readership and revenues are up."

"We owe a lot to our wonderful readers," Quip responded.

"You are being too humble," the interviewer suggested. "The great journalist Landover Scott says that many people no longer want to make the effort to determine what truth is. They've stopped reading the newspaper and instead search the computer for something to affirm their bias. But you are causing them to take another look."

"I admire Landover Scott," Quip replied. "And I don't disagree with him. But I think some people still yearn for the truth. It's just become difficult to tell it apart from falsehoods. There are people who make a good living spreading falsehoods."

Quip's newspaper purchased billboards. The only image on the large white sign was a big black "Q." Readers knew who the billboard was referring to and admired him more for it.

He was drawn to politics. And his fame had grown beyond Wisconsin. He had just been nationally syndicated. His first national story looked into a congressman from California. Quip was punching crooked politicians in the nose and readers loved it.

On board *Hilda*, Quip was putting the final touches on his investigation into Bat Bellows, a liberal congressman from Wisconsin who courted the approval of a large LGBTQ neighborhood in his district. Representative Bellows would appear at their parades and events because he needed their votes.

But Quip had been handed copies of emails sent from Bellows' personal computer. There were online discussions held with a deep-pocketed, homophobic donor to his campaign. The congressman used slurs and intolerant language to appease his patron.

The congressman's emails declared that he was "Tired of all the whining by the queers."

"But there's too many of them in my district," he impressed upon the donor. "Without the gay votes, I couldn't win re-election. But *with* the votes of those perverts, I can rise in the House to a leadership position and champion causes that you truly believe in. Stick with me. You won't be sorry."

Quip knew that Bellows' political career would be ruined when the story broke. That wasn't the journalist's concern. His concern was the hypocrisy of the congressman's behavior and the public's right to know.

Quip emailed the story to his editor back in Madison. It would appear in the next day's paper.

The sun was going down. Quip Kelly grabbed a glass of wine and flipped a switch to turn on a string of Christmas lights hanging on the boat. He unfolded a wooden chair on the bow of *Hilda*, sat down and surveyed his surroundings.

To one side, old houseboats had been pulled ashore and lined up like a trailer park. The paint was peeling and the wood was warped, but it looked like people were living inside the structures.

There were also additional neglected cabin cruisers like *Hilda* tied to the piers at the marina. Quip had never seen any of them leave the dock. He suspected they were all like *Hilda*: none of them had engines.

Quip looked over some papers that his agent had sent him. A television network wanted him to produce and star in four shows a year, breaking the same kinds of exposés he was becoming famous for. He would be paid a ton.

The network *wanted* Quip to do one show a month, but the journalist refused. He explained that his investigations required patience, time to unfold. Either way, he knew that he was approaching the kind of fame that would put his face on magazine covers.

He leaned back in his chair on the bow of *Hilda* and watched seagulls fish in the marina's still waters. It was growing darker. Lights were coming on inside housing projects that bordered a third side of his mooring.

Along the short driveway entering the marina, there were skeletons of old boats and bicycles, stained by rust and grime. They were piled on top of one another like discarded bones.

Beyond the piles of boats and bikes, there were stacked cargo containers. Tall grass surrounded them.

At least one container had been converted into a seaside getaway. He could see that the metal box had electricity, maybe a generator. He could see a lamp glowing inside, sitting on a table. Paradise was a state of mind.

He heard the metal gate scrape along the asphalt.

A late-model SUV pulled up to the cargo container with the lamp. An attractive young woman stepped out. A man inside the container greeted her at the door.

Quip believed the cabin cruiser floating next to his was lived in full-time. At night, he could see through the curtains. A big man on board watched a huge-screen TV.

The reporter hadn't met his neighbor on the boat next door. But an hour ago, Quip saw him make an uninspired effort to straighten up his floating home.

"Hi, cutie," Quip now heard, causing him to turn his head toward the dock. It was a woman's voice. He watched her climb aboard the boat next door and give the big man a kiss on the lips. It wasn't the first prostitute Quip had ever seen.

Feeling the gentle breeze skip off the water, Quip relaxed, feeling he'd had a productive day. Adding the wine and the tender rock of the boat, he drifted off to sleep. He felt safe. No one would look for him here. The last sound he remembered was the sound of satisfaction coming from the boat next door.

4

Alarge pair of eyeglasses peered up into JC Snow's bedroom. He stared down at them, and then at the naked pavement on Larimer Street below his apartment. Denver hadn't received any significant snow that season. It was overdue.

The sun was only starting to rise. In a few hours, the sidewalks would be full of pedestrians doing their Christmas shopping.

There were string lights hanging over the street, holly on the lampposts and pine boughs stretched across the pedestrian walk.

The spectacles hung outside a store at street-level. Larimer Square was one of the trendiest shopping districts in Denver. It only stretched for a couple of blocks. Short but sweet.

Robin had dropped a bag on the floor when she got home last night. It contained something she bought at a store called Garage Sale Vintage, just down the street in the building that used to house The Market.

JC's morning routine began in a trance. He climbed out of bed carefully and quietly, so as not to awaken Robin. He pulled on a vintage Denver Bears baseball team tee shirt to ward off the winter chill.

He advanced to the coffee maker and filled it with ten cups of water, some scoops of ground coffee and flipped the switch.

He filled a stainless-steel frothier with milk and then gently slipped back into bed.

Robin had moved into his Larimer Square apartment on a temporary basis in the spring. That was when JC required surgery after a painful crash during a ski race. With her help, he healed. She was nurturing, by nature.

He was even skiing again. But she never moved back to her apartment in the RiNo District. Neither of them brought up the topic of her possible departure.

"I want coffee," she said, face down into a pillow. Her voice was muffled. All JC could see was her long red curls and the beautiful curve of her back.

"I'll ask the servants to bring us some," he told her.

"And breakfast?"

"Yep," he said. "I'll ask the servants to bring breakfast too."

"You have servants?" she asked innocently into her pillow.

"Yep," he told her. "They're in the next room."

"How come I've never seen them?" she inquired, her voice still muffled.

"They're very discreet," JC advised her. "They respect our privacy."

"Where are they now?" she asked, rolling onto her side, propping herself up on an elbow and looking at him. Her beauty took his breath away, just as it did every time he saw her for the first moment in the morning.

"They must be in the other room," he told her.

"There are only two rooms in your apartment," she reminded him.

"It's an open layout," he agreed. "Yep."

"So, if I walk into the other room," she asked, "Will I see them?"

"I don't know," he said earnestly. "They might be in this room by then."

"Then *you* will see them?" she questioned.

"I can't always tell," he replied.

"Ah, you have invisible servants."

"Yep," he agreed.

"What are their names?" she persisted.

"They're difficult names to remember," he said. "But they wear name tags on their uniform."

"Their uniforms are invisible too?"

"That might be the case."

"Then, how will we know when they've brought us our coffee?" she asked with a little alarm.

"It may already be here," he told her.

"Because it's invisible."

"Yep," he said. Then he rolled out of bed. "Let me check on them. Perhaps they didn't show up for work this morning."

"I can see how it would be difficult to tell," she concurred.

"Quite so," he said as he left the bedroom.

He returned with two cups of coffee. There was white froth and cinnamon dusted across the top. Robin sat up in bed and relaxed against a pair of pillows, taking her first sip.

"Well," she said. "You can't fire them. This coffee is magnificent."

"Now you see my problem," he agreed as he slipped back into bed next to her.

JC Snow had dark hair and a dark mustache. He was in the second half of his thirties. He maintained a muscular build but was not brawny. JC actually enjoyed physical therapy after his knee surgery. It kept him around the weight room.

Robin thought JC was a gentle and energetic lover. And she felt safe beside him. She knew that he would always watch out for her.

JC believed that Robin was perfection. Her red hair curled past her shoulders. Her athletic build was the result of hard work, running and training in the gym. They both loved skiing. His was an obsession. Hers was just for the fun of it.

"Call the police," Tillison Tucker told his administrative assistant in a resigned voice.

It had been two days since the CEO of Snow Hat last heard from his able wingman. Ronny Schwartz was incommunicado. He had been under strict orders to stay in touch.

Tina Hernandez, Tucker's administrative assistant, called the county sheriff's office in Wisconsin. The resort where Ronny had been staying told her that the hotel room was empty even though Ronny's things were still in it.

The hotel told Hernandez that Ronny hadn't shown up for his complimentary breakfast for two days and there had been no charges to his room. He hadn't been seen by staff.

"The hotel is asking if we want to cancel the rest of Ronny's reservation," Hernandez asked her boss.

"Not yet," Tucker responded.

"Did you know that Wisconsin's nickname, 'The Badger State,' had nothing to do with the vicious little animal?"

The inquiry came from JC Snow's news director, Pat Perilla. They were sitting in Perilla's office at their Denver TV station.

"Badgers were the name given to men employed as lead miners in Wisconsin," Perilla continued. "They dug tunnels into the ground to keep warm when they slept."

"Are you thinking of remodeling the newsroom?" JC asked his news director. "Will we be working in underground burrows?"

"Just doing my homework," Perilla told him. "Did you know that the official bird of Madison, Wisconsin, is one of those plastic pink flamingos?"

"Makes sense," JC responded. "Real flamingos wouldn't make it through the winter."

"Well, you're going to have to do the rest of the legwork regarding Wisconsin," the news director told him. "I have something there for you. Do you have a bag packed?"

"Working for you?" JC smiled. "I always have a bag packed."

"Good," his boss said. He liked JC when he showed respect for rank, even though he knew it was conditional. "I'm sending you to Wisconsin."

"Is there a critical shortage of beer there?" JC asked.

"No," Perilla answered.

"Cheese?"

"Nothing that drastic," Perilla said with a smile that lacked commitment. "We've just learned that the number-two man at Snow Hat is missing. He was last seen in Wisconsin. His name is Ronny Schwartz. I am acquainted with him. We sometimes end up at the same functions. Nice fellow."

"So, what happened to him?" JC asked.

"That remains a mystery," Perilla told him. "And solving mysteries is something you're good at."

Perilla said that the owner of Snow Hat, Tillison Tucker, had confirmed the disappearance when Perilla heard a rumor and gave him a call. And the news director proceeded to tell JC what was known about Ronny Schwartz.

"Ronny was tending to business at Snow Hat's new acquisition in Wisconsin," Perilla said. "Tucker wouldn't disclose specifics about what business Ronny was conducting, other than it had to do with their new ski resort near Lake Geneva. But he said that Ronny's assignment wasn't expected to put him in any danger. Tucker told me that he believes whatever has happened has nothing to do with Snow Hat."

"That's what every corporate CEO says when there's bad news," JC said. "'It had nothing to do with them or their shareholders.' 'It's pure coincidence.'"

"Right," Perilla agreed. "That's something you'll have to find out for yourself. Hopefully, you find Ronny relaxing on a beach in Florida with a beer in his hand explaining that his sudden departure was a case of spontaneous retirement."

"Ah, the Great Departure."

"Yes," Perilla smiled. "Now, let's talk about who you're taking with you. Bip Peters tells me that he can't go. Something about a woman."

"Bip is always my first choice, but that is the sum of it," JC confirmed. "A beautiful Indian maiden from Utah has just moved to Denver to be closer to Bip."

Her name was Sunny Shavano. Bip met her on the Western Slope last winter. She was a raven-haired Ute with penetrating eyes and the ability to deftly handle a snowboard. It was all Bip was looking for in a woman.

But Denver was a big city, and Sunny was from a small town in Utah. She'd be alone without friends or family if Bip left now.

"Okay. Who then?" JC asked.

"Milt Lemon," the news director told him. "I know he's been trouble in the past, but you seem to get the best work out of him. He's done some great things with you. And he wants to go."

"He *wants* to go?" JC repeated. "There's something about this trip that I don't know, isn't there?"

"Probably," Perilla agreed. "But I'm not aware of what it is. He's ahead of us on this one."

"He does do good work," JC surrendered. "But he's exhausting."

"He's my choice," the news director said firmly.

"Fine," conceded JC. "Milt Lemon. And..."

"No," Perilla interrupted.

"You don't even know what I'm going to ask for," JC protested.

"Yes, I do," Perilla insisted. "And no."

"But she's my producer," JC protested. "And she's brilliant."

"Brilliant, yes," the news director began. "But she's *not* your producer anymore. Robin now might be my best *reporter* aside from *you.*"

"But who is going to protect me from Milt?" JC asked in vain.

"You *should* worry about who would protect *her* from Milt," Perilla said with a laugh.

"Where was Schwartz staying?" JC asked.

"The Geneva Grand Resort," the news director answered. "I hear that it's very nice."

"Put us there," JC said.

And the conversation ended. The news director took a phone call and waved JC out of the office.

As he closed the door to Pat Perilla's office behind him, JC was thinking about what he needed to do before he picked up and left for Wisconsin. He could be gone for weeks.

"You honestly thought you were going to go to a Playboy Club without me?"

The owner of the annoying voice was waiting for him in a narrow hallway next to Perilla's office. The hall was lined with editing bays, sliding glass doors, and Milt Lemon leaning against a wall.

"A Playboy Club?" JC asked. "I think you misunderstood."

"Ronny Schwartz was staying at the Grand Geneva Resort when he disappeared," Milt said. "I know you. That's where you're going to want to stay. You'd spend a night aboard the Titanic if you found out it was sinking that night."

"You're right," JC said. "That's where we'll be staying."

"It used to be a Playboy Club," Milt said, staring at JC.

"And?"

"There is no 'and,'" Milt spat. "It was once the most legendary Playboy Club in the country."

"And?"

"And we're going!" Milt said with animation.

"Do you think a Playboy Bunny kidnapped Ronny Schwartz?" JC asked with a straight face.

"I don't know," Milt responded. "Maybe."

"What little I know about the Playboy Resort in Geneva," JC began. "Those Playboy Bunnies would now be seventy years old. And they haven't been Playboy Bunnies for forty or fifty years. In fact, it hasn't been a Playboy Club for a long time."

"Still," Milt persisted. "Hugh Hefner once walked those halls."

JC took an impatient breath.

"And Bunnies," Milt added with a grin.

"That was a long time ago, Milt," JC said with patience.

"And Sammy Davis Jr.," Milt added.

"I thought you told me you've reformed," JC told him. "That you weren't going to be a weird pervert anymore."

"I am working on being less weird," Milt answered.

"Just stay out of trouble," JC told him. "You're a great photographer, but just stay out of trouble."

"Trouble?" Milt repeated innocently. "What kind of trouble?"

"Don't, for example," JC eyed him. "Don't try to date murdered women."

"That would be disgusting," Milt said. "That would be like necrophilia or something."

"That *is* disgusting," JC sourly repeated. "I mean don't date them only days before they're murdered."

"Be fair," Milt protested. "That's only happened twice."

"You make it sound like that's below the national average!" JC rebutted. "It's not!"

"JC, you're my friend," Milt said solemnly. "And friends are friends forever."

JC took a deep breath and exhaled.

"We leave Monday," he told Milt.

5

"My name is Mr. Knight," the man on the phone said.

The call had gone directly into the office of the politician, somehow bypassing his secretary.

"Yes, Mr. Knight," the politician said. "What may I help you with?"

"I'm calling because," Mr. Knight said, "I might be able to help solve your problem."

"I don't have a problem, Mr. Knight," the politician said.

"Oh, but you do," Mr. Knight informed him with an even voice. "A sizable problem. And I can help you solve it."

"Alright, I'll humor you," the politician said. "What is my problem?"

"It's not really a what," Mr. Knight's mysterious voice responded. "It's a who."

"And who might be my problem?" the politician asked, losing patience with the game. He cradled the phone with his shoulder and spun the ring on his finger. It was a ring with a red stone, from the University of Wisconsin.

"Quip Kelly is your problem," Mr. Knight stated.

The politician's stomach nearly slid out of his rectum. The phone dropped from his shoulder. It was not a name he expected to hear. It was not a problem he thought that he had, until now.

"Are you still there?" Mr. Knight asked after a long pause in the conversation.

The politician picked up the phone and held it to his ear.

"Yes," the politician said. "I'm still here."

"I can make your problem go away," Mr. Knight said. "If that is what you desire."

The politician checked the door to his office, to make certain that it was closed.

"How would you do that?" he asked in a voice that was not much more than a squeak.

"Why spoil your day with details," Mr. Knight answered. "I'm a professional. I help people solve their problems."

"Mr. Knight," the politician said, summoning his courage and suspicious that this call might be a trap by the news media or some law enforcement body. "And I doubt that is your real name. I do not like any part of this conversation. And if I did have a problem with Quip Kelly, which I don't, I do not believe that it is *you* who I would turn to."

"Of course not," Mr. Knight said in an even voice. "I understand. Let me leave you a phone number where you can reach me. If you change your mind, I'll be doing a little business in your area anyway. I'd be happy to add you to my client list."

The politician wrote the phone number down. He was sweating.

"We get to go to Wisconsin together," Robin sang. She beamed as they entered Denver International Airport.

"Yes, ma'am," JC said to her with a smile.

"Don't call me ma'am," Robin said. "I'm not old enough to be a ma'am."

"Yes, ma'am," JC responded, smiling. "It's a display of respect."

"It is a respectful display for your grandmother and grade-school teacher," she protested. "Not your hot girlfriend."

JC nodded his head. She had a point.

"Where you headed to?" asked the baggage handler as he took their skis.

"Wisconsin," JC told him.

"Sorry," said the baggage handler. "I meant to ask where are you flying *to* with your skis?"

"Wisconsin."

"Is this your return flight?" the airport employee asked, taking a second look at the ticket.

"No," JC told him. "We're from Denver. We're flying to Wisconsin to go skiing."

"You must know something I don't about Wisconsin," the baggage man grumbled.

"Apparently," JC said.

"It's the cheese curds," Milt yelled after him as the man walked away. "You can't get cheese curds like that if you're not in a bar at a Wisconsin ski area."

JC and Robin stared at Milt.

"I've been doing my homework," Milt said with a smile.

The only nonstop flight they could book was to Chicago. Milwaukee's airport was closer to Lake Geneva, but there wasn't a nonstop flight available from Denver. Flying nonstop to Chicago and getting a car would be a shorter trip.

"Chicagoland weather for tomorrow," the voice on the radio said, after picking up their rental car at Midway Airport. "Sunny and barely above zero."

"Chicago-what?" Robin asked.

"Chicagoland," JC told her. "They say that instead of saying 'Metro-Chicago' or 'Chicago and the suburbs.'"

"Chicagoland," she repeated. "That's cute."

"That's what Al Capone said when he was asked where he got the clap," Milt added.

Night fell as JC navigated the Kennedy Expressway and drove north, away from the airport. He was chosen as the driver because he had traveled some of these roads before.

"I thought he said 'no,'" Milt stated to Robin. She was riding in the front passenger seat.

"Who said no?" asked Robin.

"Pat," Milt responded. "The pudgy man who you work for. I thought he said you couldn't come."

"Oh, we worked something out," Robin said. "I took this week off for Christmas. I just told Pat, 'If you need me, I'll be in Wisconsin.' And I get an extra two days because New Year's Eve is a Tuesday. I've just got to go back to Denver and be ready to work on New Year's Day. But I'm going to try to use some more vacation to come back, if you guys are away too long."

"You'll miss me that much?" Milt asked with a smile.

"Yes," smiled Robin. "Desperately."

Milt was not a good-looking man. He was average-looking if he got enough sleep. He was in his forties, a little overweight, had dark rings around his eyes, gray hair and a goatee.

But he was irrepressible. He was well-practiced at overcoming his shortcomings. He pursued women who were out of his league. When his crude sense of humor made people around him wince, he simply reached deeper into the bag. He thought he was hilarious.

Milt took off his jacket inside the car. He was wearing an old tee shirt that read, "I played with myself in 2020."

"Don't you mean you played *by* yourself?" JC asked when he first saw the slogan on the tee shirt. It referred to the Covid-19 crisis.

"You spent your time doing what *you* wanted and I spent my time doing what *I* wanted," was Milt's response with a giggle.

They passed the sign welcoming visitors to Wisconsin. A few gas stations, right over the state line, lured drivers from Illinois with inordinately low gas prices.

"Did you see the price of gas here?" Milt asked.

"They also don't have any toll roads," JC informed him. "Not in the entire state."

"Wow! If it was legal to drink and drive," Milt exclaimed, "I'd move here!"

"Just because you think it, Milt," advised Robin, "doesn't mean you have to say it."

"Yes, ma'am," Milt said. Robin shook her head.

"I'm not a 'ma'am,'" she said quietly, recognizing a lost cause.

The rental SUV passed a marker saying that the Wilmot Mountain ski area was at the next exit. In the distance, they could see the lights illuminating the hill for night skiing.

"Welcome to our Midwest Mountain Tour," JC said with delight.

"Wisconsin doesn't have any mountains!" Milt exclaimed.

"Yes, they do," JC said with a smile. "They're just small mountains."

"Uh oh," Robin suddenly said. "There's trouble ahead."

Looking up Route 50, they could all see the flashing lights of multiple police units. JC applied the brakes when he arrived at the back of a line of cars at the police checkpoint.

"Hi folks," a member of the Wisconsin State Patrol said when they moved to the head of the line. His script was chipper, but his delivery wasn't.

"Where are you heading?" the trooper asked. He was bent at the waist to look into JC's open window.

"The Grand Geneva Resort," JC told him.

"Where are you from?" the trooper asked.

"Colorado," JC answered. "We're here on work."

"You just get here?" the law officer inquired.

"Yep," JC replied. "We're coming from the airport."

The trooper raised his head and saw the line of cars behind JC's rental, waiting for their turn at the checkpoint.

"Okay," the trooper told them. "Enjoy your stay."

"What's up?" JC asked. "Why the checkpoint?"

"There was a serious traffic accident along here a couple of weeks ago," the trooper informed them. "We're looking for someone who might have seen something."

"Sorry. We won't be of much help," JC told him. "Good luck."

JC pulled away from the trooper. Robin was already pulling out her tablet and searching for news of the traffic accident.

Route 50 became a dark road on a dark night. The area around them was farmland without a lot of lights.

"If you're curious," she said, reading off her tablet. "I think those police are investigating a hit-and-run. A pedestrian was killed. The car took off. Police haven't been able to find the car or the driver."

"They don't drive any better here than they do on I-70," Milt said from the backseat.

They pulled off Route 50 onto a long, winding driveway leading up to the Grand Geneva Resort. It was lined by trees and darkness. They were in the quiet country.

In the distance, they could see the lights for night skiing at the resort's own ski hill.

Pulling up to the lobby entrance, there was soft jazz slipping from the loudspeakers. Walking inside, they saw large fireplaces in three directions and heard more of the same soft jazz. The lobby was part of an open room that stretched the width of the entire building. A sunken living room was straight ahead.

"Sunken living rooms were thought to be very cool in the 1960s," JC said, admiring the retro decor.

"Hi!"

They were startled by the enthusiastic greeting from the desk clerk.

"Nineteen sixty-eight," an energetic woman behind the desk blurted. "That's when our resort was first built. But it's still shiny, like new! And there are lots of sunken living rooms here. Lots of quiet nooks."

She eyed JC and Robin like they were a couple that would be looking for quiet nooks.

"We're checking in," JC told her. "It's under the name of our television station."

"Oh, we saw you were coming," the bubbly clerk said. "A television station! Exciting! Have you ever stayed with us here at the Grand Geneva?"

"No," JC said. He couldn't help but return her warm smile.

"Well," said the clerk. "Would you like me to show you around? Someone can cover for me."

"That won't be necessary," JC said. "That's nice of you though."

"I'd like a tour," Milt told the woman. "If that would be okay."

"Of course, it would," she said in a sweet voice.

She was an attractive blonde and in her thirties. Her smile was infectious. The name plate on her brown vest that matched her brown slacks read "Branch."

"Is that your name?" Milt asked.

"Yes," she said with an embarrassed grin. "I have a sister named Twig and a brother named Leaf. My parents had an active imagination when they were young, and probably a lot of weed."

Branch laughed and they laughed with her.

JC watched Milt and Branch depart for their guided tour.

"So, where are you from?" they heard Milt ask Branch.

"I grew up on a farm in Lake Geneva," she told him.

"Which room was Hugh Hefner's?" Milt asked. Branch laughed.

"Nice people here," Robin said to JC.

"Some of the nicest," JC agreed. "People in the Midwest may be the nicest ones in the whole country."

They brought their own baggage to their room and then took a stroll through the sprawling building.

There was a maze of long hallways connecting their room to the lobby. The enclosed corridors allowed guests to roam the property without being exposed to Wisconsin's cold winters.

"Have you been to Wisconsin before?" Robin asked.

"Yep. I had an uncle who lived in Lannon," JC told her. "We'd come and visit. We'd go to a place called Sister Bay. It's up north on Lake Michigan. I was really young. I've been to the Wisconsin Dells, too. And in the winter, we'd come to Delavan Lake and stay at a place called Lake Lawn Lodge. We'd go tobogganing and skiing. It was fun."

"I see a lake out the window," Robin said. "Is that Lake Geneva?"

"Nope," JC answered. "Do you remember Milt's fixation with how this resort used to be a Playboy Club? Well, that little lake you see was built by Hugh Hefner, the CEO of Playboy, when he constructed the resort. They used dynamite to create that lake in a farm field. From the sky, it's the shape of the Playboy Bunny logo."

"Does he still live here?" Robin asked.

"Hefner passed away," JC told her and smiled. "But he lived a very active life."

"So where is the lake in Lake Geneva?" inquired Robin.

"Not far from here," JC told her. "Lake Geneva used to be the summer retreat for the wealthiest people in Chicago.

They built mansions along the shoreline. The Wrigley family, who owned the chewing gum and the Chicago Cubs baseball team, once owned six mansions on Lake Geneva."

"Why here? Hugh Hefner, I mean," Robin asked.

"Playboy got its start in Chicago," JC told her. "This was a logical place for Playboy to build a resort with a new vision."

"It's actually a very attractive structure," Robin stated. "The windows are huge. There are views in every direction."

"That's the Prairie School influence of the great architect Frank Lloyd Wright," JC said. "He was from Wisconsin."

"I love the timbers in the ceiling and walls," Robin said. "It brings warmth while the poured concrete brings a contemporary look. And there *are* living rooms everywhere."

"I read that was a trademark of Hefner's clubs," JC told her. "He liked the feeling of hanging out with friends in a living room, no matter where you were. So, all of his buildings had an abundance of living rooms."

"All this talk about Playboy," Robin observed. "I don't see a single Playboy logo or even a reference."

"I don't, either," JC agreed. "Playboy hasn't owned this property for a long time. And Hefner was a controversial figure. He ran a very successful business for many decades. But times have changed. And since his passing, we've heard two distinct narratives. Some people in Hefner's inner circle thought he was great, ahead of his time on racial and gender equality. And some say he was a control freak who used sex for power."

"I'm losing my power at the moment. It's been a long day," Robin said. "Where can a girl get a drink?"

"There might be a bar down this hall," JC guessed, following the noise that one normally hears from drinking establishments.

They entered the Igloo Lounge and settled into comfortable chairs. The room wasn't very full.

It was late. The wait staff was picking up empty bottles and wine glasses left on tables, beginning a routine that would end with the bar's closing for the night.

A few patrons remained to nurse their drinks and watch television sets above the bartender's head. All the TVs were tuned to Monday Night Football.

Two teams from the West Coast were playing, so the sound was turned down to hear the soft jazz coming from speakers in the ceiling. If the Packers were playing, the sound on the televisions would be turned up.

A porch outside the Igloo Lounge overlooked the frozen lake. There were plastic igloos on the porch, big enough to fit a table for four. There was also a large outdoor fireplace and illuminated Christmas decorations.

"I'll buy you a drink," JC told Robin. "Will you pick it up at the bar and serve me doing a Bunny Dip?"

"I don't know what that is," Robin said. "But I get the feeling my mom wouldn't like it."

6

"He has disappeared into thin air," a captain in the sheriff's office told JC the next morning. "No one saw him leave and no one saw anyone with him. He just vanished. I assure you, the sheriff and law enforcement across the state of Wisconsin are doing everything they can to find Ronny Schwartz."

"Is there any reason to suspect foul play?" JC asked. Milt stood behind JC. His camera was on a tripod and recording the interview.

"Well, he's gone," the captain said. "So, that's one reason. But he also could have gone for a walk in the woods and had a heart attack. We get a lot more of that than we do abductions."

"Is there something I don't know about Big Horizon?" JC asked.

"There's probably a lot you don't know," the law officer told him.

"I mean," JC clarified, "is there any danger that I'm not aware of because I'm not from around here? Could organized crime be involved? Is there a serial killer on the loose? Kidnappers?"

"You *are* new here," the captain smiled. "But I assume you drove here with your eyes open?"

JC nodded in agreement.

"And what did you see?" the captain asked.

"Farm fields, little houses, cows," JC offered, hoping he would pass the test. "This morning, I saw some people playing golf with orange balls that rolled across patches of snow."

"No gang tags," the captain added. "No bars on the windows of homes, no razor-wire fences built around businesses to keep burglars out."

"No murders?" JC asked.

"Rarely," the captain answered. "You might have heard about the shooting in Elk Horn. A real tragedy. Senseless. But that is not the norm. And that guy is behind bars."

"So, this area isn't crime-free," JC stated.

"What place is?" the captain asked. "But I'll bet half of the cars you passed on your way to my office, parked in their driveways, have the keys in 'em. As law officers, we don't like it, but that's how things are around here. They're nice people."

"I've noticed," JC agreed.

The low morning sun bounced off the frozen lake. It caused JC and Robin to squint as they sat inside their room. JC and Milt had returned to the resort after their interview with the captain at the sheriff's office. JC brought Robin coffee.

"What do you suppose happened to him?" Robin asked.

Robin was officially on vacation. And since they arrived late the night before, she had stayed in bed while JC and Milt went to work.

Now, they sat by a sliding glass door with a view of the lake shaped like a bunny. The door led to a porch they would probably never stand on. Outside, it was four degrees below zero.

"I don't have a clue what happened to him," JC told her. "I'm sure that Tillison Tucker has some ideas, but he didn't care to share them. Big companies try to keep their scandals in-house."

The captain they interviewed was second-in-command at the sheriff's office. He told JC that law officers across the whole Midwest were looking for Ronny Schwartz's rental car. He said that banks and ATMs were looking for any activity on Ronny's credit card.

"There are a lot of little lakes and rivers around here," Robin suggested. "Sometimes, cars just slip off the road on a dark night and sink to the bottom of a lake."

"That's one way to disappear without a trace," JC agreed. "C'mon. Let's go downstairs and get some breakfast."

Milt joined them at the café. He was wearing a red sweater and green scarf.

"It's Christmas Eve," he explained.

"Merry Christmas!" blurted the same perky blonde who checked them into the hotel the night before. "Are you hoping Santa brings you something special?"

Her holiday greeting broke the silence in the restaurant as JC, Milt and Robin studied the menu. She was wearing the same brown pants and a matching brown vest.

"Hi," Milt said to her, trying to make his voice sound like velvet.

"You work in the dining room too?" JC asked.

"Oh yeah," she said with animation. "I work at the desk, I waitress here, and I'm a snowboard instructor at the ski hill here. A lot of us have multiple jobs here. It helps pay the bills."

Branch sounded like she was singing a song when she spoke. Her voice would climb the scale for one sentence and descend back down the scale on the next.

"Branch says there wasn't anywhere to work around here until the Playboy Club opened," Milt told them.

"Oh yeah," Branch told them. "Almost everyone was happy to see them come here. *Almost everyone.*" And she laughed.

"She says families with little kids came here," Milt informed them.

"Yeah," Branch chimed in. "My mom worked here when it was the Playboy Club. She wasn't a Bunny or anything. She was a waitress. Everybody's parents worked here. And families on vacation would bring their kids! The kids loved the Bunnies! It was like being served dinner by rabbits!" She laughed some more. "It wasn't what you think. There wasn't sex going on everywhere. It was nice. Everyone behaved themselves."

"Was Hugh Hefner here a lot?" Robin asked.

"I don't think he was here very much," Branch told them. "I think he moved to Los Angeles, didn't he?"

"I think he did," JC said and changed the subject. "Did you happen to wait on a man named Ronny Schwartz a couple of weeks ago? He is a big executive in the ski industry. His company purchased Big Horizon."

"I did, yeah," Branch said as she gave it some thought. She smiled. "He was nice. Kinda flirty, but he was nice."

"And then one day he didn't come anymore?" JC asked.

"Yeah, that was strange," she said. "We were expecting him. It's not that busy right now, so we can kind of keep track of everybody. I never heard what happened. Did he check out?"

"You haven't heard that police are looking for him?" JC asked. "That he's missing?"

"Yeah, I did," she admitted. "I didn't know if I should say anything. Police came and asked us questions. I don't think we were any help, though."

"Any idea what happened to him?" JC asked.

"No," she sang.

She took their food orders and left, promising to bring them more coffee.

"Do you want to go skiing when we're done?" JC asked his two-member crew.

"You know I don't ski anymore," Milt responded. "Too old, too stiff."

"We need you to shoot some video for tonight's story. Then, you can investigate those cheese curds in the ski lodge bar," JC said with a smile. "I want to check out Big Horizon and see what they know about Ronny Schwartz."

"It's awfully cold out there," Robin cautioned. "Is it still below zero?"

"Only a little below zero," JC grinned. "Besides, they say it's not the temperature that makes you cold, it's the dew point."

"So that makes it better here?" Robin asked.

"No," JC laughed. "It usually makes it worse."

Changing into warm ski apparel, JC and Robin met Milt downstairs. He too was wearing ski clothing.

"You just told me you don't ski anymore," JC deadpanned.

"Yeah, but I want to look the part," Milt said with a smile. "You know how fashion-conscious I am. Besides, I'll blend in. Maybe I'll eavesdrop on the man who rubbed out Ronny Schwartz."

"Rubbed out?" Robin repeated.

"Yeah," Milt said. "I told you, I've been doing my homework. All the gangsters from Chicago, like Al Capone, used to come up to Lake Geneva."

"Why didn't that occur to me?" JC smirked. "Ronny Schwartz was rubbed out by Al Capone."

JC scraped a layer of frost off the windshield of their car and they drove down Route 50. They turned onto Fox River Road and passed a sign welcoming skiers to Big Horizon. The sign said, "Welcome to the Mountains of the Midwest."

Driving across a large parking lot of frozen dirt mixed with frozen snow, they parked as close to the ski lodge as possible. The complex of buildings was quickly filling with families. Children were on school break.

The new ski lodge was a big structure built to resemble a barn. There was a fresh coat of red paint on it and a silo attached. The lodge was called "The Barn."

It was part of a theme. Surrounding buildings resembled other structures you'd find in a Midwest farming community. The ski shop looked like a tractor-supply store.

Christmas music accompanied them as JC and Robin carried their skis toward racks on the slope side of The Barn. Milt carried his camera and tripod.

Facing the ski runs, most of The Barn was made of glass, to give people inside a good look at what was going on outside. And there was a long balcony on the second floor, part of the upstairs bar called The Silo.

Milt put his camera down. He lifted a snowboard from the rack to admire the radical paint job.

"Hey, gray on a tray," a young snowboarder said as he passed by. He gave Milt a thumbs-up.

Milt gave JC a confused look.

"He thinks you're an old snowboarder," JC told him. "The thumbs-up means he thinks you're cool."

"See?" Milt said with a satisfied smile. "It's my choice of skiing apparel. They think I'm cool."

JC asked an older man wearing a ski instructor's jacket where the main office might be. He was pointed to a brand-new structure built to look like a farmhouse.

"At The Farmhouse," the instructor said, pointing that way.

"It looks pretty fancy for a farmhouse," JC joked.

"That's what our new bosses make us call it," the instructor said with a knowing smile. "I guess we're in show business now."

The three journalists entered the front door of The Farmhouse and found themselves in the lobby of the main office. They were greeted by a middle-aged woman behind a desk. She wore a ski sweater with farm animals on it.

"Cute," Robin remarked, seeing the sweater.

"Thank you, dear," the woman responded. "Merry Christmas! How may I help you?"

JC introduced himself and informed the woman they were with a television crew from Colorado. He asked if anyone might be able to speak with them about Ronny Schwartz's disappearance.

"All the way from Colorado?" she said with a smile. "Welcome!" She excused herself and entered a door behind the desk.

"Is everybody in the Midwest nice?" Milt asked. "Is it in the water or something?"

"But she didn't say a word about Ronny Schwartz," Robin observed. "Not a 'What a shame,' or 'I wonder where he is.'"

"I suspect that whoever is behind that door has told employees not to say anything about Schwartz's disappearance," JC told them.

The woman reappeared from behind the door and gave them a smile.

"I'm sorry. There's no one available to speak with you right now," she explained. "You look like you're dressed to go skiing. Why don't you take some runs and come back in two hours. I think someone will be available then."

"Thank you," JC said to the compromise. "We'll do that. See you in a couple of hours."

"Can I give you three lift tickets?" the woman asked.

JC thought about this. He didn't like taking gifts while on the job. But if he was going to speak knowledgably about the Big Horizon ski resort, he was going to have to experience it. Their news director said that kind of freebie was acceptable.

"Just two," he said.

"You can buy me a beer," Milt chimed in.

"Not while you're working," JC told him.

The woman slid two beer coupons across the desk toward Milt.

"For later," she said with a smile. "It's my Christmas gift."

7

"Size Doesn't Matter!" read a sweatshirt worn by a skier at the Big Horizon ski hill.

"Eighteen seconds!" Milt shouted at JC and Robin when they finished their first run of the morning. "That's how long it took you to get from top to bottom."

"It was a good run, though," JC told him.

"It was fun," Robin chimed in. "Beautiful corduroy."

"I looked," Milt said, walking their way and holding a trail map. "It's 270 feet vertical. I told you there were no mountains in Wisconsin."

"It doesn't seem to matter," JC responded. "Look at how many people are coming here to ski and snowboard today. They know it's not Colorado, but it's what they have. And there are some really good skiers here."

They parted ways. JC and Robin headed for the chairlift and Milt went searching for another place to shoot video that would be useful for their first broadcast back to Denver that night.

JC and Robin rode the new chairlift past brand-new lights erected on towers for night skiing. Brand-new PistenBully groomers were parked next to a large shed at the bottom of the hill.

A snowboarder from Chicago rode up the chair with them. He said he belonged to the Hustler Ski Club. He talked about a trip out West he planned to take in a few weeks.

"So, you're from Colorado?" the snowboarder asked.

"Yep," JC nodded.

"You've got better snow, but Barbie lives here!" the snowboarder said with a laugh.

"Barbie?" Robin asked with enthusiasm. "You mean the Barbie doll? My best friend until I was ten? That Barbie?"

"That's right," the Chicagoan laughed. "Her storyline says she comes from Willows, Wisconsin. I don't think there really is such a place. Could you imagine the tourists they'd draw if it did exist?"

"Barbie would be a billionaire," JC said as the chairlift reached the top of the hill.

"Merry Christmas!" the snowboarder said as he pushed off the chair and headed in another direction.

"Here's something you can't get when you ski in Colorado," JC said to Robin as he pointed downhill. "I can see our car in the parking lot, no matter where we are on the mountain."

They could see their car, The Barn, The Farmhouse, a restaurant called The Kitchen, the access road and beyond.

She laughed and said, "Stop, I like it."

"I do too," he agreed. "There's no such thing as bad skiing. I should put a lid on the Colorado hubris."

"Yes, you should," she said. "Don't be a snob."

On the next run, they paused at the top and watched young racers training in a slalom course. A man on skis pulled up next to them.

"Pretty impressive, aren't they?"

"The racers?" JC asked. "Yeah, they look great. What age are they?"

"U-fourteens," he said. "Under fourteen years old. They have a great racing program here. That's my daughter in the yellow helmet."

"Is this the Buck Hill of Wisconsin?" JC asked with a smile.

"You know Buck Hill? In Minnesota?" the man asked. "We're similar in size. Buck Hill has put racers on the Olympic Team, like Lindsey Vonn, Kristina Koznick and Paula Moltzan."

"Maybe we'll be saying that about your daughter in a few years," JC told him.

"I'd love to see my little girl get a shot," the man said proudly. "It gets political, though."

"What do you mean 'political'?" JC asked.

"You know," the man said. "Sometimes, it's who you know. And certain parents can *buy* a spot for their kid on the A-team here, while better racers languish on the B-Team. Right?"

"I hope not," JC said. "Your daughter looks great."

"Thanks," the man said and pushed off. "Merry Christmas!"

"Does that really happen?" Robin asked JC.

"Beats me," he said. "I just got here."

They took another run and waited at the bottom for Milt as he walked their way.

JC and Robin studied a cleared patch of land next to the small hotel. Signs told them construction of a big addition to the hotel was coming in the spring.

"The new owners are pouring money into their acquisition," JC noted.

Milt arrived and looked at the lift tickets hanging from their jacket.

"I remember these!" he said.

"Old-school lift tickets," JC said, taking a closer look at the adhesive paper. "It's like being back in the 1970s."

Their lift tickets were white with purple polka dots. They hung on a metal wicket run through the pull tab of a zipper on their jackets.

"Tomorrow, the tickets will be different, like white with green stars on them," JC told Milt. "It's the way they prevent customers from using today's ticket tomorrow or the next day."

"What are they using in Colorado?" Milt asked.

"Now, most of the bigger ski areas across the country run on RFID tickets. They have computer chips and barcodes. We get scanned every time we ride up the lift, like a frozen pizza at the grocery store."

Some skiers with the tickets on metal wickets wouldn't take them off their jacket for the entire winter. The collection became an archive of their skiing experience, forming a ball of wickets and tickets at the end of their zipper.

JC and Robin took another run. The top of the black diamond slopes all had interesting plunges built into them, an extremely steep drop made possible by bulldozers when they added elevation to the hill. Sometimes, the plunge was followed by a roller coaster ride over large mounds and knolls. In skier parlance, they were called "animals" and "whales."

"How are your knees?" Robin asked JC.

"They're fine," he told her. "I still need to gain confidence in my ACL knee. It feels like someone replaced my knee with an elbow. But I'm stable. You don't have to worry about me anymore."

"No," she said dismissively. "Not at all."

It had been over a year since Landover Scott had cried. It was dark then. His wife climbed into bed. He would follow, just happy to be in her company. They exchanged a kiss and told each other, "I love you," as they had each night for the last forty-five years. Then, he turned out the light.

"Are you working tomorrow?" she asked in the dark as she lay close to him.

"Just a little magazine article," he told her. "Why, do you need me?"

"It will wait," she said sweetly. "I have my eye on a new living room chair. I saw it in Sturgis. But I want you to see it before I buy it."

"How about the day after tomorrow?" he asked.

"That will be fine," she assured him. "It will wait. I wonder if I'm coming down with a cold or something."

"Do you want me to get you something?" he asked.

"No, a good night's sleep will take care of it. Good night, honey."

Sleep was sometimes hard to come by for him. About twenty minutes had passed. He could hear his wife breathing, enjoying a sound slumber, when he heard a much louder noise. It appeared to have come from outside, perhaps in their yard.

"Scotty, where are you going?" she asked, stirring as he climbed out of bed.

"Did you hear that?" he asked. "It sounds like a tree fell or something. I'm going to go take a look, make sure it's not leaning on our house."

"In the dark?" she asked with alarm.

"If we had a forest *inside* our house, I'd check there first," he kidded her. "I'll be fine."

"My husband," she said in a sleepy but adoring manner. "Always on guard. That's why I sleep so well. I love you, honey." He gave her a kiss on the head that had already slipped back onto her pillow, and he headed outside.

After pulling on some work boots to protect his feet from the snow, he picked up a flashlight and followed its beam out the door.

He circled the house. There was a lake on one side and trees on the other three sides. A few times, he pointed the flashlight into the woods. But he found the trees standing erect at their appointed posts.

He found nothing leaning against the house and no explanation for the noise he had heard from bed.

"I'll look again in the daylight," he told his wife as he sat back down on their bed. "I'd guess that a tree fell in the woods. It sounded like a tree falling. I'm just glad that it didn't hit the house."

His wife didn't answer and he smiled to himself, glad he hadn't woken her up again.

As his head hit the pillow, he reached over and gave her a pat. She didn't stir.

He knew he was imagining the worst, but he switched on the light and gave her a look. She still didn't move.

"Babe," he whispered as he gave her a gentle shake. Still, she didn't move.

He pulled himself closer to her and spoke louder as he called her name. She didn't answer.

He rolled her over to face him and saw the sweet face he always saw when she slept. So gentle a face, she still looked like the girl he'd fallen in love with, many years ago.

But she didn't wake. She was gone.

8

" A sheriff's deputy up in Door County found the car," the captain at the Kenosha County Sheriff's Office told JC while Milt aimed his camera at the two men. "No sign of Ronny Schwartz, though."

"Where in Door County?" JC asked.

"Gills Rock."

"What's in Gills Rock?" JC asked.

"A lot of water," the captain told him.

JC, Milt and Robin, when they returned from two hours of skiing, were told by the woman at The Farmhouse to go see the sheriff. She still had a smile on her face and the Christmas music was still playing, but something was wrong.

At the sheriff's office, the captain told them that Ronny Schwartz's rental car had been found a few hours north of Lake Geneva.

"Any evidence of foul play?" JC asked.

"We've only just begun to process the car," the captain said. "I'll tell you this, we don't see any bullet holes in the windshield. And no one reported any disturbance. We're not even sure how long the car has been there."

News of the car's discovery was also delivered to the offices of Snow Hat in Colorado, where Ronny Schwartz worked.

"Cancel the rest of Ronny's hotel reservation," Tillison Tucker instructed his administrative assistant, Tina Hernandez. "And Tina, get me a flight out to Wisconsin for tomorrow."

"Yes, Mr. Tucker."

JC, Robin and Milt drove back to the Grand Geneva Resort to prepare for their live shot. The discovery of Ronny Schwartz' empty rental car would be big news. They would get pictures of the car from a network TV affiliate in Green Bay.

A light snow began to fall as Milt drove back to the hotel. JC was riding in the front passenger seat, writing a script for his broadcast. Robin was in the back, doing research on her tablet.

Snowflakes fell on tilled rows in the frozen dirt where corn had been harvested last fall. Dairy cows were making a slow march from their pasture to the barn, where they would find warmth and food.

"America's Dairyland," Robin said as she looked up to watch the cows. "Did you know that nearly a quarter of the dairy farms in the United States are in Wisconsin? And about ninety percent of the milk from Wisconsin cows goes into cheese? This is the only state where you can be recognized as a master cheesemaker."

"Is that what the Green Bay Packers packed?" Milt asked. "Cheese?"

The famous National Football League franchise in Green Bay was founded back in 1919. But they needed money to pay for their uniforms.

"Cheese packers would make sense. But it was a meat-packing company," JC told them. "Canned meat. The Indian Packing Company paid five hundred dollars for the football team's uniforms, so they named the team after the company."

Following their live shot back to viewers in Denver for the evening news, they strolled into the Igloo Lounge at the Grand Geneva. They ordered dinner from the bar.

"Where are you from?" the bartender asked.

"Colorado," JC told her.

"What brings you here?" the bartender asked.

"We're skiing," Robin informed her.

"You came from Colorado to ski in Wisconsin?" the bartender asked. "You must know something I don't."

"Apparently," JC smiled.

"Are you from Barbie's hometown?" Robin asked the bartender. She smiled at her joke.

"No, I am from Poynette," she told them proudly. "That's where the world's tallest horse used to live!"

"*Used* to live? Did he move to Hollywood?" Milt asked.

"No," the bartender laughed. "He died. He was twenty-years old. His name was "Big Jake. His rear end towered over most men."

"To Big Jake and his big rear end," JC toasted with his new glass of old Lagavulin.

Robin took a sip of JC's single malt Scotch and grimaced.

"Yeech," she squealed. "How can you drink that stuff?"

"It's like drinking mother's milk," JC smiled.

"Was your mother a drunk?" she asked.

They peered out at the snow piling up on the porch of the bar.

"So," Milt asked JC. "Was Ronny Schwartz murdered?"

"Somebody got murdered?" a man asked. He had been sitting quietly at the bar next to JC.

"That's where I would put my money," JC responded casually. "We just don't know who, what, where and when."

"Ah, the tenets of a great journalist," the man said. JC judged him to be in his seventies. His eyes were bright and JC guessed they had seen things.

"Landover Scott," the man said as he extended his hand. JC took it.

"Holy cow!" JC exclaimed suddenly. "I should have picked you out as soon as we entered the room! I must be blind."

"No," the man said in a forgiving tone. "I'm older and balder and fatter than I was when you last saw me on television."

"Well, it's an honor, Mr. Scott," JC said.

"The honor is all mine, JC," Landover Scott replied. "I'm a great admirer of your work. And call me Scotty. All my friends do."

"He knows who you are, JC," said Robin. She was proud of her boyfriend.

"Well, I'm not in your league," JC told him.

"Oh, you're a big-leaguer, JC, whether or not you want to admit it," Scott said.

"This is Robin Smith," JC blurted, embarrassed that he hadn't introduced his friends earlier. "She's also a reporter at our television station. A fine one. And this is Milt Lemon. He is our talented photographer."

"A pleasure to meet you all," Scott said as he shook hands.

"I'm surprised to see you here," JC said. "I've heard that you've become something of a hermit."

"Not really a hermit," Scott said. "I just preferred to spend my time at home on Klinger Lake. I wrote articles and a couple of books and spent time with the only person I really *wanted* to spend my time with, my wife."

"That is so sweet," Robin said.

"I heard that she passed away last year," JC said. "I'm very sorry."

"A heart attack," Scott murmured. "After we turned in for the night."

"That is so sad," Robin said.

"Where's Klinger Lake?" JC asked, changing the subject.

"Not that far from here," Scott replied.

"You're from Chicagoland?" Robin asked, pleased to utilize the nickname she liked.

"No, no," Scott chuckled. "I'm from Michiana."

"Michiana," Milt repeated. "Is there a fifty-first state I wasn't told about?"

"Not unless I missed that one too," Landover Scott laughed. "Michiana describes the area along the Michigan and Indiana border. Have you heard of Sturgis?"

"South Dakota?" Milt inserted. "Where they hold the motorcycle rally?"

"No," Scott smiled. "It is a source of constant confusion. But we're in Michigan. The part they call 'The Mitten.' It's about four hours from here. We really have a White Pidgeon mailing address. But that's even smaller."

"A lot of small towns in the Midwest," Milt offered.

"There are small towns all over the country," Scott agreed. "That's where the cream rises to the top."

JC bought a round of drinks. He wanted to try some local beers and ordered a Mello Rillo, a sour beer brewed in Waukesha.

"Anyway, it has begun to get lonely on our lovely lake," Scott said as he accepted their condolences. "So, I thought I'd come here for a while. My wife and I liked to come here for brief getaways. We saw Bob Hope and Sonny and Cher perform here. But maybe I *am* a bit of a hermit, these days."

"We're probably disturbing you," Robin said.

"No, not at all," Scott waved his hand. "I enjoy the company of the fourth estate."

Scott intercepted the bill when the bartender placed it in front of JC.

"So, you don't know *why* he was murdered," Scott ruminated. "None of it is any good if you don't know why."

Landover Scott was tall and bald and soft around the beltline. Seventy-seven years old, he seemed younger than that.

He was a former network television reporter. JC had watched film of him reporting from battlefields overseas and civil rights marches in the South.

"Mr. Scott is a legend," JC began to tell Robin and Milt. "He covered the Democratic Presidential Convention in Chicago in 1968. The one with all the combat between protesters and the cops."

"I was still wearing diapers when I got that assignment, just out of college," Scott said. "And please, call me Scotty."

"He covered Richard Nixon's resignation," JC added.

"All the good reporters were at lunch," Scott grinned. "I was the only one they could send."

"Viet Nam," JC said.

"I was only there at the end," Scott told them. "It was a mess."

"9/11," JC uttered.

"Yes," Scott sighed. "After all those decades of struggle, I wondered if mankind had learned anything. I'm not so sure."

They all quietly sipped their drinks. It wasn't a very hopeful message from a witness to their times.

"So," Scott interrupted the silence. "Who died?"

"*If* he's dead," JC responded. "His name is Ronny Schwartz."

"Tell me," Scott asked. "Why would someone want to kill him?"

"I'm not sure," JC told him. "We haven't been on this story very long."

"Well, you're the Sherlock Holmes of television reporters," Scott declared. "Have you got a list?"

"A list of what?" JC asked. "Reasons to kill him? Including a list of people who would *like* to kill him? I suppose it's time to put a list together."

"Here's what I do. I like to walk around in the other guy's shoes," Scott told them. "Come up with a list of people *you'd* like to kill. And then ask yourself how you'd do it."

"You have a list of people you'd like to kill?" Robin asked with a horrified look on her face.

"Everyone has a list of some sort," JC said.

"*You* have a list?" she asked JC, raising her eyebrows.

"Relax," JC said. "It's a short list."

"Am I on it?" she asked in dread.

"Hardly ever," he responded.

"I'm on it occasionally?" she asked, alarmed.

"Occasionally is overstating it," he said. "Really, it's rare."

"Once a month?" she pressed.

"No, no," he said. He started laughing. "We're kidding you. No, I never think of killing you." Scott was laughing too.

"Do you expect me to believe that you *don't* have a list of people you'd like to see dead?" Scott asked Robin. "See, I'm giving you a break. I'm not saying you have to *murder* them. Maybe you'd like them to fall off of a skyscraper. Same end result."

"No!" she protested. "That's horrible. I certainly do not have a list of people I want to see dead!"

"Would you like one?" Scott asked. "Mine is unbearably long. If you'd take half, I'd consider it a favor."

JC, Scott and Milt enjoyed a loud laugh. They assured Robin that they were just having fun at her expense.

"You are awful people," she scolded them, but with a smile.

"So, how long are you staying at the Grand Geneva?" JC asked Scott.

"I'll be here long enough to enjoy the brumal scenery of winter in Wisconsin," he said.

"Well, I'll get to work on my list," JC told him. "Who would want to kill Ronny Schwartz? I'll give you an update the next time we bump into each other."

"I look forward to it," Scott told them.

They all pushed away from the bar, Scott picking up the night's tab.

"It's sad about Scotty," Robin said when she and JC had returned to their room. "He misses his wife."

When they were in bed and turned out the light, Robin slept that much closer to JC, careful not to let him slip away in the night.

9

"How, precisely, do you propose to solve my problem?" the politician asked the mysterious Mr. Knight when he called on a burner phone.

"If you want details, I can give you details," Mr. Knight responded. "But I don't think you want details. It should be enough that I overheard Mr. Kelly having dinner with his wife at a restaurant in Madison. I heard him list the targets of his next few investigations. You are one of those targets. That is what I thought you should know. And I can solve your problem."

"So, you are going to approach everyone whose name you heard?" the politician asked.

"Let us just talk about you," Mr. Knight responded. "You are my concern, at the moment."

"When would it happen?" the politician asked.

"Soon," Mr. Knight responded. "I am in your area now. That's why I am talking with you. These things usually take more planning."

"How much?" the politician asked.

"What is the value of your reputation?" Mr. Knight asked. "How much will you do to prevent your life from being ruined?"

"What am I going to do?" Amanda Taylor asked. "I can't hide forever. But Raff will tell them I was driving. And I wasn't."

"Senator Raff Swensen?" Quip asked.

"Yes," Amanda answered.

They sat in the living room of a Gulf Coast condo on the water in Florida. The curtains were pulled shut, even though they were on the second floor. Quip didn't think the curtains needed to be closed, but Amanda felt more comfortable that way.

Her family owned the condo. They were well-off.

"That's how I got my internship at the state capitol," she told Quip. "My parents had connections. Then I met the senator."

"How old are you?" Quip asked, sizing up the situation.

"Twenty-one," she answered.

"Was something going on between you and Senator Swensen?" Quip asked.

Amanda Taylor looked away. She faced the curtains as though she could see the Gulf on the other side of them.

"We were just having fun," she said as she began to cry. "Me and a few of the other interns. We hooked up with senators and they'd take us to nice dinners and out on boats and to nice resorts."

"So, the night in question," Quip said to her. "Who was driving the car?"

"Raff was," she quickly answered.

"Senator Swensen," Quip clarified. Amanda nodded in agreement.

"And what happened?"

"We were driving on a dark road near the exit for the ski area," she answered. "It was dark. There was someone walking along the road. I saw him but I don't think Raff did. He never even touched the brakes. He hit the person hard with the fender of our car. The guy just disappeared."

"Why didn't the senator see the pedestrian?" Quip asked her.

"He was sort of busy," she said, smiling and then not smiling.

Quip waited.

"He was, um, fondling me," she said with restraint.

"Where were his hands," Quip asked.

"His right hand was on my breast," she said. "Under my bra."

"While he was driving?"

"Yes," she told him. "Then we hit the man."

Her voice trailed off as she recounted the impact.

"Which fender of the car?" Quip asked. "Right or left?"

The question brought Amanda back into focus. She thought for a moment.

"The right side," she told him. "The side I was on. I was in the passenger seat."

"And what did the senator do then?" Quip asked.

"He said, 'Oh shit,'" she responded. "And then he took off. He went like a bat out of hell. He just wanted to get out of there."

"Did he call police?" Quip asked.

"No," she said. "He told me to keep quiet about it, not to say a word to anyone. He dropped me off at the resort where we were going to spend the night. We were going to go skiing the next day. But he told me to get a good night's rest and get an Uber back to Madison the next morning and he'd pay me back."

"And where did the senator go?" Quip asked.

"I don't know," Amanda answered. "He dropped me off in the parking lot. I had to walk a little way to the front door of the lobby. I don't think he wanted anyone to see the bent fender. I didn't see him again."

"He told you to say nothing, not to contact the police?" Quip asked.

"That's right."

"Did you see him at the capitol after that?" Quip inquired.

"Yes. He pulled me aside into a conference room that wasn't being used," she replied. "He asked me if I would say that I was driving the car. He said that he could take care of everything and that I wouldn't go to jail. But I refused."

"How did he take your refusal?"

"He got angry," she told Quip. "That's when I got scared. The next day, I came here."

"Florida."

"Yes."

Quip looked at his notes and the tape recorder that was running.

"Had you and the senator been drinking?" Quip asked. "Before the accident. Had the senator, specifically, been drinking?"

"Yes," Amanda told him. "We'd had dinner at a club. We had champagne. At least a couple of bottles, maybe more."

"How many rooms?" he asked her.

"What?" she said. "I don't understand."

"How many rooms had the senator reserved for the two of you at the resort that night?" Quip asked.

"One," she said. Her posture, sitting there on the coach, deflated like air being let out of a balloon. "One room."

On Christmas morning, JC and Robin exchanged small packages in their hotel room. They agreed to leave their real presents back in Denver, to be opened when they returned.

But in their hotel room overlooking the lake shaped like a Bunny, Robin opened the small box JC gave her. She pulled out a snow globe. She shook it and a blizzard ensued. And standing in the blizzard inside the globe was a reporter with red hair, holding a microphone.

"It's a reminder," JC told her. "If you weren't with me in Wisconsin, they'd have you out in a snowstorm on I-70 reporting on traffic jams."

Robin gave JC a present. It was a CD called *Ski Songs* by Bob Gibson.

"Bob Gibson was a folk singer in the 1950s," she said. "He recorded songs like 'Super Skier,' 'Bend in His Knees,' and 'Super Skier's Last Race.' They're really fun."

"Merry Christmas!" The waitress exclaimed. It wasn't Branch, but she commenced pouring coffee for JC, Robin and Milt.

"Merry Christmas," JC and Robin replied.

Holiday music played from speakers in the ceiling. The dining room was mostly empty.

"Where's Branch?" Milt asked. He did a poor job of masking his disappointment.

"I'm filling in for her," the young woman told them. "Branch gets to spend Christmas with her family in Lake Geneva. My name is Sheepy. Can I get you some orange juice or something?"

"You're not local?" Milt explored. "No one to share Christmas with?"

"No, I'm local. I'm from Elkhorn, not far from here," she told them. "I'll go visit my family when my shift ends. I'm part-owner of a café, but we closed it for today."

"Sheepy, what a great name!" Robin said.

"I grew up on a farm near Elkhorn," Sheepy explained. "I loved sheep. I still do! Everyone started calling me Sheepy. It's really Elizabeth. But most people don't even know that's my name. They know me as Sheepy."

Sheepy Johnson had red hair piled on top of her head in a bun. She was probably in her late twenties and her face was covered with freckles. She looked slightly odd, except when she smiled. That brought out a radiance.

"I like your red hair," Robin said with a smile.

"I like *your* red hair," Sheepy replied with a laugh.

Sheepy took their breakfast orders, Milt flirted with her a little, and she disappeared through the door to the kitchen.

"I thought you had your eye on Branch," Robin asked Milt.

"A good fisher isn't trying to catch a specific fish," Milt told her. "He casts his line in the water unsure which fish will bite."

"You're so romantic," Robin said sarcastically.

Sheepy emerged through the kitchen door with their orders.

"Are things slow right now?" Robin asked their server.

"They are," Sheepy told them. "It will pick up right after Christmas. By New Year's Eve, it will be pretty crazy."

"When is the busy season here?" Robin inquired.

"It's pretty steady," Sheepy stated. "The busiest time every year is in March, when thousands of *Dungeons and Dragons* fans come for a convention here. A lot of them are dressed in costumes. And they have games going on all over the building."

"That actually sounds kind of fun," Robin exclaimed.

"It is! Especially the costumes." Sheepy smiled. "There's also a big Soberfest here each year. People who have given up alcohol. It's huge."

Sheepy left them to their breakfast.

"Do you think she likes me?" Milt asked Robin.

"What about Branch?" Robin asked. "Women talk to each other, you know."

"Yeah, I don't like that," Milt said. "There should be a vow of silence."

"I think those only work in monasteries," Robin told him.

"So, what are we going to do today?" Milt asked JC.

"First, I'm going to give you this," Robin said, handing Milt a gift-wrapped package.

"What's this?" Milt asked.

"A Christmas present," Robin said. "Merry Christmas!"

Milt opened the package and found a hardbound copy of Harper Lee's *To Kill a Mockingbird.*

"It's about a lot of things," Robin said. "But part of it is about a good man. Something I think every man should aspire to."

"You think I can be a better man?" Milt asked.

"I think you *want* to be a better man," she told him.

"Thank you," he said.

The rest of the morning was spent on the telephone. Robin spoke with her father and her brother in North Carolina. JC called his brother and his sister. Milt was on the phone with his six-year-old daughter, Jayne.

"What are we going to do for the rest of the day?" Robin asked as she and JC sat in their room.

"We have the day off," he began. We should ski at Wilmot. Or we can do nothing. We don't do that very often. We won't work, but I do want to call the sheriff's office and see if there's anything new in the Ronny Schwartz search."

"That didn't last long," she pointed out. "That's work, you know."

The phone at the county sheriff's office was answered by a deputy who sounded like he didn't want to be working.

"Anything going on?" JC asked after identifying himself as a journalist.

"Just crimes of the day," the deputy reported. "Nothing much. A few domestics. And someone's furnace stopped working."

"They called you because their furnace broke?" JC asked.

"Yeah. I think they want us to come over and shoot it," the deputy said.

"Just a quiet Christmas," JC summarized.

"Mostly. The action is all up in Door County," the deputy said.

"What's going on up there?"

"Some Polar Bear Plunge for charity," the deputy told him. "But one of the shivering beauties submerged herself in the water and saw a body."

"A body?" JC repeated.

"Yeah," the deputy responded. "Divers pulled the poor guy out. You ought to call up there. Now *that's* a story. I guess that woman drank half the lake, screaming underwater. Just about drowned herself."

"Did you call your sheriff about this?" JC asked.

"I've got two years until I can retire," the deputy answered in a snarky tone. "And I'm going to get fired on Christmas Day for disturbing the sheriff at home?"

"Could this man in the water be the guy your sheriff is looking for?" JC asked. "The guy whose car was found empty up in Door County?"

The deputy was silent on the other end of the phone line. Then JC heard a click.

"Do you want to go over the river and through the woods for a Christmas ride?" JC asked Robin as he placed his phone back on the table.

"In a sleigh?" Robin said with glee.

"Someone already got slayed," JC told her. "I think we should drive up to Gills Rock."

It was a long drive to Gills Rock for JC, Milt and Robin.

"But traffic is light," JC pointed out with optimism.

"Everyone else is celebrating Christmas," Robin grumbled.

It was a longer drive than JC expected, nearly four hours up I-43 and then State Route 57. They listened to Christmas music as they passed through Milwaukee and Green Bay. JC apologized to his friends more than once for the long drive.

The welcome sign as you entered the unincorporated community of Gills Rock had a boat and a seagull on it. The coastal town was built for summer. It *endured* the winter.

It was at the northern tip of the Door County Peninsula. Gills Rock sat on a 120-mile stretch of Lake Michigan known as Green Bay. At one end was the hometown of the Green Bay Packers football team.

They were at the other end.

There had been a lot of shipwrecks off Gills Rock. The nickname of that particular body of water was "Death's Door."

A little collection of homes and boats belonging to commercial fishmen sat along the shore. The water close to land was frozen, but there was lots of open water further out.

The man's body had been removed by the time the journalists arrived at the lakeside community. But there was still a skeletal presence of sheriff's deputies.

Milt shot video of them.

And JC's fear that the long trip would be a waste of time evaporated as they found witnesses to interview. People who had been at the Polar Bear Plunge were still milling about the park near the beach. They were eager to tell colorful stories about their experience.

"The one who found him during the Polar Bear Plunge," an older woman told the camera, "she came out of the water screaming. She had fully submerged herself under the water. You know, to do it all the way. Then, she came to the surface shrieking! I don't think anyone paid much attention, at first. They thought she was just reacting to the cold water."

They approached a man in his forties. His adolescent daughter clung to him. JC introduced himself to the man and asked for an interview.

"Your name is JC?" the man asked.

"It is," JC answered with a smile.

"Happy birthday," the man said.

"That's another JC," the reporter responded.

"I'm so proud of you," Robin told him and looked at the other man. "He doesn't always admit that."

The man laughed. He asked if he could get his daughter on television. They said it was okay with them if he wanted her to stand alongside him.

"He was wearing ski boots," the man then said into the camera. His adolescent daughter stood in front of him with both of his hands on her shoulders. "He looked like he was wearing a suit and tie. But he was wearing ski boots. There's no mistaking ski boots."

"Ski boots?" JC asked, disbelieving.

"I know it sounds crazy," the man said. "But they were ski boots. I was probably ten feet away when they pulled him onto the beach."

Milt shot visuals from the beach where the Polar Bear Plunge had taken place. He shot the sand beach and Victorian houses that overlooked the water. There was a motel that looked like a lighthouse.

And everything was frozen. The wind came unobstructed from the north, the Upper Peninsula of Michigan and Canada.

The lake water, when it sprayed over its banks, had hardened on objects nearby. Benches, rocks and flagpoles had become ice sculptures. It was one of the few things that would draw visitors to town in the winter.

The sun set during their long drive back to Lake Geneva. Steam rose from the rivers that weren't frozen.

"If that is the body of Ronny Schwartz," Milt said, "then it wasn't an accident."

"No," JC agreed. They recalled witnesses saying that the body pulled from the water had ski boots on.

"I don't think you can swim wearing ski boots," Milt stated.

"Ugh, so he was thrown in the water while he was still alive?" Robin asked.

"It might surprise you what people can do wearing ski boots," Milt interjected. "There are guys intent on setting the world record for running the fastest hundred meters wearing ski boots. A German ran it in fourteen seconds and change. Then an American ran it in thirteen seconds and change. The boots weigh four or five pounds, and I can't even *walk* in them!"

"Why would someone do that?" Robin asked.

"Run in ski boots? Probably had to go to the bathroom," Milt suggested.

On Christmas Day, the Door County sheriff was not confirming that the body belonged to Ronny Schwartz, but speculation had begun. And the headline on the weekly newspaper there read, "Murder at Death's Door."

10

From the peak of the Mountain Top ski area, the lodge below was designed to look like two snowflakes.

Mountain Top was a five-minute drive from JC and Robin's room. The ski hill was built in 1968, part of the 1,300 acres that was then the Lake Geneva Playboy Club Resort and now the Grand Geneva.

It was 211 feet vertical with three chairlifts. But the expert runs were steep, with a quick acceleration from zero to thirty-five mph. In twelve seconds, you were back at the chairlift with a smile on your face.

"It's like only skiing the best part of a longer hill," JC said. "Over and over."

JC suggested they should go skiing on the morning after Christmas, because they worked well into the night on Christmas Day, traveling to and from Gills Rock.

"I'm not sure about this whole Hugh Hefner and Playboy thing," Robin said as they rode up a chairlift.

"You mean the propriety of it?" JC asked.

"Yes," she confirmed. "But everyone here seems to be grateful for the experience. They say it was a nice club."

"It's all history now," JC said.

JC and Robin enjoyed the short trip up the chairlift. The low December sun cast their shadows on the trees as they passed. There was a brief flurry. But the sun's reflection caused snowflakes to look like fireflies.

"It's really beautiful," Robin said.

A tele-skier sitting next to them said he belonged to "The Wisconsin Hoofers," a ski club at the University of Wisconsin.

"It was started by Norwegians in the 1920s," the man said. "Now, we have six-thousand members."

"It's Pineapple Powder," a snowboarder declared as he rode up the chair with them on the next trip. "I'm from Hawaii. Whenever it snows on me, it's Pineapple Powder."

"You came here to ski from Hawaii?" Robin asked.

"No," he laughed. "I live in Chicago. Most of the skiers in this part of Wisconsin come from Chicago. But the first time I ever skied was in Hawaii, on top of Mauna Kea."

"You can ski in Hawaii?" Robin reacted with surprise.

"Yeah!" the Hawaiian answered with a broad smile. "It can snow on a few spots in Hawaii. But the most snow falls on Mauna Kea. It's not steady enough to build chairlifts or anything. You drive to the top in something with four-wheel drive and then you ski down."

"Wisconsin is the speed skating capital of the United States," another snowboarder told them on another chairlift trip to the top. "Milwaukee often hosts the U.S. Nationals and Olympic time trials. Pretty much all the best long-track speed skaters come here to train."

JC and Robin stopped halfway down their next run to watch younger skiers running gates, training to race. The course was pushed to one side of the trail.

"Want to jump in?" a man said to them as they watched. He was eyeing JC's racing skis. "I see your gear. Those Fischer Slaloms are the best."

JC agreed. But he declined to join the gate training.

"So, these kids race for Mountain Top?" JC asked.

"They do," the man said. "It's a nice group of kids and parents, not like some other mountains. We used to belong to the Big Horizon race program. But the parents there were pretty cliquish. If you were not in their circle of friends, they made it pretty clear that they didn't want you to speak at their meetings. I got the feeling they didn't even *want* me at their meetings. They just wanted to collect my money. We pulled our kids out and put them here. It's much more fun."

JC, Milt and Robin ate lunch back at the Igloo, the bar that was off the main hall of the Grand Geneva Resort. The television was on. Quip Kelly was being interviewed after this latest triumph.

"Our great country has some work to do if we're to be as great as we say we are," Quip told the interviewer. "There is too much greed. Greed fueled slavery when our country was founded, and greed is still guiding too much of our politics."

"So, how do you pick the targets of your investigations?" the interviewer asked.

"It starts when someone gives me a tip," Quip responded. "Then, I figure out if the complaint is true or whether the tipster just has an axe to grind. I just try to separate the good guys from the bad guys. I don't care what their politics are or what political party they belong to. And I don't care *where* they are. I'm working on cases across the country now, not just Wisconsin. If they break the rules, they might get caught by Quip."

That slogan was becoming Quip's brand. His television show, now in production, was going to be called "Caught by Quip."

Quip Kelly had returned from Florida. His unmasking of Congressman Bat Bellows created quite a stir.

But Quip was already moving to a new hiding place. He felt he was only days away from getting his story on Senator Raff Swensen on the front page of his newspaper.

And it would come at a time when Senator Swensen was a growing commodity in political circles. Influential people were taking notice of him.

Swensen was a handsome fifty-two years old. He and his beautiful wife were young and hip, by political standards. He won re-election easily. There were even whispers about a run for governor.

His given name was Ralph. When he entered politics, Swensen changed it to Raff. He thought it made him sound younger and more energetic.

Quip's new hiding place was a lonely run-down, three-room house in Silver Lake. It was near the Wilmot Ski Resort. There was faded brown aluminum siding peeling off the front.

Inside, there was a bed in one room. A swayback couch sat in the living room with a table and chair near the front window. There was a soiled bathroom, and a kitchen with a dented refrigerator and chipped cabinets.

It was dirty and beyond saving. But the space heater worked, and Quip could spread out his notes on the table in the living room. No one would ever look for him there.

JC's live shot that night rehashed much of what they had said regarding the discovery of the body at Gills Rock. Their news director impressed upon them that hardly anyone watched the news on the night of Christmas, so it would be new news to them.

They were doing their live shots each night outside of the front door at the Grand Geneva Resort. JC stood with a large lighted arch in the background. It looked like a fortification left behind by the Roman Empire.

Snow was falling, making it a beautiful setting.

At the end of their workday, they drove a few miles to a place they could get brats and cheese curds for dinner. The atmosphere was local, and they were served with a smile. Wisconsin was a friendly place.

Returning to the vast lobby of the Grand Geneva, they found that the number of guests at the hotel was starting to swell. Christmas was behind them, and New Year's Eve was approaching.

JC and Robin retired to the Igloo and found more people there than they had been accustomed to. Milt said that he would join them after talking to his daughter on the phone. She was back in Denver, staying with the parents of Milt's dead ex-wife. The little girl's grandparents were not fond of Milt. But, after they lost a custody battle in court, they exhibited court-ordered tolerance.

JC went to the bar and was greeted by the barkeep from Poynette. She was middle-aged with dirty-blonde hair. She wore the company uniform, a brown vest and matching brown pants.

He asked her about local craft beers. She poured him something brewed in Milwaukee called a Lakefront Riverside Stein amber. He ordered a prosecco for Robin.

"Do you see many bear around this part of Wisconsin?" JC asked her as he looked out the window at the woods. "In the summer?"

"Not many around here," she replied. "But more than we used to. They saw two of them in Elkhorn over the summer. And up north, there are bear everywhere."

JC gathered up their drinks and returned to the table.

"Did you ever throw a boomerang?" Robin asked when he got back to the table. They sat on overstuffed chairs at a table in a dark corner. A boomerang decorated the wall over their head.

"Once," JC answered.

"Did it come back?" she asked.

"Not yet," he said. "But I keep looking over my shoulder."

"Ha-ha," she said, mocking him.

They sipped their drinks and watched the crowd. Some were on the dance floor in the middle of the room. The music was growing louder.

"It must be going well."

"What?"

"Milt's conversation with his daughter. It's been a half hour."

"He loves his daughter," JC told her. "She's his best friend. They're both about the same age."

"Is he crude around her?" Robin asked.

"He would say he is not," JC told her. "But, in a more innocent way, it's still crude. She'll have stories to tell when she grows up."

Robin finished her drink and held the empty glass in JC's line of sight. He rose and carved a path through the crowd, pushing past some dancers to get to the bar.

JC wondered if there had been a wedding. Many of the men on the dance floor wore sport coats without ties. Some of the women were dressed in gowns that plunged in both the front and back.

After paying for their refills, JC held the drinks high as he squeezed around the dance floor, hoping a dancer wouldn't knock the glasses from his hand. He saw Robin's red hair at the edge of the dance floor. Her back was turned to him.

He worked his way in behind her and pressed the cold glass of prosecco against her bare back.

"Oh!" she blurted. She jumped and spun to face him. It wasn't Robin.

"Oh shit," he said, realizing his mistake.

It was Shara.

"Oh shit," she said.

He looked over Shara's shoulder and saw Robin's eyes, trained on the two of them.

"Hello, JC," she said as she regained her composure.

JC choked.

Shara Adams Kelly was once the love of JC's life. They met in college on the ski team at Colorado State. He thought they would be married and ski off into the sunset.

Then she left him, without explanation. She got married and divorced.

He won her back when they crossed paths in Montana. Again, marriage seemed to be in the works. Again, it fell apart.

Now, she was married to Quip Kelly. And Robin was eyeing the two of them from her table in the dark corner.

11

Milt came down to the bar to join JC and Robin. He saw them standing by the dance floor. It was crowded. He squeezed between dancers to claim a spot behind his two friends.

"Wow," Milt shouted to Robin over the crowd. He eyed the low-cut back of her dress. "Are you sure you don't have that on backwards?"

The beautiful redhead turned to face Milt. It was Shara.

"Oh shit," he babbled. Some beer drooled out of his mouth.

"Hi Milt," Shara said with a patronizing smile. "I see you've been working on your social graces."

"Armsorrysherbeth," Milt replied, both choking and wiping the drooled beer from his chin at the same time.

"What are you doing here?" JC tried to ask casually. Then he peeked at the table where Robin sat, alone and captivated by the scene unfolding across the room. "Wait, I'm sure that Robin would like to hear this too. We should join her."

Milt was the first to arrive at the table where Robin sat. She had a forced smile on her face.

"Hey, Robin," Milt said. "You look a lot like JC's old girlfriend, Shara. Has anyone told you that?"

Robin's forced smile was frozen on her face.

"This is a lovely turn of events," JC said to himself.

He slid his chair as close to Robin's as possible and sat down. He put his hand on her knee and handed her the prosecco. Robin looked at him with that forced smile.

"I thought it was you," JC explained to her. "That's why I did that, with the cold glass and the exposed skin and everything."

"But it wasn't," she said in a tone too civil to actually be civil. "And I'm not wearing a party dress with a plunging back."

JC chose silence as the astute option of diplomacy.

Robin's eyes turned to Shara. A genuine smile formed on Robin's face.

"Hi Shara," Robin said. "It's nice to see you again. Pretty dress by the way. I love the color."

"Hi, Robin," Shara said with a smile. "Thank you. It would look great on you."

JC looked at the floor as the two stunning redheads spoke to each other like old friends.

"What *does* bring you here?" Robin asked innocently.

Shara looked around the room and then eyed all three of them.

"I shouldn't say anything," she cautioned. "But you won't blab, right?"

"I'm a reporter," JC stated the obvious in a disarming manner. "Who would I tell?"

Shara smiled at his joke.

"Quip, my husband, is doing his disappearing act again," she said.

"That's right," Robin remarked. "You're married to Quip Kelly. We love his work."

JC noted that Robin said "we." He didn't know if it was just reflex, since they were a "we." Or, he wondered, was Robin marking her territory, making it clear to Shara that *he* was a part of *her* "we."

"I'm really proud of him," Shara continued. "Anyway, this is where he came to disappear."

"A crowded bar?" Milt asked.

"Not quite," Shara replied. "But near here."

"Considering the people he's picking a fight with," JC said. "He's probably right about hiding. What's the saying? 'You're not paranoid if they're really after you.'"

Shara gave him a worried look. It was not lost on her that someone might try to harm her husband.

"Anyway, he knows I don't like it when he goes off alone for a month. I understand, but I miss him," she said. "So, he's trying something different. He got me a room here and he rented another place that's typical of where he usually hides out. He says it's a total dump and I wouldn't be comfortable there. But he slips through a side door here, each night, and we get to spend the night together and have room service breakfast. It's not perfect, but it's a big improvement over what we were doing before."

"Where are you two living?" JC asked. He spoke with Shara while keeping an eye on Robin. It wasn't a balancing act that he particularly enjoyed.

"We live in Madison. Here in Wisconsin," Shara said. "That's where Quip got his first newspaper job. I was in Montana, of course. I still owned the bar at the Grizzly Mountain Ski Resort. Quip came to Grizzly Mountain during one of his disappearing acts. No one in *Montana* knew who he was, so he could live normally while he worked on his next exposé. He came into the bar and that's how we met."

"How's Jumper?" JC asked. Jumper was Shara's black Lab. He and JC adored each other.

"He died over the summer," she said with sadness. "Poor guy. He got cancer. He had just turned ten."

"I am crushed," JC said honestly. "One of the best dogs of all time."

"He loved you," she told him.

"Are people nice when you go out together?" Robin asked. "Quip must make a lot of enemies."

"He's a rock star when we go out," Shara said with a smile. "True, some people dislike him. But the average Joe, the voters, love him for what he's doing. You *know* that there are politicians in every capital in the country who are taking advantage of their situation."

"Some of them play it straight," Robin pointed out. "Some of them just try to do a good job."

"Of course you're right," Shara answered. "But there are others who take bribes or cheat on their wives. And rarely does someone call them out. They get away with it! Quip doesn't let them get away with it. Most Americans love what he's doing."

Outside a big window by the bar, they could see the snow outside. It was coming down harder. Snow was covering cars and sidewalks and the rural roads that surrounded Lake Geneva.

The Grand Geneva Resort was going to have a good night, selling rooms to guests who just came for dinner or a drink and now wouldn't want to drive home through the storm.

One septillion snowflakes fall in the United States each winter. That's a one followed by twenty-four zeros.

The largest snowflake ever recorded, says the *Guinness Book of World Records*, was fifteen inches across.

Rain falls to the earth in a hurry. It drops at about thirty-two feet per second. Snowflakes take their time. The speed of a falling snowflake can be as slow as a single foot per second. Rain is autocratic. Snow is art.

Quip Kelly leaned over the table where all his notes and accumulated evidence were spread out. It was cold in the small house he rented.

He saw the snow piling up outside. He didn't see any snowplows. He didn't want to risk driving to the resort that night. He called Shara but was pushed to voice mail.

If he wasn't going to spend the night with his wife, he decided he'd continue working.

Quip had promised Shara that they would spend more time together after his story about Swensen hit newsstands. It wouldn't be long.

The light in the living room spilled out the window of the shabby house and into the countryside that was quickly being covered by a thick layer of snow.

"Who would be stupid enough to pose for these pictures?" Quip muttered to himself. The photographs captured Raff Swensen with his arm around two young women who were topless. They were all on a boat. One of the girls was Amanda Taylor.

12

"Ronald Schwartz, forty-one years of age, was discovered in roughly three feet of water in Gills Rock on the day before yesterday, December twenty-fifth," the sheriff announced. "The cause of death has been ruled to be drowning."

A news conference had been called by the sheriff. It was held at the Big Horizon Ski Resort in The Farmhouse. That was the Wisconsin corporate headquarters for Snow Hat and where Ronny Schwartz had first been reported missing.

Outside The Farmhouse, families were unaware of the tragic news. They glided down their small mountain and then rode to the top again.

It was Christmas week. Children didn't have school. Lift ticket prices were elevated to holiday rates, but more skiers and snowboarders came regardless of the cost. Time was harder to find than money.

The owner and CEO of Snow Hat and Big Horizon, Tillison Tucker, had come to Wisconsin. He joined the law enforcers in attendance at the press briefing.

"Ronny loved Wisconsin," Tucker said into the microphone on the table at the front of the room. "He insisted that Snow Hat have a presence here. While we are still a new member of this community, I can see that Ronny was right."

"Are you investigating this as a homicide?" a reporter in the audience asked the sheriff.

"There are aspects of this case that cause us to consider foul play," the sheriff answered.

"Like the ski boots?" another reporter inquired.

"We're not in a position to offer specifics of our investigation," said the sheriff.

"Are there any suspects, Sheriff?" a reporter shouted.

"There are no suspects that we're prepared to discuss at this time," the sheriff responded.

That meant there were no suspects, JC thought to himself.

"Is it true that he was found wearing ski boots?" another reporter asked.

The sheriff paused and looked toward his investigating officer. They probably had been debating just how much they wanted to release to the public. But that particular cat was already out of the bag. JC had aired an interview with a witness who said that he saw the deceased wearing ski boots when he was pulled from the water.

"I can confirm that," the sheriff said. "He was wearing ski boots on each foot."

"Was he otherwise dressed to go skiing?" JC asked.

Another pause as the sheriff and his subordinates looked at each other and communicated in some unspoken language.

"No," the sheriff said. "He was not."

"What was he wearing?"

"He was wearing a coat and tie," the sheriff disclosed. "And an overcoat."

"Were his hands tied?" a reporter inquired. "Was he bound up in any fashion?"

"No," the sheriff responded.

"Was he alive when he entered the water?" the sheriff was asked.

Another pause.

"We believe that he was," the sheriff said. "We would like to ask anyone who saw Mr. Schwartz anywhere between Kenosha County and Gills Rock, to please contact us. No matter how insignificant it may seem, we'd appreciate a call. Thank you. That's all we'll have to say on the matter, right now."

"Were there signs of a beating?" one reporter asked as the sheriff, his deputies and Tillison Tucker rose from behind the table and headed for a door behind them. The question went unanswered.

"Was he drugged?" a reporter shouted. That question also went unanswered.

"Could this have been a suicide?" another reporter asked.

The sheriff stopped and turned.

"We do not believe this to be a suicide," he said. He turned and left the room, closing the door behind him.

"Someone buckled him into ski boots and threw him into the water to drown?" Robin said. "What a horrible way to go."

"I would guess that someone took him out on the ice to the open water and tossed him in. In that cold, struggling to stay afloat with heavy ski boots on and an overcoat soaking up the water, he only lasted a short time before he slipped under."

"Wouldn't someone hear him if he screamed?" Milt asked.

"It's twenty-three miles from Gills Rock across the water to the state of Michigan," JC said. "So, it's over ten miles in each direction from the middle. Could someone hear *you* if you yelled ten miles away?"

"Poor man," Robin said. "Was he married? Did he have children?"

"Neither," JC told them. "He lived for his job."

"And maybe died for it," Milt added.

"Mr. Snow," came a voice behind JC. He turned and saw that it was Tillison Tucker.

"I don't believe that we've met," Tucker stated as they shook hands. JC introduced Milt and Robin to the tall businessman wearing cowboy boots and a Stetson.

"I *am* familiar with your work," Tucker said with a smile. "I believe you led police to the New York senator who was arrested at my ski resort."

"John Buford," JC said in confirmation.

"What's become of the senator?" Tucker asked.

"Still in prison," JC told him.

"That was a difficult winter," Tucker mused. "That poor woman from Vermont also died in one of our hotel rooms."

"Bitsy Stark," JC reminded him.

"Happily, I can report that those are not everyday occurrences at our ski resorts," Tucker stated.

"I'm sorry for your loss," JC said. "Mr. Schwartz was with you for quite a while."

"He was," Tucker agreed. "He was a friend and my most-trusted employee. He was from near here, just over the border in Illinois. He has no family in Colorado, so his family wants him buried in his hometown, Evanston. His parents and a sister still live there. I'll accompany the body to Evanston when law enforcement tells us he can go home. Hopefully in a day or two."

"Any thoughts on who would kill him?" JC asked. "Or why?"

"None," Tucker said. "It makes no sense. Maybe it was a robbery or a carjacking."

"Why was he sent to Wisconsin?" JC asked. "His office is in Colorado, down the hall from you, right?"

"He was in *my* office as much as his own," Tucker chuckled. "He was just here on routine matters, getting our new ski area up to speed. Nothing extraordinary."

JC and Milt proceeded to shoot an interview with Tucker on camera. Tucker mostly steered his remarks toward complimenting Ronny Schwartz, rather than speculating on who took the man's life.

"Are you going to do any skiing at your new resort while you're here?" JC asked, making small talk after the interview was over.

"Maybe I will," Tucker said with a smile. "I don't get out enough. I think I'll do that."

Tucker took his leave while Robin helped Milt break down his lights and tripod.

"So that was Mr. Bigshot, huh?" a woman said, standing in the doorway that Tucker had just exited through. "You're that newsman from Colorado, aren't you?"

JC confirmed her suspicions and introduced Robin and Milt. The woman looked to be in her forties. She had dark hair and looked like she had just been to the hair salon. She wore a fleece vest and a turtleneck. The vest was embroidered "Big Horizon Ski Racing."

"They catch anyone for killing that other Snow Hat guy?" she asked.

"No," JC said.

"Well, good riddance," she said. "They're ruining this place."

"And your name is?"

"Linda Smith," she said. "I'm vice president of the ski racing program here." She said it as though that position came with a lot of gravitas.

"I've seen your kids out gate training," JC said to be nice. "Some of them look very good."

"Well, some of them aren't as good as they think they are," she said in a snide voice.

"How so?" JC asked her.

"The new rules," she said. "The new people. Some of them just show up and think they should race for the top group."

"Are they faster than the other kids?" JC asked.

"How fast they are isn't important," she said.

When it came to racing, JC thought, how fast a skier raced kind of *was* important.

"I work my butt off for this club," Linda Smith told him. "I arrange the bake sales to pay for the ski jackets and these vests. The board and I arrange where we race and where we stay when we race. We put a lot into this club. My kid deserves to race in the top group. Everything was fine until someone complained and Snow Hat gave us new rules to follow. Some of those parents are just out to get my kid. I really hate those Snow Hat guys. They should all go back to Colorado."

JC would write Linda Smith's name down as soon as they parted company. He excused himself and caught up with Milt and Robin at the car.

"Do we have breaking news?" Milt asked sarcastically. "Are the eighth grade skiers picking on the smaller skiers?"

"I think we'll leave it alone for now," JC answered. "There goes your Emmy."

"She was kind of grumpy, wasn't she?" Robin said.

"Yep," JC agreed. "Remember that parent we talked to whose child used to belong to the Big Horizon ski team?"

"Yes," she recalled. "He said it wasn't fun because of some of the parents. Kind of a clique, I think he called it."

"I think we just met the very woman he was talking about," JC speculated.

A pickup truck with a shovel on the front was plowing the parking lot as they left Big Horizon. And there were dozens of rogue footpaths, packed down by ski boots, through the new snow.

On the way back to the Grand Geneva Resort, Robin looked out the window of their rental SUV at people shoveling their driveways. Some wore old ski goggles and ski gloves as they pushed shovels and snowblowers across the asphalt. One used an old tractor with a plow on the front.

"Do you think Tillison Tucker knows what Ronny Schwartz was working on when he was killed?" Robin asked.

"Of course," JC said. "And I don't know why he's lying to us."

13

"**Y**ou came!"

Sheepy seemed delighted to see them inside her restaurant. She held a pot of coffee in her right hand.

"Welcome to Rainbows," she said. "Our restaurant is owned and operated by the LGBTQ community. I am a co-owner. That's my partner over there, Cyndi."

Sheepy pointed at another woman, serving a table in the corner, a beautiful Black woman with dark skin and dreadlocks.

"Do you want to know something?" Sheepy asked and then told them without waiting for an answer. "The oldest existing gay bar in the country is just up the road in

Milwaukee. It's called 'This is It!' A lot of us call it 'Tits."
She laughed and departed to get them menus.

JC, Robin and Milt sat at a table by a big window looking
out on Lake Geneva. The frozen body of water was just
across Wrigley Drive.

The sun was breaking through the clouds. It glared off
the crystals left by the new snowfall. Business owners had
dutifully shoveled their sidewalks first thing in the morning.

Rainbows restaurant was decorated with rainbows on
every wall. There were more rainbows on the storefront.
The colorful display stood out in a line of restaurants and
bars on either side of their building. It was a prime spot. The
beach was just across the road.

Sheepy came back to take their lunch order. Her red hair
was piled in a bun on the top of her head, the same working-
woman's hairstyle as the last time they saw her. She bit her
lip as she wrote down their orders.

Milt asked her about Christmas and followed with a
couple of semi-personal questions before Sheepy left to
place their order.

"My gosh, you're hitting on her," Robin said.

"I think she digs me," Milt said with a confident smile.

"The restaurant is named Rainbows," Robin reminded
him. "Sheepy told us it is owned by the LGBTQ
community, and she's a part-owner."

"She just pointed out her partner, Cyndi," JC added.

"I know," Milt responded. "You're my partner."

"I'm not your partner," JC said softly and solemnly.
"There's nothing wrong with that, and I'm flattered."

"Milt, honey," Robin said and gently put her hand on
top of his. "She just informed you that she prefers to be with
women."

"That doesn't mean she isn't into me," Milt said after thinking a moment.

"It kinda does," Robin told him. She gave JC a looked of bewilderment. He returned the confused look.

"Besides," JC said to him. "You're old enough, she could be your daughter."

"No," Milt protested. "My daughter is six years old."

"That's because you already slept with a girl who could have been your daughter," Robin schooled him.

Milt looked out the window and gave all this some thought.

Lake Geneva's mansions and country estates had bubblers to keep the water from freezing around piers and boat houses that couldn't easily be removed from the lake. The first ice fishers of the season were just bringing their huts onto the ice for the winter.

Looking up the shoreline, you could see some of the Gilded Age manors on Snake Road. The common explanation for the road's name was that it snaked along the shoreline. After a few beers, some said it was where all the rich snakes lived.

"One of the estates recently sold for thirty-two million dollars," Sheepy told them after bringing their food. "It has thirteen bedrooms, thirteen fireplaces and a boathouse. The mansion looks like the White House, only it's red brick."

In Lake Geneva, the Wrigleys were neighbors to the Maytag washing machine family, who were neighbors to movie stars, who were neighbors to founders of great Chicago banks.

"A man who lives in one of the mansions spent one million dollars on his birthday party!" Sheepy informed them. "And the artist, Claude Monet, visited here."

They turned their attention to their food as Sheepy walked back to the kitchen.

"I don't know where you parked," a mysterious voice said from the next table. "But if your car is in those angled parking spaces by the water, if you park over the line, it's a twenty-five-dollar ticket."

"For parking over the line?" Milt exclaimed.

The man at the next table was sitting alone, looking at them. He wore an EMT's uniform.

"Tourists can be the pits," the man continued. "But so can some of those people up in the Queen Anne estates."

"Give us some dish," Robin urged him with a broad smile.

"You'll need a big spoon," the man smiled back. "For all the dish I can give you."

"GET OUT OF HERE, YOU FUCKER!"

The shouting came from another end of the restaurant. It was Sheepy's voice.

She was screaming at a man who sat by himself at a table. Blond hair and good-looking, the man's eyes grew with his embarrassment.

"Get out of here!" Sheepy yelled at him. Her pale freckled face was red and wet. "You're the asshole who thinks we're perverts! Get the fuck out of here!"

The man slowly rose from the table and walked for the door.

"I'm sorry," he muttered.

"I know who he is," Robin said to JC and Milt. "Isn't that Bat Bellows? That's the congressman who was just caught saying all those rude things about gays and lesbians."

"Wow," JC said. "Good eye. Quip just went public with Bellows' emails, calling the LGBTQ folks all sort of names."

There wasn't a peep inside the restaurant. The sound of Bellows closing the door behind him resonated like a gunshot.

Then, a smattering of applause broke out from some of the restaurant's tables.

"Way to go, Sheepy," a customer said.

"Thanks, Sheepy," another told her. "He deserved that."

Sheepy now stood over the empty table. She looked emotional. Her pale face was still red. Cyndi came over and gave her a hug from behind.

"You did good, honey," Cyndi whispered in her ear.

"Sorry," Sheepy said in a quiet voice to her customers as she lifted her head slightly to look at them and walked back to the kitchen.

"Well, my gossip will have to wait," the EMT said from the table next to Robin, JC and Milt. "I can't top that."

He rose and walked to the exit. As he moved past the big windows, he pulled out his cell phone, eager to tell his friends what just unfolded at Rainbows.

That night, on Denver's evening news, JC was live and provided details of Ronny Schwartz's unsolved murder.

It was Friday night. JC and Milt would have the weekend off. Robin's vacation would end after New Year's Eve.

They walked into the Igloo Lounge and took the table with comfortable chairs in a corner. A television over the bar had the sound up. The bartender and a customer were watching Halley O'Brien's show, "The Snow Report." Halley's brand of humor had them laughing.

"Did you catch the rabbit yet?" a booming voice inquired of the journalists. It was Landover Scott. He was standing over their table.

"Which one?" JC asked with a smile. "There are so many rabbits, I feel like a greyhound at the dog-racing track in Loveland."

"That's not open anymore, is it?" Scotty asked.

"Nope," JC said. "I think there's a hospital on that spot now."

They made room so Scotty and a woman alongside him could also sit down. JC thought the woman appeared to be from Scotty's era, probably in her seventies, still attractive.

"This is Ruth Kilde," Scott said. "But call her Bunny."

"Bunny? How fun!" Robin laughed.

"That's been my nickname since I was twenty-five," the woman laughed. "That's when I got a job here as a Playboy Bunny."

"Really!" Robin expressed. "Give us the scoop."

"You'll probably be disappointed. It was a lovely place to work," Bunny said. "Lots of fun. But there wasn't any debauchery. We weren't even allowed to go on dates with the customers! They were strict with us."

"How did you get the job?" Robin asked.

"I was a small-town girl," the woman explained. "I needed a job, like everybody else. I lived down the road in Burlington. I asked them for work, they said 'okay,' and they taught me the Bunny Dip."

"That was the way Bunnies were trained to lower themselves to table level, to serve food and drinks?" JC asked.

"Yeah," she laughed. "It was so we wouldn't fall out of our costumes!"

"My wife and I met Bunny when we used to come here," Scotty said. "Bunny and I have been friends for decades."

107

"His wife was a wonderful woman," Bunny said. "Such a dear." Scotty gave her a smile of thanks.

"Are there any other former Bunnies living around here?" JC asked.

"There are three or four of us," she said. "They have an annual Bunny reunion here. That is a hoot! We have a lot of laughs, a bunch of old Bunnies."

JC and Milt got up to buy another round of drinks. That left Robin alone with Landover Scott and Bunny.

"I hear there's some bad paper going around," he said.

"Bad paper?" Robin asked.

"That was one of the old terms for counterfeit money," Scotty laughed. "Actually, I'm hearing about fake lift tickets at one of the ski areas."

"Really?" Robin said. "I'll have to keep my eye out."

"It's not a big deal," Scotty said. "I'm just making conversation."

JC returned with wine for Scotty and Bunny and a prosecco for Robin. JC drank a smooth, fifteen-year-old Glenfiddich. Milt had a Schlitz.

"There used to be a swimming pool next to where you have breakfast," Bunny said, pointing in the direction of the café.

"Really," Milt said, consuming every word the former Bunny uttered.

"And they used to have a recording studio on the grounds," she told them. "Some big stars used to sneak in here to record, like David Bowie, Nine Inch Nails, and John Mellencamp."

"Oh my gosh," Robin said to JC as she clutched his arm. "That man over there. Isn't that Bat Bellows?"

The congressman looked like he hoped not to be recognized as he slipped into a seat at the bar.

"Stars used to pop out of the woodwork here all the time," Bunny said. "Is he famous?"

"Infamous," Robin told her.

"Well, we had those too," Bunny laughed.

Landover Scott took an interest in the fellow identified as Congressman Bat Bellows. JC told him about the incident that day at Sheepy's restaurant.

"Good for her," Scotty said.

Bellows was trying to hide his face behind a Packers ballcap and sunglasses at nighttime.

"People have always come here to hide," Bunny said. "It must work, because they keep doing it."

"I'm going outside for a smoke," Scotty told them. Bunny said that she'd join him.

"Can I give you a few sawbucks?" Scotty asked when JC scooped up the bill before the older journalist could.

"A few what?" Robin asked, giggling.

"Sawbucks," Scotty repeated. "Ten bucks. Well, a sawbuck is ten bucks. I offered him a few, that's three. That would cover the drinks for me and Bunny."

"Sawbucks?" Robin repeated.

"Go ask your grandmother," he teased as he and Bunny rose from the table. "I want a cigarette."

"I'm going with them," Milt said as he got out of his seat. "I want to hear more of Bunny's stories."

That left JC and Robin alone at the table. She stared at him.

"What?" he finally said.

"Do you want to see her?" Robin asked.

"Who?" JC said, looking around the room and wondering who Robin had spotted.

"Shara," Robin stated. "I mean, it would be natural to want to see her after all this time. She probably wants to see you too. Maybe you still have feelings for each other."

"Oh," JC said with dread. "I guess I knew that we were going to have this talk. No, I don't need to see her. I'm with you. I'm right where I want to be."

"You said you don't *need* to see her," Robin told him. "But I asked if you *want* to see her."

"Honestly, I don't think about her," JC insisted. "I think about you."

"I wouldn't stand in your way," she said. "If that's what you want, you should go to her."

"Why are we having this conversation?" he asked her. "Listen, do you remember the first time we kissed? We were in Lake Placid. You amazed me from the start. You have amazed me ever since. You have always been there for me. I don't ever want to be anywhere without you. I am crazy in love with you."

She smiled a sweet smile and put her hand to his face and kissed him.

"But if you want to be with her," she said, with a smile that he couldn't quite read.

"I could use a drink. Would you like a drink?" JC interrupted. "Or should we go to the room?"

She gave him another kiss and looked at him seductively.

"I love you too," she said. "Let's go to our room."

14

"I remember, like it was the death of my own child."

Tipper Jones nursed a can of Miller Lite. He held it in hands with dirt under cracked fingernails. He stared into the past.

"I couldn't turn down the money," Jones said, full of reluctance. "I would have lost her anyway. I didn't have any choice."

Jones was dressed like he was about to work on a broken snowmobile. He wore layers to keep warm. Grime was pressed into the tan outer overalls. It would never wash out. Hard work put that grime there. He was never ashamed of hard work.

"We still did it old-school," he said as he spoke of the days when he owned the Fox River Runs ski area. "We survived by offering an affordable lift ticket and a place where kids were safe. Parents could drop them off on the way to work and know they'd still be there at the end of the workday when they came to pick them up. Everybody looked after each other."

A couple of years ago, Tipper Jones sold the Fox River Runs ski area and it became Big Horizon.

"My dad started the ski area. He ran it for almost forty-five years," Jones said. "I came aboard after leaving high school. Then I ran it for another thirty years. Dad didn't sell it to me. He gave it to me. It was like adopting a free dog at the pound. It was the most expensive free thing I ever got."

"Did you make any money doing it?" JC asked.

"You don't own a small ski area to make money," Jones answered. "You think you're going to make money, in the beginning. Then, you realize that you're just doing it to preserve a way of life."

It was Saturday. JC, Robin and Milt had the day off. They had decided to explore another of Lake Geneva's ski resorts.

The day started with breakfast at the café at the Grand Geneva.

"Good morning!" Branch Olson had chirped as she came to pour them coffee. "I hear that Sheepy took good care of you while I had time off for Christmas."

Robin informed Branch that they had lunched at Sheepy's restaurant in Lake Geneva.

"I heard about that," Branch said like she was singing. "I mean, Sheepy telling that congressman off. Good for her."

"Yep. What's your pin say, on your vest?" JC asked.

"Oh, it's the way they used to spell Wisconsin," she said, smiling. "It used to start with an "O." It was O-u-i-s-c-o-n-s-i-n." I think it was what French explorers wrote down when the Indians talked about this area."

"So, do you work here all year?" Milt asked. "If I came back on vacation this summer, would I find you here?"

Her eyes grew big, and she smiled.

"I pick up some shifts here during the summer," she told him. "And in the summer, I'm a mail jumper!"

"A mail jumper?" JC repeated.

"Alright, so this is how it works," she began. "It's easier to deliver mail by *water* to people who live on the lake than by driving the twisting roads. It's a lot faster on the water. So, each cottage or mansion on the lake has a mailbox on their pier. I ride on the mail boat, it slows down at each pier, I jump out and run to the mail box and stuff it with mail. Then I have to run back down the pier and jump back on the boat, because the boat doesn't stop!"

"Seriously," Robin asked. "This really happens?"

"Yeah! It's really fun," Branch said. "We can do the whole lake in two and a half hours."

"Do you ever miss the boat?" Milt asked. "Do you fall in the water, trying to jump back on?"

"I've never missed the boat," she smiled. "I fell down on the dock once. I cut up my leg, but I got back up and just barely got back on the boat."

Following breakfast, JC and the others headed to the Alpine Valley Ski Resort, near Elkhorn, where Sheepy told them she grew up.

Alpine Valley opened in 1964. It was similar in vertical and pitch to the other Wisconsin ski areas they had visited. Only, Alpine Valley had more trees. It was more…alpine.

The ski lodge and a hotel there were built Bavarian-style. There was gingerbread trim everywhere. The little faux-Bavarian village greeted skiers and snowboarders when they pulled into the dirt and gravel parking lot. This was a weekend, so the parking lot was filling up.

"I'll see you in the bar after you have your little fun," Milt said and departed.

JC and Robin adhered the blue-striped lift ticket to a metal wicket they hung from a zipper of their jacket and proceeded to the chairlift.

"Old-school," JC remarked of the lift tickets. "I kind of like it."

"Fun souvenirs," Robin agreed.

Riding up the chairlift, they passed a tree where a dozen colorful strings of beads and some bras hung from the limbs.

"A bra tree," JC noted. "A staple of American ski areas."

"Do you think they remove their bra when they're passing the tree and just toss it?" Robin asked.

"*You* would have a better handle on the logistics than I would," JC told her.

"They probably stuff an old one in their jacket when they leave home that morning," she said.

"That's what I would do, if there was a men's underwear tree," he said.

"That would be gross," she grimaced. "Like whitey tighties? Blech."

They took a ski run that lasted twenty-nine seconds and arrived back at the chair lift.

"I'm a backcountry skier," one young man said as he rode up the chairlift with JC and Robin.

"Are you backcountry skiing today?" Robin asked curiously.

"No," the man said seriously. "It's all lift laps in Wisconsin. But you can go green some places around here."

"And 'going green' means to the uneducated?" JC asked with a smile.

"Tree skiing. Happy New Year!" the man said, arriving at the top of the hill and pushing away.

Following their next run, a snowboarder joined them on the chairlift.

"Does my face look like roast beef?" he asked, turning his face toward them.

JC was speechless. Robin gave it a try.

"Maybe honey-roasted ham?" she suggested.

"Yeah," the boarder agreed. "I took a spill. I scraped off my good looks."

At the top of the hill, he wished them a happy new year and went his way.

"We need to work on our ski lingo in Wisconsin," JC said to Robin.

On their next lift ride up, it was just the two of them. JC remembered something and looked over his shoulder at the bottom of the hill.

"Do you want to see something weird?" he asked her.

"What gal doesn't?" she replied with a smile.

They arrived at the top of the lift and he told her to follow him. They skated to the precipice of the hill.

"See that place down there?" he asked, pointing in the direction of a large structure. "That's an outdoor stage, a music venue. In 1990, the great blues guitarist, Stevie Ray

Vaughn, performed at a concert there. Then he hopped on a helicopter to fly to Chicago. But there was thick fog and his helicopter crashed into this hill. He was killed."

"That's really sad," Robin said. "This better not be a joke."

"It's not a joke," JC told her. "It is sad."

After one more run, JC and Robin skied to the lodge, grabbed their boot bags and joined Milt in the upstairs bar. It was called the Valley View Lounge.

Milt had saved them a table. He sat there eating cheese curds and drinking a Leinenkugel Bock.

That's when and where they crossed paths with Tipper Jones.

"Lake Geneva is like Summit County in Colorado," Milt said. "They've got ski areas all over the place."

"On a different scale, yes," JC agreed. "There's a bunch in Michigan too."

"Wisconsin has the third-most ski resorts in the United States."

That was how Tipper Jones engaged them in conversation from a seat at the next table.

"We're tied with Colorado," he added. "We both have thirty-one."

They learned that Jones was the former owner of the ski area that was now Big Horizon. They stayed to listen to his story.

At their invitation, Jones joined them at their table and snacked on cheese curds. JC and Robin ordered a local beer called Spotted Cow.

Tipper Jones turned out to be a born storyteller. He had a friendly face, despite being beaten red by the wind and sun. A sparse beard covered his chin.

"You don't make money running a small mountain ski area," Jones lectured them. "You'd have a better chance of getting rich if you played the lottery. But you know what you do?"

"What do you do?" Robin asked.

"You do it anyway," he said. "Because people in town want something to do. They want somewhere to work. I had a guy driving one of the groomers. He was seventy-five years old. What do you think happened to him when Snow Hat bought the place? He got a pat on the head and was sent home."

"And you regret selling your ski area now?" JC inquired.

"I had to do it," Jones told them. "The cost of snowmaking, the cost of insurance, the cost of everything."

"And you choose to drink here at Alpine Valley instead of the place where you grew up?" JC asked.

"Yeah, I guess I do," Jones said. "Maybe it hurts a little to see what they've done to Fox River Runs. They're ruining the place. I like this place better."

"So, what are you going to do with all that money you got for selling it to Snow Hat?" Robin asked.

"I have plans," he said proudly. "Plans that will knock your socks off. I'll tell you some time, but not now."

"Holy crap!" exclaimed Milt.

They looked at Milt for an explanation. He just gestured to a woman walking a few tables away.

It was Sheepy Johnson. Her red hair hung down below her bare shoulders and she was wearing a cocktail dress. The awkward woman with her hair in a bun had vanished. She was stunning.

"Sheepy!" Milt yelled.

She turned and smiled and worked her way over to them. She said that Cyndi was taking her out to dinner. They had just stopped by Alpine Valley for a drink. Cyndi wanted to celebrate Sheepy's brave scolding of Congressman Bellows the other day.

She gave them a smile and a wave and left the bar, with Cyndi at her side.

15

One man's ruins would build another man's castle.

Quip Kelly's popularity was growing. He was climbing up the stacked bodies of politicians whom he had taken down.

The crusading newspaperman was becoming a phenomenon. And that made him a growing commercial product.

Shara became his gatekeeper. She kept an eye on his popular social media accounts. She responded to fans with a thumbs-up or a heart, on Quip's behalf.

Quip wasn't very interested in the daily internet discourse with his legion of fans, but Shara answered their questions and comments. If she was stuck for an answer, she would consult her husband.

But Quip's chief concern remained his initial mission. He saw himself as the journalist who could turn the tide against greed and hypocrisy in politics. He thought that public servants used to be better than this. He wanted them to be better again.

His wife told people that Quip was a "regular guy." He found fame flattering, but beyond that, not very interesting.

The sun was dawning on a new day. He took one more sip of coffee and rose from his chair by the window in their hotel room that looked out over the Bunny-shaped lake.

"Back to the rock pile," Quip told Shara.

She was disappointed to see the time of day arrive when her husband would leave her to return to the shack where he worked, even on a Sunday. Quip told her he would be back in time for dinner.

Shara thought that she might go skiing. She was also toying with another idea, introducing JC to her husband. She thought they would have a lot in common.

After kissing his wife, Quip climbed into his car in the parking lot of the Grand Geneva. He was headed for his hiding place.

"I don't live in a cave," he recently told an interviewer on television about his occasional disappearing acts to work on a story. "I just go somewhere you don't expect to find me. I can still go out to dinner. Most of the time, I can still sleep next to my wife. I just live in the shadows for a while."

He stopped at the nearby Piggly Wiggly supermarket to pick up cheese curds for lunch and a large coffee.

Fox River Road was busy. Skiers were headed for their small mountains. He didn't look to see if anyone on the road was following him. If he had, he might have noticed.

Quip drove toward the tiny community of Wilmot, near the ski area. He passed the high school and the ·dirt track where they raced cars in the summer. And he passed the Kenosha County fairgrounds.

He passed the turnoff to his rental house and drove south. Before long, he crossed the border into Illinois.

Quip consulted a piece of paper with directions written on them. He had received a tip.

Taking a right on a nondescript rural road, he pulled up at an abandoned barn and two outbuildings.

The roof of a farmhouse on the property had caved in. Scorch marks gave Quip the impression there had been a fire a long time ago.

He looked at the barn and the pair of smaller sheds, faded gray by time and the weather.

Getting out of his car, he looked in the barn first. It was empty. He walked in and watched dust dance in the light that squeezed between slats of the wall. The building still smelled like manure.

He stepped back outside to check the sheds. They were each the size of a two-car garage. The first shed was filled with everything one might find on a farm. A flatbed with flat tires, cans, buckets and attachments to work the soil. Everything was rusty and it all had more things piled on top of it.

The second shed had a newer sign that read, "Do Not Enter." There was a chain and a padlock on the door. Quip walked around the side until he found a dirty window.

Rubbing the dirt off with his sleeve, he peeked through the glass.

"The smoking gun," he said to himself.

There was a car, late-model and recently washed. But on the right front fender, the paint was flaked and there was a significant crease in the metal.

By breaking the glass of the shed's window, Quip had been able to lean in and take clear pictures of the dented fender. He wasn't officially trespassing, he could explain, he had merely leaned in an open window.

Now, heading back to his temporary home, Quip's mind went over the short list of things necessary before he sent his story to the newspaper.

As his car re-entered Wisconsin, he drove past modest homes and farm fields. A sign hung outside The Stage Stop Restaurant saying it had been open since 1848.

Quip glanced down 114th Street at the Wilmot Riverside Bar and Grill. He had come to enjoy visiting that humble tavern, from time to time, to have a beer and get normal.

Taking a left and heading out County Route C, he passed a small airport and pulled into the dirt driveway outside of his rental. He called the house his "rent-a-wreck."

If there had been any concrete left where there used to be a sidewalk, it would need shoveling. But there wasn't, so his coming and going had pressed down the snow into a firm dirty white path.

Unlocking the door and pushing it in, some snow fell on the linoleum floor. He grabbed a paper towel to wipe it up. Old linoleum could get as slippery as ice.

It was a small house. The couch, the only comfortable place to sit, was only ten feet away from the front door that it faced. The upholstery was brown and it sagged in the middle. He threw his coat on top of it.

The journalist stood at the table and sifted through photographs. There was the one with the topless women. Another captured the senator with his hand under a table and on a young woman's bare knee.

"Leading the lamb to slaughter," he said to himself.

He stared at the photo of the two young women posing with Swensen. Quip would instruct the newspaper's photo editor to obscure their breasts and faces.

He pulled a new photo off a printer that sat on the table. The picture was of Swensen's car, hidden inside the shed with a bent fender.

In a few days, Quip thought, the photos would be paraded across the internet. That was the power of the pictures. This was going to be a public execution.

One last photo showed Swensen arm in arm with his wife. She was waving at the crowd at a campaign rally. The senator's wife looked at Raff Swensen with adoration.

The image brought Quip sadness. He looked at the senator's bio. It told him the couple had been married for two decades. Quip thought about the sacrifices she made to help elevate Swensen's career.

Either the senator's wife was a practiced actress, or she really was clueless to her husband's dalliances. Either way, Quip doubted that she deserved that kind of betrayal.

Of course, Quip thought, the first shoulder that Senator Swensen would try to cry on when he was caught would be his own wife's.

Quip thought about the sacrifices made by Shara, so that *he* could become a crusading truth-teller. He thought about his wife's loneliness. And sometimes, *she* had to endure the ridicule that came from *his* enemies.

He was happy that they were starting to see a tangible reward. Some serious money was promised. Many newspaper reporters weren't particularly well-paid. He was on the verge of becoming rich and Shara would be well taken care of.

Quip thought about what lay ahead when his exposé on Senator Swensen was published. His journalism had to be airtight, flawless.

His article would come under attack by those who felt threatened. His credibility would be called into question. But if the stories were airtight, if they were accurate, the accusers would fall silent.

The newspaper reporter worked past noon and decided that he wanted more for lunch than cheese curds. He put the package of cheese in the refrigerator, grabbed his coat and headed for the car.

Within minutes, he pulled up to the Wilmot Riverside Bar & Grill.

He greeted the man behind the bar as he climbed onto a stool. He ordered a beer and a hamburger.

Quip had told the bartender that he was a ski instructor at Wilmot Mountain, just down Fox River Road. He didn't want anyone knowing his true business.

The tavern was dark, but friendly. The walls were covered with pictures of cars racing at the nearby dirt track. He thought it was odd that he didn't see any pictures of snow skiers.

There were a handful of people sitting in the bar wearing ski gear.

"We go skiing for a bit," one man told Quip, "Then we get in our car and drive here for lunch and a beer, and then we drive back and ski for the afternoon."

Sipping his own beer, Quip thought about the photos lying on the table back at his rent-a-wreck. He didn't pay a photographer for the incriminating images. But he wondered if someone else did.

Somehow, pictures like that made their way to him. They showed up when they were slipped under his door, or placed in brown paper envelopes and left in his mailbox, or sent to his email.

Quip did enough research to confirm that the images were not phonies. One way to do that was to identify everyone in them, and be certain that the room and the circumstance were authentic.

New technology allowed so many pictures to be photoshopped, altered to serve one's purpose, and sent to unsuspecting voters. He had come to doubt the authenticity of any image until he had fact-checked it himself.

But employees who worked in state capitols weren't idiots. From the legislative staff to the maintenance department, they knew what was going on around them. Quip used those people to confirm his findings.

At the Wilmot Riverside Bar & Grill, Quip had his back to the rest of the room. He was minding his own business, eating his hamburger and drinking his beer.

One set of eyes, at a table across the room, rarely looked away from Quip's back. He was studying the journalist. He had been all day.

16

"Do you know that we used to have pink margarine in Wisconsin?"

Bunny, Landover Scott's friend, was quizzing JC and Robin. They sat in a sunken living room off the main hallway of the Grand Geneva Resort. The time had just passed five p.m., so it was wine-o'clock. They all enjoyed some red.

"Wisconsin saw margarine as a loathsome competitor with their true dairy products," Bunny told them. "So, the state banned any substance that looked like butter but wasn't actually real butter from the real milk of a real cow."

"So that banned margarine," JC concluded.

"Yes," Bunny told them. "Until a clever food company made *pink* margarine. No one could say anything pink looked like butter." She laughed.

"Is there any progress in the hunt for Ronny Schwartz's killer?" Scotty asked JC and Robin.

"No," JC told him. "I think the police are stumped on the motive. If they figure that out, then they can figure out who did it."

"It will be hard to catch someone if it was a random killing or a robbery," Scotty speculated. "Those were always the hardest, the ones that had no rhyme or reason."

"I agree," said JC. "But the ski boots must have been a message."

"Does anybody hate the fact that an outsider turned the ski area into Big Horizon?" Scotty asked.

"*Anybody?*" JC laughed. "There's a long line of people who resent Snow Hat's acquisition of that ski area. People don't like change."

"The sheriff should make a list," Scotty smiled. "Like I told you to do."

"I'm working on mine," JC said.

"I hear that Quip Kelly is getting ready to lower the boom on another deserving public servant," Scotty stated. "I wonder who he caught in his skivvies, this time?"

"In his what?" Robin asked.

"His skivvies," Scotty repeated. "That's underwear. Sorry, I sometimes talk in a language that will die with the people of my age."

"For the sake of argument, do you ever question whether Quip is going about it in the wrong way?" JC asked.

"Going about what?" Scotty asked.

"Catching the bad guys," JC said.

"Is there a bad way to catch bad guys?" Scotty asked. "Aren't we all better off the moment they're caught?"

"Normally, I believe that," JC said studiously. "And I'm not saying Quip is wrong. But it taps into the worst side of social media. He uses public ridicule to carry out the sentence. He embarrasses the target of his investigation to the point that there is no going back. No trial, no 'innocent until proven guilty.' The senator, or whoever, is shunned. He's ruined. His family sometimes abandons him."

"Yeah," Scotty agreed. "It's a pretty thorough scrubbing."

"On the other hand," JC said. "The targets Quip picks are people who *chose* to steal money or cheat on their wife. Life is about choices. Quip didn't force those guys to do something rotten, he just caught them doing it."

"But I know what you mean, JC," Robin offered. "We've all stumbled. Maybe we started an argument that cost us a friend. Maybe we broke a boy's heart. Maybe we stole cable TV."

"Neither of those are against the law, except the cable TV one," Scotty added. "Politicians are easy targets, these days. But aren't they supposed to be held to a higher standard? I've always thought that if a man will lie to his wife, then he won't have any trouble lying to people he barely knows, like taxpayers."

"True," JC said. "Those politicians chose to do the underhanded things they did. They shouldn't whimper, only because they got caught."

"But they do whimper," Scotty said with a smile. "And they blame the media."

"Yes, they do," Robin agreed. "When will people get wise to that tactic?"

"By the way, do I sense a guilty conscience?" Scotty asked JC.

"He tortures himself," Robin responded. "He works so hard to be fair. But he also feels guilty about every dog who died in his care. He still feels guilty for something he said to a friend in seventh grade. He has an amazing memory."

"A good memory can come in handy," Scotty told them.

"It's a blessing and a curse," JC advised. "Robin is right. I sometimes remember stuff that happened twenty years ago. And it still keeps me up at night."

"Do you remember the first United States president to be impeached?" Scotty asked.

"President Johnson," JC told him. "That's Andrew Johnson. Abraham Lincoln's successor."

"Yes, it was," Scotty agreed. "Do you remember which president shocked reporters by lifting up his shirt and showing off his fresh scar?"

"Same name, different president," JC responded. "That was Lyndon Baines Johnson. Almost one hundred years after Andrew Johnson. LBJ had just had his gall bladder removed."

"Good memory, indeed," Scotty declared. "Do you remember Bunny's first name?"

"Ruth," JC answered.

"How sweet," Bunny exclaimed. "You remembered!"

"A good memory can come in handy," Scotty smiled. "If nothing else, you can impress the girls."

"JC, can I speak to you for a moment?"

JC turned around to see Shara standing there. It was clear that she wanted to speak to him alone, apart from his friends.

"Sure," JC said, looking at Robin and climbing out of his seat.

They walked to the other side of the sunken living room where no one would overhear them.

"Can I get you a drink?" he asked.

"No. Thank you," she answered. "This won't take long."

Shara sat down on a chair and JC sat on a chair facing her.

"Would you like to meet Quip?" she asked. "I'm sorry that I'm being so secretive, but that's how it has to be, right now."

"I understand," JC said. "Where?"

"And I need it to be just you," Shara said. "It's nothing against your friends. He just needs to be very careful."

"I think I get it," JC told her. "When?"

"Is now alright?" she asked. "He just got back to our room. He's taking a quick shower."

"Yep. Now is okay," JC told her. "Does he need me to scrub his back?"

"That's my job, wise guy," Shara said with a smile.

JC and Shara returned to Robin and the others. JC explained that he had to go somewhere. He'd be back in less than an hour. He leaned over and kissed Robin.

"I'll tell you everything," he whispered into her ear. "When I get back."

"There had better not be lipstick on your collar," she whispered back to him.

Robin watched as JC and Shara walked from the room.

Shara led him down familiar hallways at the resort to Building Two. The hallways connecting the buildings were saving them from another cold winter night in Wisconsin.

"You're just down the hall from us?" JC asked with surprise.

"I guess so," Shara told him.

"It's me, hon," she said as she knocked on the door and then swiped a room key to let them both in.

Quip Kelly stood on the other side of the room. JC saw that he was a sturdy man. He looked like he worked out to stay in shape. He had a large jaw and brown hair that was neither short nor long.

"Hi JC," Quip said, reaching out as they shook hands.

"Glad to meet you, Quip. I admire your work," JC said. "We were just talking about you in the bar. Do you remember a great old reporter named Landover Scott?"

"I remember him," Quip said.

"We were just sitting with him, sharing a drink," JC said.

"Wow," Quip remarked. "I'd like to meet him sometime."

"That can be arranged," JC told him. "I thought you were in hiding."

"I am," Quip smiled. "But I only hide from the bad guys. I'm sure you'll keep our secret?"

"Of course," JC answered. "Though I should warn you, Landover Scott told me tonight that he heard that you're close to going public with the misdeeds of another politician."

"He did?" Quip wanted to learn more. "Did he name any names?"

"No. He didn't give me any specifics."

"Could you ask him to keep that under his hat?" Quip requested after giving it some thought.

"Sure," JC said. "I'm certain he can be trusted. Though, I can't speak for whoever told him."

"No, of course not," Quip answered. "Well, it will be over soon."

"If you don't mind my asking," JC said. "Where are you hiding when you're not hiding here in the lap of luxury?"

"My other hiding place is far from luxury," Quip laughed. "It's out by Wilmot."

"I hope you're not chasing Willmott's ghost," JC said.

"There's a ghost at Wilmot Mountain?

"No," JC smiled. "I just stumbled across the story when I was doing research on Wilmot. I came up with a story out of Seattle about a Willmott's ghost. It's the name of a restaurant there. It's named after a woman who used to sneak into the backyards of friends or public parks to plant flowers. They'd never see her. But when they saw the new flowers she had planted, they'd blame Willmott's ghost."

"That's a friendly ghost," Shara interjected. Until now, she had been watching the two men interact. It was a little weird, she thought, but they were the same man in many ways.

"Do you want to see what I'm working on?" Quip asked JC.

"If you think that would be alright," JC answered.

"You'll keep it quiet until I break the story, right?"

"Yes, I promise."

"Good," Quip clapped. "I question whether it is always good to work in a vacuum. I'd like to see what you think when I throw down my evidence in front of you. I'll tell you everything then. Give me one more day. Can you come, day after tomorrow?"

"I'll make a point of it," JC said. "You know, I had a great-grandfather who was a newspaperman. A bit of a muck-raker, I'm told."

"That's the best kind," Quip smiled. "Did you happen to meet him?"

"No," JC replied. "He lived in Upstate New York for a while, then he moved back to Scotland. His name was Clarence Julius Snow. His son, my grandfather, moved back to the United States."

"We should look him up," Quip said. "We should see what he was up to."

"That would be fun," JC smiled. "Let's do it."

They shook hands and JC departed.

Before returning to the living room where Robin sat with Scotty and Bunny, JC stopped by the bar. He sat on a chair next to Milt.

"Dare I ask what you're up to?" JC quipped.

"I'm talking with Paula," Milt told him. "The bartender from the town with the big horse."

The bartender, whose name was Paula Peterson, returned from a trip to the supply room with three bottles in her hands. She asked JC what he wanted to drink. He ordered a twelve-year-old Glenfarclas single malt Scotch whisky.

"Paula is a snowboard instructor at the Mountain Top ski area here," Milt told JC.

"You are all multi-taskers," JC said of the staff at Grand Geneva.

"Most of us grew up skiing or snowboarding," Paula said. "In high school, it was the dating scene. We skied or went snowboarding or went snowmobiling."

"That sounds like a fun winter to me," JC told her.

"It was," she responded. "But there wasn't much else to do. Summers are really busy around here. There are so many lakes. But in the winters, it's a really good place to hide."

JC was getting that impression.

17

Quip Kelly was out the door early the next morning. He wanted to look from afar at another target he was zeroing in on.

State Representative Vic Brown was attending a breakfast for disabled skiers in downtown Lake Geneva. Quip watched from afar, unnoticed.

Brown was a dashing figure, Quip thought. He wore blue jeans and a stylish winter coat with subtle colors that would photograph well.

His brown hair was about halfway to gray, but his smile made him look twenty years younger. The smile was both sincere and a little mischievous. Older women gazed at him and patted his hand when he walked by. On his finger was a ring with a red stone.

Quip had learned that Brown possessed a talent for steering tax dollars to charities of which he was the sole beneficiary. Brown's day would come, Quip thought to himself as he slipped out the exit.

JC and Robin walked into the hallway of Building Two, headed for breakfast. They nearly collided with Shara Adams Kelly as she was emerging from her room. She was carrying skis.

"I'm going to bring Quip some breakfast at his house and then do some skiing at Wilmot," Shara told them. "He was out early."

"Thanks for introducing me to him," JC said. "He's a nice guy."

"He likes you too," Shara responded. "I can't believe he invited you to his house. You gained his trust in a hurry. But wait until you see the shack he's rented. It's really disgusting."

The three of them stood in the hallway, smiling in silence.

"I'm glad you like him," Shara then said to JC. "I love him so much. This may sound strange, but I wanted your approval."

"We have a lot of history, you and I," JC said.

"Do you mind?" Shara said, looking at Robin. Then she leaned in and gave JC a kiss on the cheek. "You and I are both so lucky," Shara said to Robin.

Shara turned and walked down the hallway toward the stairs, her skis balanced on her shoulders and her poles held in her other hand.

While JC and Robin joined Milt at breakfast, Shara stopped to pick up a breakfast sandwich and coffee for Quip. He was on the phone when his wife pushed open the front door of his hideout.

"State police confirmed the make and model of Senator Swensen's car," Quip told her as he hung up the phone. He picked up the picture of the damaged automobile. "I'm meeting with them tomorrow. I'll tell them what I saw and where to find the car."

The drive from Quip's rental house to the Wilmot ski area took Shara all of five minutes. She located a parking spot close to the lodge and locked her skis to a rack.

Wilmot had been open for skiing since the 1930s. But the small mountain had been waiting for skiers to arrive for fifteen thousand years. It was a glacial moraine left behind by the Ice Age. The mountain had few trees on it and looked bigger than it was because it was surrounded by flat cornfields.

Shara was an excellent skier, with a racing background. She found that the short expert slopes wasted no time getting to the point. She enjoyed the steep plunge to the bottom. It was thrilling.

After a short chairlift ride, she was back at the top and ready for another plunge. It was fun, she thought. Wilmot did a lot with a little. She did lift laps until lunch.

She noticed the chairlift operators greeting many of the skiers by name. She sensed that the older lift operators worked at the hill winter after winter. She wondered if they didn't even watch the children grow into adults. Maybe they even watched those adults have children of their own.

Shara thought about children, about having some with Quip. She liked the thought.

From the top of Wilmot Mountain, she could see a great deal of Kenosha County. She saw smoke rising nearby. Probably a farmer burning debris. Maybe an old shed.

When she heard sirens, she thought the fire may have burned beyond its desired boundaries. What would we do without volunteer firefighters, she thought.

After buying a tee shirt at Wilmot's gift store, Shara loaded her skis and backpack into the car. She planned to visit a friend just over the state line in Illinois. She was surprised that it was so close. She'd be back in time for dinner with Quip.

"Have you been listening to your police and fire scanners?" It was Landover Scott's voice on the phone.

"Scanners?" JC responded. "I don't have scanners for Wisconsin. In my hotel room?"

"Oh, right," Scotty laughed. "I have an app on my phone that gets the local scanners. Some habits are hard to break. I slept with scanners on in my bedroom at home for thirty years. My wife learned to sleep right through them."

"What are you hearing on your scanners?" JC asked.

"There's a house fire in Wilmot," Scotty said. "Did I hear that Quip Kelly is renting a house out there?"

"You didn't hear that from me," JC said defensively. In fact, Scotty *hadn't* heard it from him. How, JC wondered, does Scotty get his information?

"Well, no matter," Scotty said. "But there's a pretty good fire burning out there."

"Where is the fire in Wilmot?" JC asked.

Quip had given him directions to the house, in advance of tomorrow's visit. It was by an airport on County Route C.

"County Route C," Scotty told JC. "By some little airport."

JC grabbed a coat and locked the hotel room door behind him. Robin was in Milt's room. They were editing footage for that night's live shot. He didn't disturb them.

The rental car swayed on the winding road that followed the Fox River. JC knew he was driving too fast. But he also knew that every available patrol car would be at the fire. There wouldn't be any law officers left to give out speeding tickets on Fox River Road.

He pulled up to a volunteer firefighter who was directing traffic away from that section of County Route C. JC couldn't even see Quip's house from there. But he could smell the smoke.

JC explained to the volunteer that he might have information important to the investigation. He needed to get to the fire scene.

The volunteer refused to let JC drive down the road. He tried again to explain. Again, the volunteer told him to turn around. He would not be allowed access to the fire scene.

JC drove around him.

He parked behind a white 4x4 Ford Interceptor with gold lettering declaring it was a patrol car belonging to the county sheriff's office.

On foot, JC walked toward the house. The fire was out. But he recognized the smell. He had smelled it before, sickly sweet like burned flesh.

A white tent had been erected outside the house in the front yard. There were a few evidence markers in the snow and on the road. Investigators concentrated on a spot where a car had parked.

"SIR!" The voice was booming, a no-nonsense voice.

"Stop!" the voice ordered. The deputy's bark would have stopped a herd of bison. "Stop right there!"

JC stopped. He had reached yellow police tape that blocked his advance up the driveway.

The stern deputy approached, carrying a clipboard. JC hoped he wasn't going to be hit with it.

"I was supposed to have a meeting with the man who is renting this house," JC said quickly. He didn't bother mentioning that the meeting wasn't supposed to happen for another twenty-four hours.

"Well, you're going to have to move back," the stern deputy ordered. "There's nothing you can do here."

Two figures in white hazmat suits brushed by JC and the deputy. Their outfits made a crinkling noise as they walked past.

"Whoever your boss is," JC said to the deputy. "He's going to want to speak with me."

"Alright," the deputy responded. "Leave your phone number with the man at the barricade of the *road* you were *not* supposed to come down. You'll be called at an appropriate time."

JC wanted to get into that house. He wanted to see what had happened in there.

"They're going to want to talk to me now," JC insisted. "Do you know who rented this home?"

"A Mr. John Adams," the deputy said, looking down at the clipboard. "That's what the rental agreement says."

"The occupant of that house was not the second president of the United States," JC said with a smile. "That house has been rented by Quip Kelly, the investigative reporter. You know, 'Caught by Quip?'"

"And if that's Quip Kelly," another booming voice asked. "Who does that make you?"

JC turned around to face a man in a thick trench coat. He wasn't tall but he was solid. He looked like he could make a formidable obstacle.

"I'm JC Snow. I'm a television reporter. Quip asked me to come out to look over the work he was doing."

"Is this his house?" the man in the trench coat asked, looking skeptically at the unsightly shack.

"He was hiding here," JC informed him.

The man considered JC's answers.

"I'm Agent Aurek Nelson," the man finally stated, without offering a handshake. "I'm with the state Division of Criminal Investigation. Come with me to the door. Do *not* enter the house unless you are told you may enter. Do you understand me?"

"Yep," JC replied.

"Deputy?" the agent said to the deputy, asking to pass.

"Certainly, Agent Nelson," the deputy confirmed and walked away.

The agent and JC proceeded past the white tent set up in the front yard. A dog was waiting for his turn to enter, pacing in the back of a car marked "State Fire Marshal."

The front door to the house was open. Only those in hazmat suits were inside, still collecting evidence.

Standing at the entrance, JC could see an incinerated old couch. At the foot of the couch, he could see two burned limbs. JC thought they were a pair of feet and portions of two lower legs. They still had shoes on.

It was a gruesome scene. Hands attached to portions of forearms laid on the couch. A scorched skull was perched on the back of the furniture.

"What the hell are you doing here?" a terrifying voice came from a man who had three stars on his epaulets.

"Sheriff," JC said nervously. "Have you determined who is renting this house?"

"What business is that of yours?" the sheriff responded tersely.

"Hi, Sheriff," the DCI agent then spoke up.

"Oh, hi Aurek," the sheriff said in a much friendlier tone and pointing at JC. "Is he with you?"

"For the moment," the agent informed the sheriff.

"It's not John Adams," JC said. He pointed at the incinerated body. "I can't tell who that is, but this house is being rented by Quip Kelly, the newspaper man. 'Caught by Quip?'"

The sheriff looked at the corpse.

"Oh shit," he said.

141

18

"Let go of me!"

There was a struggle going on, just across the yellow tape at the end of the driveway.

Sheriff's deputies, in their dark navy-blue jackets, were wrestling with a woman who was trying to push her way toward the house.

"I need to see him!" she screamed as she wiggled out of their grip.

JC turned to see Shara rushing toward the doorway of the house. He took three steps before she reached him, still running. She tried to push JC out of her way.

He caught her in his arms.

"I want to see my husband!" she screamed at JC.

"No, Shara," he said. "You don't want to go in there."

"I want to see him!" she screamed, crying.

"No, you don't, Shara," he said in a comforting voice. "Not like this."

JC gathered her into an embrace. She seemed to understand. A shriek forced its way out of her lungs and she sank to the snow-covered ground, sobbing.

A crowd had gathered on the edge of the road. Something like this didn't often happen in Wilmot, population 442.

Shara was led away from JC by two deputies and into a large mobile-command center that had arrived. It was black and as big as a tractor trailer, with two slide-out rooms.

"You!" a lieutenant sneered and gestured to JC from inside the fire scene. "In here," he commanded.

JC took a moment to prepare for the grisly scene he would be returning to and entered the house.

The air held onto the scent of smoke and burned flesh. A large fan on the floor was blowing the smoke outside. Those in hazmat suits moved about, studying things and picking things up.

JC glanced again at the charred corpse on the charred couch. There appeared to be no torso. It had vanished amidst the flames.

Looking around him, JC could see very little damage to the rest of the room. A bare table and wooden chair remained intact, untouched by the fire. Only the corpse, the couch, a spot behind the couch and a smudge on the ceiling were marked by fire.

"Strange, huh?" the DCI agent said to him. "The deputy state fire marshal says that with the door and the windows sealed tight, there was no oxygen to feed the fire. It ignited, burned the guy, and then was snuffed out for lack of oxygen."

JC remained silent. It was a shocking scene to survey around him.

"Quip Kelly, huh?" the agent asked. "Can you identify him?"

"I can't tell," JC said as he looked at the human remains. "Not like that."

"Not surprised," Agent Nelson answered. "Is that his wife out there?"

"Yeah," JC responded.

"We can collect a DNA sample. Maybe we can get a fingerprint," Nelson told him. "If it's him, we'll have a positive I.D. in very little time."

"Hi Kuzyn!" the deputy fire marshal greeted Agent Nelson.

"Hi Jakub," the agent said as they shook hands.

"We're both of Polish descent," Nelson explained to JC. "This is Jakub Williams. We're not cousins. There are a lot of Polish-Americans around here."

JC ran his finger down a wall. It was covered by a thin oily film.

"That's body fat," Deputy Fire Marshal Williams told him. "It's on the windows, everything. It's what happens in a fire like this. That's why his torso is gone. We all carry a lot of fat in our torso, a fire like this just cooks it until it disappears."

"Did he smoke cigarettes?" Agent Nelson asked JC.

"I don't know," JC told them. "You'll have to ask Shara, his wife."

JC was ushered out of the house by the same lieutenant who ordered him inside. Led back beyond the yellow ribbon at the end of the driveway, he was released.

Agent Nelson proceeded to the sheriff's mobile-command center, parked on the street in front of the fire scene.

Shara sat inside the mobile-command center. She had been given a seat and wrapped in a blanket and handed hot tea.

She answered their questions in a monotone.

"Quip doesn't smoke cigarettes," she told the same stern lieutenant who had escorted JC in and out of the house.

"How about marijuana?" the lieutenant asked. He held up a plastic bag with the remains of a joint.

"No," Shara told him.

"I just found this in an ashtray," the lieutenant told the DCI agent. "It looks like a roach, what's left of a marijuana cigarette."

"He didn't smoke pot," Shara told him, slowly moving her eyes to the bag of evidence. "Yes, that is certainly what that looks like." She smiled slightly.

"The fire marshal says that this fire looks like something started by smoking," Agent Nelson tried to tell her. His voice was more compassionate. "Are you sure? He won't be in trouble. And you won't be in trouble, if it's pot."

"Thank you," she said and tried to muster another smile. "No, he didn't like pot. He drank alcohol, but he didn't smoke anything."

The agent and the lieutenant exchanged puzzled looks.

"Is it possible that he kept it a secret from you?" the agent asked. "I've been married twenty-five years. There are a few secrets that I keep from my wife."

"It's possible," Shara said. "But I don't see how. I know what weed smells like. I wash his clothing. I have never smelled it on his clothing."

The agent and the lieutenant looked at each other again. Her answer wasn't going to change.

"Thank you, Mrs. Kelly," Agent Nelson said. "We're sorry for your loss."

The agent excused himself and headed back for the house.

"Can you find remains of a cigarette in the couch?" he asked the deputy fire marshal.

"I doubt it, Aurek," the fire expert said. "The couch burned pretty completely. A cigarette, or a joint, usually gets dropped onto the couch or between the cushions and it imbeds itself into the material. It smolders and burns. That generally destroys the cigarette. Once in a blue moon, we might find some plastic from the filter. But if it's a joint? What's going to survive a fire?"

"So, how do you rule smoking as a cause of any fire?" Nelson asked.

"Usually, the fire looks just like this," the fire marshal told him. "And we'll find a pack of cigarettes or some other indicator that he was smoking. And family members will confirm that he smoked."

"Well, they found a joint in an ashtray," the agent reminded him.

"And that's where we'll start," Williams told him. "Why don't we all meet tomorrow? I'll take a further look around here. And maybe you'll find some guy at the bar down the street bragging about how he started the fire."

"Arson?" The sheriff was jolted by the new possibility entering the investigation. "If it was arson, it was a murder. Are you saying this was a murder?"

"No, no," the fire investigator said. "I'm just not ruling it out. I'm not ruling *anything* out."

19

"His notes are all gone, JC," Shara said. "Where did they go?"

She was anxious.

"I was given sedatives to get some sleep last night," she told them.

But she was still jittery when JC and Robin responded to her call after breakfast and walked down the hall to her hotel room.

"All of his work was there at that house," Shara said. "I've already asked the sheriff if they took his paperwork away, or if it burned in the fire. He told me that the table was empty when he walked into the house. He tells me that he didn't find paper, notebooks, photographs, anything!"

"Could he have hidden it?" JC asked.

"No. I have already been out there this morning," Shara told him. "I was allowed to go in to collect his things. After I had a good cry, a deputy even helped me search. I looked everywhere. It's gone."

"What exactly is missing?" Robin asked.

"All the evidence. A man named Swensen and a man named Brown." Shara spat when she said the words, as if their names had a sour taste. "The notes, the stories he was writing, the photographs."

"And who is Swensen? Who is Brown?" JC asked.

"Raff Swensen is a state senator. Brown is a state representative," Shara said. "Quip was making arrangements to break the story about the senator this week. You should see the photographs!"

"And he didn't make duplicates?" JC asked.

Shara instinctively looked both ways. She looked at the door, suspicious that someone might be listening on the other side. Then, she stepped to the desk provided in the hotel room. She scribbled something on a pad of paper that had the hotel's brand at the top. Deliberately, she did not say a word. Scribbling on the pad, she wrote, "He told me he did. I just don't know where they are."

Still without saying a word, Shara crossed the room and opened a box. It held things she was able to salvage from Quip's hideaway that morning. But it was mostly empty.

There was a toothbrush and toothpaste and a hairbrush. There were sunglasses and a ballcap that said, "Wisconsin Football."

And there was a 1911 A1 Colt .45 revolver.

"It was his grandfather's," Shara told them. "He carried it during World War ll."

"Let's go for a walk," JC suggested. He understood Shara's concern about being overheard. He didn't know if it was a realistic concern, but why take chances?

They walked out through the lobby. Hotel employees were hanging decorations for the New Year's Eve celebration that would take place that night.

Newspapers were stacked off to the side of the check-in desk. The headline of the Lake Geneva paper was about Quip Kelly's fiery death. State Representative Vic Brown's visit to the charity breakfast was pushed to the second section.

JC strolled with the two redheads on a sidewalk that took a winding path around the grounds of the Grand Geneva Resort. They wore their winter coats and pushed their hands into their pockets to protect them from the wind.

"I must say," JC told them. "I don't know many burglars who would resist the temptation of walking away with a gun."

"I thought about that too," Shara said.

"That's a collector's item and in pretty good shape," JC said. "He could sell that gun for a thousand dollars."

"So why didn't he take it?" Robin asked.

"Because that's not what he came for," JC surmised. "Someone was being very careful."

As JC, Robin and Shara walked back toward the building, they saw a number of vehicles parked at one end of the sprawling main building. Law officers and fire investigators had chosen a conference room at the resort to discuss their findings regarding the fire that killed Quip

Kelly. Visitors, Including the widow and especially two television reporters, were not welcome.

The sheriff and DCI Agent Nelson sat at the head of the table in the conference room.

"Positive identification has come from DNA on a hairbrush that Mrs. Kelly gave my deputies," the county sheriff told the others inside the room. "The body is that of Carol 'Quip' Kelly. We have informed the widow of that fact."

"His name was Carol?" one law officer remarked. The others gave him a look suggesting that he quit being a wiseass.

"We found what remains of what we think is a melted butane lighter," the sheriff continued. "It was in amongst the ruins of the couch. Maybe it was dropped there."

"By Mr. Kelly, lighting a joint?" asked another law officer.

"Or whoever," Deputy Fire Marshal Jakub Williams chimed in. "We've taken the initiative to cut out a piece of the home's floor. There was a hole in the linoleum covering of the floor, right by the body. The hole was about a foot long and it pre-dated the fire. It may have absorbed a flammable liquid, if any was used.

"Any flammable poured on the couch would have burned. But if some dripped onto that wood in the opening of the linoleum, the wood may have absorbed it. Fire burns upwards. So below, we might find a trace of the flammable."

"While we're on the subject of pursuing suspicions," the sheriff said, "Mrs. Kelly says that there were important papers in that house. But we've found none."

"Money? A will and testament?" a law officer asked. "What is missing?"

"I think we all know who Quip Kelly was," Agent Nelson began. "Mrs. Kelly tells us that, as a habit, Mr. Kelly chose a hiding place to finish work on a news story that might expose someone powerful. She says he was working on such a story, and this house that burned was his chosen hiding place."

"Are we looking at that as a motive, if the fire was set?" a local fire chief inquired.

"First," Agent Nelson said, "we're going to see what the fire marshal discovers about the cause. It could be a coincidence. Second is what Mrs. Kelly tells us is missing, Quip's notes would tell us who he was writing about."

Outside, Shara had been spotted. Members of the news media were staking out the resort and hustled in her direction.

"The only way you'll get them to leave is if you give them a little bit of what they want," JC told her. "Collect your thoughts and tell one of them to spread the word. Tell them you'll hold a news conference in an hour."

"Thank you for coming on such short notice," Shara said, an hour later. She stood in front of a bank of reporters and microphones. "I have a prepared statement and then I hope you will respect my privacy and allow me a chance to grieve the loss of my wonderful husband."

She spoke in front of the same arch on the grounds of the resort where JC had been reporting live to Denver each night.

Milt was among the news photographers in a collection of television cameras aimed at Shara.

JC had prepared Shara to see Milt there. They had a job to do. It might not be their desire, but it really wasn't their choice. Viewers in Denver were also interested in details of Quip's death.

Shara told the reporters what a wonderful man her husband was. She described his dedication to readers and viewers who followed his stories.

"Quip rarely sat still," Shara told them. "As a result, he was working on a number of news stories of importance. I do not want to see his work end before it is completed. Therefore, as soon as I can organize the material, I plan to turn over all of Quip's investigative notes to the journalism school at the University of Wisconsin in Madison."

Shara told the reporters that she expected to turn over Quip's records in a week or two. She said it would be her priority.

She stated that any questions regarding the investigation into the fire should be directed to the sheriff.

"Please remember my husband as a good and decent man," Shara said. "He was dedicated to helping those who are vulnerable and honest. And he was determined to get the bad guys."

Then, she again asked the news media for privacy and walked away from the microphones without taking questions.

Robin stayed behind and helped Milt wrap up his equipment. He said he was in a hurry to go somewhere after editing JC's package for that night's broadcast. It was New Year's Eve.

JC also had somewhere to go.

He climbed into the car and followed Fox River Road. He turned left on 114th street and parked in front of the

Wilmot Riverside Bar and Grill. The signs outside advertised Old Style Beer and Schlitz.

The tavern was decorated for that night's New Year's crowd. JC took a seat at the bar and ordered a Pabst Blue Ribbon. He looked up at a sign that said, "Beer: So Much More Than Just a Breakfast Drink."

JC struck up a conversation with the bartender, a man in his fifties with an easy disposition. His name was Walter Schroeder, one of the many descendants of German settlers who came to Wisconsin.

The conversation turned to the day before. The day of the fatal fire.

"What are the local folks saying here?" JC asked.

"They are saying what a shame it is," Walter said. "Not too many knew the fella. He was new around here. But he'd come in here sometimes. Kept to himself, but he always behaved."

"This is a local bar," JC said. "You must know just about everyone who comes in here."

"I grew up in Wilmot," laughed Walter. "I also work as a lift operator at the ski mountain. Between skiing and serving beer, I pretty much know everyone who lives around here."

"Did you see anyone you didn't know in the bar yesterday?" JC asked.

"Give me just a minute," Walter said. He walked out from behind the bar and took a food order from a table.

"I guess I did see a stranger in here yesterday," Walter told JC after giving the food order to the kitchen. Walter leaned on the bar and got himself comfortable.

"A fellow came in and ordered a beer," Walter said. "He sat here at the bar, next to the seat where you are."

"Did he tell you what brought him here?" asked JC.

"Usually, if a stranger comes in during the winter, he's here to ski," Walter answered. "But this guy wasn't dressed to ski."

"Anything unusual about him?" JC inquired. Walter thought about this.

"No, I got him a bottle of beer," the bartender told him. "I noticed that he had a sore hand. It was red. It was his right hand."

"What did that hand injury look like to you?" JC asked.

"I don't know," Walter told him. "I asked him how it happened. He said it got caught in something mechanical he was working on. He just slipped that hand into his coat pocket and finished drinking his beer with his left hand."

"Did it look like it could have been a burn?" JC asked.

"I grew up on a farm," Walter laughed. "I have burned my hand on a tractor engine, burning fields, burning old sheds, burning debris and working on cars at the racetrack. Yeah, I guess it could have been a burn."

"And when did the man leave?" JC asked. The bartender gave it some thought.

"That's hard to say," Walter told him. "All the excitement broke out. The fire, you know. I guess I didn't see him after that."

"And haven't seen him since then?" JC asked.

"No."

"That was the strangest New Year's Eve I've ever experienced," JC said.

Robin sat next to JC, leaning on him in their dark hotel room. They had enjoyed dinner at the hotel together and brought a bottle of champagne back with them. They hadn't seen nor heard from Milt.

They pulled the couch over to the sliding glass door so that they could look outside. There was a bright moon illuminating the landscape. They could hear inebriated New Year's Eve revelers howling outside.

In the distance, they could watch the celebration going on at the resort's small mountain. Skiers lit the night by carrying torches down the slopes. There were people dressed as a cow on skis. And there were fireworks.

Look there!" JC said softly, pointing to the edge of the lake. He'd spotted three white-tailed deer.

"Do you think they know that it's a new year?" Robin asked as she moved over to the bed and pulled the covers over her without undressing. "Do you think they make New Year's resolutions?"

"Yeah," JC said, sliding into bed next to her, also not undressing. "Their New Year's resolution is not to get shot."

"That was last year's resolution," she said, speaking soft and lazy like she did just before falling asleep.

"Oh yeah," JC said. "This year's resolution is not to get hit by a car."

"Yeah," she said as she drifted asleep. "That's a good one."

They were awakened by an alarm on JC's phone only a few hours later.

Robin had to meet her driver in the lobby and take the hired car to the airport.

"Let me drive you to the airport," JC had pleaded with her.

"No," Robin told him. "You'll be too tired. And you have to work today. I'll sleep in the car and on the plane. I'll take a quick shower at home and get to work just in time."

He walked her down to the lobby to meet her driver.

"Thanks for coming with me," JC told her. "How many of your old boyfriends packed skiing and a murder into one vacation?"

"Poor Quip," she said. "Poor Shara."

"Shara said that she's going home to Madison to get things in order," JC told her as they waited for her car to arrive. "She'll have to return, though, to collect Quip's remains and have them cremated. But that can't happen until the sheriff releases them."

When the car arrived, JC and Robin embraced.

"Happy New Year," Robin said quietly.

"Happy Hogmanay," JC responded. That was the Scottish New Year celebration. The night they fell in love followed a Scottish Burns Supper.

"Take care of yourself, Jean Claude," Robin said softly.

"Yes, ma'am," he replied softly.

"Don't let anything happen to you while I'm gone," she told him.

"Why?" he asked. "You want to be there to see it when something happens to me?"

She gave him a look and he smiled.

20

"She keeps staring at me," the deputy said.

"Who?" another deputy asked. "The new woman in the forensics unit? The one just out of college?"

"I wish," the first deputy answered. His name was Anderson. "Not her. The redhead."

"The victim?" his friend, a deputy named Krueger, asked. "She's staring at you? You know she's dead, don't you?"

"I don't mean she's into me," Deputy Anderson told the other deputy. "She's like the Mona Lisa. Her eyes are open and they're following me wherever I go."

"The Mona Lisa of the Midwest," Deputy Krueger remarked. "Don't let the press hear you. That'll be their headline."

"She's kind of smiling at me too," Anderson continued. Now, Krueger studied her.

"Well, she is your type," Krueger responded. "She just lies there. Nothing to say. Lets anybody touch her."

"Have some respect," Anderson snickered. "That could be somebody's sister."

"Well, she'd have all that in common with *your* sister," Krueger replied.

"You're an asshole," mumbled Anderson.

The two deputies were told to stay with the body, in a cow pasture near Dryer Lake. It was a quick drive from Lake Geneva, down 50 and then a left turn on County Route P.

With the sun just coming up, the sheriff directed the other deputies to form a grid and search the scene. The murder weapon had already been located. But who knew what they would find if they took a look around. A dropped wallet? A cigarette smoked by the killer? Or maybe the killer himself, or herself, after taking their own life in a fit of remorse?

The body of the dead woman was unclothed. There was only underwear found near the woman. There was no purse, no form of identification.

Presuming she began the night carrying a purse or identification, it was either in the field presently being searched, or the killer absconded with it.

The field was covered by about a foot of compacted, glazed-over snow. Only one set of footsteps led to the body. A forensics unit was making an effort to capture a shoe print from the tracks.

"The killer carried the woman to this spot," a detective said to the sheriff as they gazed at her.

"So, she was probably already dead," the sheriff responded.

The victim was lying on her back. Her red hair was tousled, lying on the snow under her head like a pillow.

A fork protruded from the victim's chest.

"That's forked-up, man," Deputy Anderson said.

"Shut up, Anderson," the sheriff said. "Or you'll be back answering the phones *next* Christmas."

White Ford 4x4 Interceptors with gold lettering were parked in a long line on the nearest road. The road had been plowed of snow down to its dirt surface. It didn't get a lot of traffic, but there were patrol cars parked at the closest intersections to prevent anyone from driving by the crime scene.

"Do you know the fork has seven different parts?" the detective asked the sheriff. "There's the point, tine, slot, root, neck, back and the handle."

"How would you come to know this?" the sheriff asked.

"I was a dishwasher at a restaurant," the detective told him. "That's one of the few jobs a fourteen-year-old kid can get. That fork might lead us somewhere. There's got to be other forks, spoons and knives that look a lot like it. Maybe in someone's house. Maybe in a restaurant."

Their breath rose like smoke from their mouths. After a cold night, they were grateful as the first flash of sun warmed their faces.

The same large mobile-command center that had been at the fire in Wilmot arrived. It was already being set up on the road next to the cow pasture. Coffee was brewing inside. It would make the morning a little more tolerable.

"Anybody know who she is?" the sheriff asked the detective.

"There's an EMT over there," the subordinate replied. "He hasn't been allowed near the scene. But from where he was looking, he thought he knew who she was. He said he had a brief conversation with her a few days ago at that Rainbows restaurant in Lake Geneva. They were sitting at the next table."

"Well, who does he think she is? Did he give you a name?" the sheriff asked.

"Not a name," the detective reported. "But he said she was with the reporter who is in town from Colorado. He said there was a redhead in his news crew."

JC was still lying in bed. He gave Robin a call. He thought he could catch her at Midway Airport in Chicago before her plane took off for Denver. She didn't answer her phone.

He wished he had driven her to the airport. But she was adamant about getting herself there. She said that she would come back next weekend, if he hadn't wrapped things up. She said he could drive to Midway then and pick her up.

There was a knock at JC's door. He threw on a tee shirt and blue jeans.

He opened the door to a pair of sour-faced law officers. One was in street clothing, and one was in a dark navy blue uniform.

"Mr. Snow?"

"Yes," he replied. "How may I help you gentlemen?"

The law officers stood in the doorway of the room. They made no effort to enter and didn't seem interested in an invitation.

"Are you acquainted with a Robin Smith, Mr. Snow?"

"I think you know the answer to that question," JC said. "She is a co-worker of mine in Colorado and my girlfriend. What does this have to do with Robin?"

JC got a sinking feeling.

"Is she alright?" he asked urgently. His heartbeat grew rapid. He was anxious to hear that she was fine.

"A body has been found, Mr. Snow," the plainclothes detective explained. "We'd like you to come with us. Perhaps you can clear up the identification."

JC felt a pain in his stomach. He was dizzy. It was hard for him to concentrate. He couldn't even remember sitting back down on the bed.

"Why don't you come with us," the plainclothesman said after a minute.

JC had no recall of locking his hotel room door, or grabbing the jacket he was putting on. He walked down the hallway with the two law officers.

"When is the last time you spoke with Ms. Smith, Mr. Snow?" the deputy in street clothes asked.

"Earlier this morning," JC said, struggling to remember anything at all. It was still early in the morning. "She caught a ride to the airport. She's flying back to Denver. She has to work later today."

JC found that stringing four sentences together left him breathless. And he grew fatigued after walking the length of the hallway.

He didn't remember walking outdoors, but the cold air stung and stirred his cognition.

He was steered into the backseat of a white Ford Interceptor. He recognized the gold-block lettering that said "Sheriff."

In foreign surroundings, he suddenly felt helpless. He desperately wanted Robin by his side. He felt exposed and frightened without her.

"How did she get to the airport?" the investigator asked, breaking the silence.

"She hired a car," JC said from the backseat.

"Did you see the driver?" JC was asked.

"Yes, I did," he told them. "He was tall, heavyset. But he was flabby. He was just overweight, not much muscle. Balding. Dark hair. I wrote down the license plate too."

"Good," the plainclothes deputy said.

JC wanted to ask the question but was afraid to hear the answer.

"It isn't her, is it?" he asked, and hid his head in his hands. He didn't want to be seen crying.

21

"Where are we going?"

JC asked the question from the backseat of a Ford Interceptor driven by the uniformed sheriff's deputy.

"We're going to the morgue, Mr. Snow," the detective in plain clothing turned around and said from the passenger seat. "We'd like you to try to make an identification."

JC thought he was going to be sick. The thought of losing Robin. The thought of her suffering, of her being frightened. The thought that he wasn't there to protect her. The thought of her being alone in a refrigerated drawer.

He vomited into a paper bag moments after the detective handed the bag to him between the cage and the window panel of the vehicle.

The backseat he was riding on was uncomfortable. It was made of stiff plastic or vinyl. The choice of upholstery was probably because that seat had to be washed a lot. Suspects did foul things back in the cages of cop cars. They would sometimes spit, throw up, urinate, bleed.

It occurred to JC that he would be a suspect. At the moment, that didn't matter much. But it occurred to him.

Kenosha was the largest city he had seen since arriving in Wisconsin. The medical examiner's office was only a few blocks from Lake Michigan.

JC pulled his cell phone from his pocket and dialed a number.

"Who are you calling?" the detective asked in a controlling voice from the front seat. It occurred to JC that his escorts didn't want him making any calls.

"I'm calling Robin," JC told them. He didn't ask for permission.

As the phone rang, he thought that this nightmare could end in an instant, as long as Robin picked up the phone. The call went to voice mail.

He thought he might throw up again and pushed the phone back into his pants pocket.

The patrol car pulled around the back of the building and parked. The detective quickly opened the door. JC wondered if *he* had tried to open the door, would it have opened?

JC felt like he was in custody as he was walked into a hallway of the building. He wasn't in handcuffs and the deputies weren't holding onto him, but he felt like they were keeping an eye on him. He wondered how they would react if he suddenly ran. He was, he was certain, a suspect. He suddenly felt too warm.

He was steered into a room which led into another room. This one was clean and white. JC had been in a morgue before.

"Are you ready?" the detective asked.

The question punched JC in the chest. There weren't going to be any more formalities. There wasn't paperwork to sign. Time was up.

A stainless steel table had a sheet draped over it. The detective touched one corner of the fabric and gave JC another glance, looking for permission to proceed. JC nodded silently.

The sheet was only pulled down to her chin. JC's eyes fell on the pretty face and then the long red hair. He took a deep breath, but his eyes never left her face.

"Do you recognize this woman?" the detective asked.

"Yes," JC answered, barely able to get the word out.

The detective waited impatiently for JC to make the formal identification.

"Well," the detective finally said. "Who is it?"

"I can't remember her real name," JC told him without removing his sad eyes from her face. "Everyone called her Sheepy. Sheepy Johnson."

JC thought that he'd be sick again.

In the hallway, the detective asked JC to tell him everything he knew about Sheepy Johnson.

"She was our waitress at the Grand Geneva Resort," JC said. "She also is a part-owner of the Rainbows restaurant in Lake Geneva. We saw her there too. She waited on our table. She's really a delight."

"Anything else?" the detective asked.

"I think she is from around there," JC told him. "I think she said she grew up on a farm outside of Elkhorn."

"That will help," the detective responded.

The detective's demeanor had changed. JC felt that the distance between them had closed.

"Can you tell us where you were last night?" the detective asked of him.

"I was with Robin," he replied. "We had dinner at the Grand Geneva and went back to our room."

"Does Robin have red hair?" questioned the detective.

"Yes."

JC's likelihood of being the killer had just statistically fallen a metric mile. Now, he was someone who might be of use to their investigation.

The body having been identified and the interview complete, the detective was satisfied. He asked the uniformed officer to drive JC back to the Grand Geneva. This time, JC rode in the passenger seat in front. The seats were more comfortable.

Remaining behind at the sheriff's office, the detective easily found a Johnson Farm near Elkhorn. The family had three boys and one daughter, Elizabeth.

He reported to the sheriff that he had a positive identification on the victim found in the field.

"Who is it?" the sheriff asked, sitting inside his office.

"An Elizabeth Johnson," the detective said. "She was twenty-nine years old and from Elkhorn."

"The next county over," the sheriff responded. "Who reported her missing?"

"Her girlfriend," answered the detective. "Someone in a car spotted the body first and called 9-1-1. But at about five, Larsen called and reported her missing."

They both sipped coffee in cardboard cups. It was purchased at a shop down the street.

"Do they live together?" the sheriff asked his detective.

"Yes. But the girlfriend, a Cyndi Larsen, says she slept at her parents' house. Her father is ill. She became worried when Elizabeth didn't show up for work this morning. They both planned to get there pretty early to prep for breakfast. They open at six."

"Have we confirmed that?" the sheriff wanted to know.

"Yes sir," replied the detective. "Larsen's parents confirm that she was with them."

"It still doesn't mean she didn't kill her," the sheriff pointed out.

"No sir," the detective replied.

"Elizabeth Johnson?" the sheriff repeated. "Who the hell is that?"

Elkhorn was just inside the next county. The sheriff had over a hundred fifty thousand souls to worry about in his own county. Many of them were voters and it paid to know them. But he knew the sheriff in the next county and knew about many of the affairs going on there, too.

"The family owns a farm. The victim has a nickname," the detective said to his superior. After looking at his notes, he said, "Sheepy, sir. Sheepy Johnson."

"Oh no," the sheriff said sadly. "I know that family. Sheepy was a nice girl. Alright, call the sheriff there. Let him know we're going to take a drive out to the farm and talk to the family. I'm not looking forward to this."

JC experienced a wave of relief. But his body was weak. He wanted to sleep.

He envisioned the events of the last hour, as the sheriff's patrol car drove up the winding road returning to the resort. JC made another call to Robin's phone. It was pushed to voice mail again.

He wanted to hear her voice. He was *desperate* to hear her voice. He wanted any doubt to be removed.

With emotions in overdrive, he felt guilt. The corpse was not Robin's. But the gratitude he sensed was tied to the fact that another young woman, Sheepy Johnson, was dead.

JC hadn't heard from Robin since she left his bed in Wisconsin. If she was alright, where was she? His stomach began to turn again.

The deputy dropped him off outside Building Two. Climbing the stairs to their hotel room, JC thought about the similarities between Robin and Sheepy. They were both attractive women of about the same age with wonderful long red hair. One *could* be mistaken for the other, JC thought. The idea heightened his anxiety. Could the killer have been after Robin?

When his phone rang, he jumped a little. He didn't want to be interrupted by Milt or the newsroom in Denver or the front desk. But he picked up.

"JC?" the voice at the other end of the phone said.

JC held the phone to his ear but said nothing. The phone felt heavy in his hand.

"Are you going to say something?" the voice asked. "Or are you just going to breath into the phone like a pervert."

"Hi, Robin," JC finally responded.

22

"Listen," Milt said. "I have something to tell you."

He was waiting for JC downstairs in the café to have breakfast together. JC was late.

"Sheepy is dead," Milt informed him.

"How do you know that?" JC inquired.

"A member of the hotel staff told me," he responded. There was sadness etched on his face. The dark rings around his eyes seemed darker.

"I'm sorry," JC answered. "I know you liked her. We all liked her."

"You don't seem very surprised," Milt said.

"Alright," JC replied. "I guess I have something to tell you, then."

Milt had no idea that the murder victim lying alone in a field was first thought to be Robin. JC proceeded to describe the worst hour of his life.

JC actually found that he felt better, talking about it. He was able to discuss it in the past tense, a terrible false alarm that was behind him.

"I would have freaked out," Milt said.

"I did," JC admitted. "I threw up in back of the deputy's car."

Milt thought that was funny.

Milt and JC then discussed the murder of Sheepy Johnson as they ate breakfast. Their server that morning was an unfamiliar face, but they stopped talking whenever she approached their table. It felt like a measure of respect.

"What are all the reasons someone would kill a pretty, hardworking waitress who grew up nearby on a farm?" JC asked when the server walked away.

"She taught snowboarding too," Milt told him. "At Big Horizon."

"How do you know that?" JC asked.

"I saw her last night," Milt answered, grinning a new toothy grin.

"You saw her?" JC asked with surprise. "When?"

"New Year's Eve," he said matter-of-factly, then flashed his teeth with another smile.

JC studied Milt's face, especially the lower half.

"Wait a minute. Before we go any further," JC said. "Did you beat someone up and steal their teeth?"

"Why do you ask?" Milt responded with another shiny grin.

"Because the mouth on your face this morning looks better than *your* mouth," JC replied.

"I went to the dentist," Milt told him.

"This is what you look like when you brush your teeth?" JC inquired.

"I had them whitened," Milt answered, still grinning. "They gave me key-lime-flavored floss. It's delicious. I'm reinventing myself."

"Is there a limit to how many times you can reinvent yourself?" JC asked.

"I don't think so," Milt replied. "And don't try to spoil my feng shui."

"I don't think that's possible," JC smiled.

"After I went to the dentist, I came back looking for you," Milt said. "I figured you and Robin had hit the fartsack, so I went out. It was New Year's Eve, for goodness sake!"

"The what?" JC asked.

"The fartsack?" Milt answered, struggling to know which question JC wanted him to answer.

"What is a..." JC began. But he preferred that word never to pass his lips.

"A bed," Milt told him. "That's what we called a bed in the Army."

"Please tell me that you do not use that word around women," JC implored.

"Fartsack? They think it's funny," Milt said, laughing and showing his new teeth.

"You did, didn't you," JC asked.

"What?" the smiling man asked.

"Did you ask Sheepy to join you in the fartsack?" JC gulped.

"Not in so many words," Milt told him. "Okay, yes. In so many words, I did. She told me that she preferred women. I'm okay with that."

"But that didn't stop you, did it?" JC asked, feeling defeated.

"Well," Milt said, "I pointed out that she said she *preferred* women. It didn't sound like she was absolutely ruling it out."

"I think she was," JC said. "Oh no. Don't tell me she..."

"No," Milt responded. "But she laughed."

"She was probably feeling giddy relief that she was a lesbian," JC told him.

"Women think I'm cute," smiling Milt stated.

"Women think you were born with a mental disability," JC sighed.

JC thought back to Milt's brief marriage. For a short collection of days, Milt had been married to a beautiful younger woman who was intelligent and normally way out of his reach. But her one night of weakness, sex with a strange awkward man, resulted in a child.

As soon as Jayne was born, the woman divorced Milt. A few years later, she was struck and killed by a driver that police suspected Milt had hired to kill her. Milt was eventually cleared.

"I might remind you," JC said to his photographer. "You were also investigated in the murder of a young woman from Vermont who came to Colorado to ski. You were seen on a security camera, hitting on her just a day before her life was taken."

Milt remained silent. This was how these conversations usually went. JC now felt sorry for pointing out the terribly flawed man's terrible flaws.

"But we're friends, right?" Milt finally said.

"Oh, God," JC groaned. "Of course, we're friends, Milt. I just worry about your judgment sometimes."

"But never when I have a camera on my shoulder, right?" Milt pursued.

"No, oddly enough," JC agreed. "You are a great photographer. You really are."

Milt flashed that new white grin of his.

Following breakfast, JC came to Milt's room to draw up a plan for the day. The Ronny Schwartz murder and the death of Quip Kelly, not yet declared a murder by investigators, were going to require a lot of digging.

The Schwartz investigation, according to law officers, seemed to have no suspects and no motive. Because he drowned, the death actually took place in Door County. A kidnapping, though, may have happened anywhere between here and there.

The unfortunate Sheepy Johnson was not really of concern to television viewers back in Colorado. At the moment, there was no reason for JC to report details of her death back to Denver.

Discussing their options, they were interrupted by a knock on the door of Milt's room. JC was closer, so he opened the door into the hallway.

JC recognized the pair, the same uniformed officer and detective in plain clothing that had knocked on his door earlier that morning.

"Is there a Milt Lemon in this room?" the detective asked JC.

"Not again," JC lamented.

"Why do you say that, Mr. Snow?" the detective questioned.

"Wait until you meet him," JC told them. "You'll understand."

"Would you collect your jacket, Mr. Lemon," the detective said, looking past JC. "And come with us?"

"Oh, and Mr. Snow," the detective said. "That DCI agent would like to hear from you with a phone call in the next hour." He gave JC a card with the agent's phone number.

Milt slowly rose from the video-editing setup where he sat. He grabbed his jacket and walked for the door.

"Try to have him back by dinner, boys," JC said as the three of them walked down the hall. "If he doesn't eat, he gets hangry."

The uniformed deputy gave JC a puzzled look.

"If he gets hungry," JC explained. "He gets angry."

"You're not helping, JC," Milt said over his shoulder in an elevated voice.

Robin Smith lived in a section of Denver called River North, or RiNo. It was artsy and trendy. Once full of warehouses and small industrial buildings, those structures were filling up with new bars and restaurants and art galleries.

She was staring out her window at a building across the street. It had a large mural of a woman clutching a cat. Robin was watering plants when her phone rang.

"Of course, he has," Robin said when JC told her that Milt had been taken away by sheriff's deputies. "How long do you think *this* will take?"

"I'll give it a few hours," JC told her. "Then, I'll call the TV station and inform them we might have a problem getting video for our story tonight."

"They won't let you off the hook, you know," she said. "They'll just have you sit in a chair and tell them insightful things."

"I guess you're right," he said with a smile. "But not if I don't have someone to point a camera at me sitting in a chair."

"They could hire someone local," she suggested.

"Yeah," he agreed. Then he got to the real reason he called. "Are you alright?"

"JC, I'm fine. You don't have to keep asking me that. I was never in danger. I had an uneventful drive to the airport and an uneventful flight back home. Though, it doesn't seem like home when you're not here."

"You're right, hon," he said. "But I'm not going to forget that feeling for a while. I'm just so grateful."

"JC stop," she said. "I love you too. And I'm fine. So, what else is going on there?"

"Does a fork seem like the weapon of choice in a well-thought-out murder?" JC asked.

"Was it a big fork?"

"Yep."

"But you don't think a premeditated murder would be carried out with a fork," she assumed.

"Nope. It seems more like something you'd use when you're looking for a weapon on short notice," he told her.

"Where did the fork come from?" she asked.

"They haven't told us that," he answered.

"You're thinking it came from the kitchen in Rainbows?" she asked.

"Of course, I am," he responded. "I'm sure they have a selection of large forks."

"And that makes someone at the restaurant look guilty," Robin added.

"If it is a fork from the restaurant? I guess," he said. "The problem is, if you want to make someone *innocent* look guilty, like her girlfriend Cyndi, that's also a good reason to use a fork from the restaurant."

"Maybe it *is* Cyndi," Robin speculated. "Maybe they argued over meat tenderizer. Or, more likely, they had a lover's spat. Police see a lot of lovers' quarrels end that way."

"Yeah," JC agreed. "And then undressing the body would be a ruse, to make it look like a sexual assault."

JC told Robin that the DCI agent was expecting his call. Robin said that she needed to get dressed and get into the TV station. She told him that she had booked a flight back to Wisconsin after work on Friday night. She would see him soon.

"Is the fork from the restaurant?" JC asked as soon as Agent Nelson answered the telephone.

"You know," the agent responded. "I didn't ask you to call me because I was worried that all your questions weren't being answered."

"I know that wasn't the *whole* reason," JC said. "I just thought we'd trade."

"I want to know about Bitsy Stark and Milt Lemon's ex-wife, both of whom are dead," the agent said firmly.

JC told Nelson everything about those two murder investigations. He also provided the names and phone numbers of the investigating officers in Colorado, so that he could speak law-officer-to-law-officer.

"Now, my turn," JC declared. "The fork was from the Rainbows restaurant, I understand."

Actually, it was a guess on JC's part. But he wanted to sound more informed than he was.

"I don't know who told you that," the agent said. "But yes, the fork is from the restaurant."

"And Cyndi, from the restaurant, was in a relationship with Sheepy?" JC asked.

"Why would you say that?" Agent Nelson asked.

"I'm guessing that's why you wanted me to call," JC said. "To see what I know. Sheepy told us they were a couple. And we saw Sheepy and Cyndi together at the bar at Alpine Valley a few days before she died. Sheepy was all dressed up. She looked great."

"Yes, we know that Cyndi Larsen was in a relationship with Sheepy Johnson," the DCI agent confirmed.

JC jotted down Cyndi's last name. He hadn't time to look into her background at all, including her last name.

"So, Cyndi Larsen is a suspect?" JC asked.

"Who isn't a suspect, at this point?" the agent asked. "Alright, I'm done answering your questions. Answer a few of mine."

"A few *more*," JC corrected, reminding the agent that he provided everything he knew about the deaths of Bitsy Stark and Milt's ex-wife.

"Don't think you're so smart," the agent told JC. "The sheriff has already talked to the detective that handled those investigations, Trujillo. Nice guy. And he says you can be useful, as long as you know when to stay out of the way."

"I'll have to send Detective Trujillo a thank-you card," JC smirked.

"What do you know about Milt Lemon?" the agent asked.

"He's a great photographer and actually sensitive and kindhearted," JC told the law officer. "He's just spent a lifetime trying to disguise that."

"He shows up on security video with Sheepy Johnson the night she was killed," the agent said bluntly. "He looks to me like he was attracted to the woman, like he was trying to put the moves on her."

"Where was this?" JC asked.

"At a bar in Lake Geneva," Nelson said. "Were you with him?"

"No," JC told him. "I was with my girlfriend back here at the resort."

The agent asked for and was provided with a phone number for Robin. He would want to confirm JC's story.

"It looks like Milt Lemon tried to kiss Ms. Johnson," the agent said.

JC just sighed and rubbed his face with his hand.

"Then, they walk away in different directions," Agent Nelson summed up the episode on security video. "That doesn't mean he didn't stalk her."

"Listen, Agent. Despite his ill-advised advances, Milt seems to be practiced in taking 'no' for an answer. And women seem to find him amusing," JC said. "He's like a really ugly puppy."

This time, JC heard the *agent* sighing over the phone.

"A sheriff's deputy will be dropping him off back at your hotel soon," Agent Nelson said. "We have no reason to hold him, at this time."

"I'll make certain he's fed and bathed," JC said.

"Let me ask you," Agent Nelson added. "Does he understand the meaning of lesbian?"

"I was hoping you had a book or something he could borrow," JC sighed.

"Keep a closer eye on him, would you?" the agent asked. "We may want to talk to him again."

"I'll lock him in his crate tonight," JC responded.

23

"Farmers are charmers!"

Milt had just asked Branch, as she was pouring them coffee, who she usually dated in Lake Geneva.

"Do you want to go out?" Milt asked.

"Sure!" she answered as she finished with the coffee.

JC just about spit his coffee onto the table when he heard the pretty blonde say she would go out on a date with Milt.

"There should be a Lemon Law," JC mumbled. "A five-day cooling-off period before you can date, after being questioned in another woman's murder."

Milt gave JC a look that suggested now was not the time for that discussion.

"I'll tell you all about it," Milt said to Branch. "It's a funny story."

"Where do you want to go?" Branch asked Milt.

"Do you want to show me around Lake Geneva?" he asked her.

"Oh yeah," the perky waitress answered. "I know all the spots in Lake Geneva."

"Do you own a gun, Branch?" JC asked.

"I do!" she answered.

"You might want to bring it on your date," JC said.

The sun outside was bright, but a fierce wind was blowing. Through the window, they saw old leaves skipping across the top of the snow. Tall trees were groaning as they bowed in the gusts.

"I am fuller than a tick!" Milt announced as he pushed himself away from the breakfast table. Branch laughed, picked up his empty plate and headed back to the kitchen.

"Fuller than a tick. What a quaint saying," JC told Milt. "Sort of like announcing, 'Hey everyone, I'm gonna pop a big blister! Wanna watch?'"

"Branch enjoys my urban wit," Milt protested.

"You may see my urban vomit," JC responded. "Everyone in the Midwest is nice. You're simply the first rude person she's ever met. She's intrigued."

"Yes," Milt grinned. "She thinks I'm worldly."

"The cops say they might want to talk with you again," JC informed him.

"Why?" Milt asked him. "I liked Sheepy."

"That's what murderers always say," JC responded.

"They only looked at me because of what happened to my ex-wife and Bitsy," Milt complained.

"Yes," JC agreed. "It is unfair to be suspicious of a guy who leaves a string of dead bodies behind him on date night."

"Exactly," Milt concurred. "It is an ongoing saga of suck."

"So, if the killer isn't you," JC asked, "we have two suspicious deaths two days apart. This, in a place where every single resident could win 'Miss Congeniality' in a beauty pageant."

"Nice people," Milt agreed. "That's for sure."

"I do wonder," JC said. "Are the murders of Quip and Sheepy related?"

"Not to be a Debbie Downer," Milt told him. "But they haven't ruled Quip's death a murder."

"No, but they will," JC said. "Shara insists he didn't smoke cigarettes or weed. And the killer fled with all of Quip's notes."

"What about the story we were sent here to cover," Milt reminded JC. "Are those deaths connected to Ronny Schwartz's murder?"

"That's a good question," JC admitted. "And the cops say they have no idea why Ronny Schwartz was killed. If we figure out the motive for killing him, will we figure out who killed the others?"

A stately woman with gray hair walked by their table and seated herself on the other side of the resort's café.

JC and Milt had already paid for breakfast and pushed their chairs away from the table to leave.

"Do you know who that is?" Branch said in a whisper when she rushed to their table. She poured them more coffee, as if to have an excuse to stop there.

JC glanced past her hip to take another look at the woman.

"You have to help me," he said, after failing to recognize her.

"That's Gretta Miller," Branch said with a secretive smile. "That's the wife of Senator Miller, who was forced from office after that story by Quip Kelly. The senator used to bring girls here. He'd say they were his nieces. He had a lot of nieces, I guess. And they always shared a room!"

"Close family," Milt said.

JC looked past Branch's hip again, with additional interest.

"What's she doing here?" JC asked.

"I'm told she checked in two nights ago, New Year's Eve," Branch told him. "And she checked in alone. Her husband is not with her."

"Quip caught him having a bunch of affairs," Milt said, smiling. "They might have agreed to separate vacations."

"I have a feeling that she didn't consult the senator on this one," JC added. "She looks like a tough lady. She might be considering how to finish off her husband."

"This is too funny," Branch giggled, looking toward the entrance to the café. "Look who's coming in now."

JC and Milt both looked at a man entering the café and walking down the next aisle of tables. It was Congressman Bat Bellows, choosing the Grand Geneva to secrete himself away after being disgraced by Quip Kelly, as well as Sheepy Johnson.

"Now that is someone the police should be talking to," JC said.

"Goodness," Gretta Miller grumbled as the congressman passed her table. "Is this the only place in Wisconsin to hide?"

The wind made for a bitter chill when JC and Milt walked outside. The snow was covered by small branches where they fell from the trees. JC made his way to their car in the parking lot of the Grand Geneva and Milt placed his camera and batteries in the backseat where they'd remain warm.

Driving to Spring Lakes, they passed snowmobilers powering along the edges of farm fields. Their rental SUV pulled up a driveway in front of a single-level home that looked like many of the homes along that stretch of road.

Tipper Jones was in front, pulling Christmas lights off of the shrubs.

"I am nearly losing the function of my hands," he complained to his visitors as they approached. He reached for another cord of lights and pulled it toward him, careful not to damage anything.

"Why can't we just keep the lights up until a warm day?" he grumbled.

"Because they lose their magic after New Year's Day," a woman answered from the front door that was cracked open.

"She's lending moral support," Jones said to JC and Milt.

"Hi," she said with delight, stepping onto the porch. She was in her sixties and wore a heavy coat, hat and knit gloves.

Tipper Jones's hands were bare, to more easily coax strands of lights off the shrubs.

"Let's go inside," Jones said to them, gathering up the lights he had removed and leaving the rest of them hanging on the shrubs.

"Man, that stings," Jones grimaced as he rubbed his hands at a fireplace in the living room. "What brings you here?"

"You said you had something else to tell us," JC replied.

"So I did," Jones answered with a smile. "So I did. Come with me. Thank you, darling," he said as he grabbed a cup of hot chocolate off a tray his smiling wife was holding. JC and Milt also took a cup as she extended the tray toward them.

They entered an office stuffed with artifacts from skiing history, especially Big Horizon.

"We still call it 'Fox River Runs' in this house," he said.

The office was decorated with old black and white photos of the ski area. They hung on the wall and stood up in frames on every table and shelf. Some of the skiers in the pictures wore knickers, thick wool socks, and lace-up boots.

In the oldest photographs, skiers wore neckties under their sweaters, and their pants were billowy. The skis held next to them towered over their heads.

Jones pointed out a picture of his father, standing next to a groomer from the 1960s.

"They've come a long way since then," Jones said in a homespun way about the groomers.

"You asked me what I was going to do with the money I made by selling Fox River Runs," he reminded JC with a smile.

He pulled a package of blueprints, permits and conceptual drawings off the top of a desk and handed them to JC.

"Look at this," the older man said with pride.

"Indoor skiing?" JC guessed, after taking a moment to study the drawings and a description on one of the permits.

"You bet," Jones said with excitement. "Right in the middle of Chicago. Eighty percent of the skiers that come here to Wisconsin are from Chicago. Why not bring the mountain to them?"

"I've skied at one in New Jersey," JC told him. "It was fun. It was August and I was skiing."

"Exactly!" Jones said with excitement. "They can ski in August, and they can ski after work in November! They'll still want to go visit Vail and Sun Valley and Jackson Hole. But in Chicago, they can have skiing right down the street."

"I have to admit," JC said, "I think this is a great idea."

"I've got it all figured out," Jones said, taking the paperwork back from JC and pointing at it. "It will have 250-feet vertical, a chairlift, and it will be a constant twenty-eight degrees, so the snow never melts. I'll have lockers, and season-pass holders can keep their skis and their ski clothing there. They can leave the office at five o'clock wearing three-piece suits. And by five-thirty, they're wearing ski pants and a jacket and making turns on perfect snow."

"Do you have a site picked out?" JC asked. "You have to build the ramp and install the refrigeration."

"I nailed down my spot!" Jones said. "It's in an industrial area where the land isn't too expensive. We had a hiccup, but we're past that now and ready to forge ahead."

"I'm really impressed," JC told Jones.

"Why drive to Wisconsin when you can take the "L Train" a stop or two and get off at a ski area?" Jones told them. He was glowing.

"You're going to out-'Snow Hat' the 'Snow Hat' company," JC told him.

"Yep," Jones crowed. "And I'm going to do it with the money they paid me."

24

"JC, I need your help."

That was the email message he received from Shara. She was back in the condo in Madison, Wisconsin, that she had shared with Quip. The message explained nothing. There were only two more words, "Please come."

JC rose in the morning and drove away from Lake Geneva. It would take an hour and a half to drive to Madison. Milt stayed behind at the resort to catch up on editing.

The directions into the center of town, near Shara and Quip's condo, took him down Ski Lane. No one seemed certain why the road was named that. One of the few articles that JC could find on the subject said there might have been a ski jump in that neighborhood in the 1940s. There had been another ski jump nearby on the University of Wisconsin campus.

He pulled up to a three-story building. It was constructed in recent years to resemble an older fashionable brownstone. From there, a walk of five blocks would take you to the state capitol building, near trendy State Street, and Lake Mendota.

That address in that neighborhood cost more than a newspaperman earned, JC thought, and Quip died before the big payouts began. Shara must have helped pay for the condo, using money from the sale of her bar in Montana.

Inside the vestibule of the building, he pushed a button, a buzzer sounded, and the door unlocked. Climbing up to the second floor, JC saw Shara leaning out from an open door.

They exchanged a long hug. Her form felt familiar to him. But it was also awkward. They were the same people, but the hugs were different than they had been, years ago.

He walked into the condo and saw the shining hardwood floors. It was an open layout with two bedrooms off the living room and kitchen. And it was a mess.

"I've spent most of my time crying," Shara told him. "It looked like this when I came home."

"It was ransacked?" JC asked.

"Yes. I don't know what they were looking for," Shara said, tears rolling down her cheeks again. "But nothing seems to be missing."

"Then they didn't find what they were looking for," JC told her as he began to walk through the condo and examine the chaos. "They were looking for paper. Look at what they disrupted. Drawers, bookshelves, anything that could hide documents. They were looking for what Quip was hiding."

"Is that what this is?" Shara asked, wiping her eyes. "They weren't looking for jewelry or money or drugs?"

"You said he didn't do drugs," JC reminded her.

"He didn't," she said meekly.

"Did they take any jewelry?"

"No," she whimpered.

"So, if they were after Quip's notes to an investigation, did they find anything?" he asked.

"They already took those from the house in Wilmot," she told him.

"Were there duplicates here?" he asked. "They might have been looking for the duplicates, to wipe clean any evidence of what Quip had discovered."

"No," she said.

"No, what?"

"The duplicates weren't here," she replied. Shara looked at him with her moist eyes. She had something to tell him.

"They were in the boat," she said.

"You own a boat?" he asked.

"No," she answered. "But Quip had rented one, in Florida, as a temporary hideout. And he started hiding things there."

"Have you been there?" JC asked her.

"No," she said. "But about a day after Quip died, I received a phone call from a man I didn't know. I guess he lives on a boat near the one Quip rented. Quip must have trusted him. He said Quip had told him that if anything ever happened to him, to retrieve a box from the boat and mail it to me."

JC looked around the condo and saw an open box on a table, the sticky tape that once sealed it hung from the open top.

"It only arrived today," Shara said. "It wasn't here when whoever broke in and did this."

"Have you called the police?" JC asked, realizing he hadn't seen any police presence.

"Not yet," she said. "I have to make sure that Quip's secrets stay a secret."

"You don't trust the police?" he asked.

"I don't know who to trust, JC," she said in resignation. "People will protect their friends when things get political, even police. Besides, I'm a suspect."

"You're suspected of breaking into your own house?" JC asked. "But you said police don't even know about this."

"I'm a suspect in the death of my husband," she said, tears forming in her eyes again. "The sheriff called and asked if I was coming back. I said that I would be, to pick up my husband's remains. That's when they said they would want to speak with me."

"That doesn't mean you're a suspect, Shara," JC told her.

"JC, they asked me where I was when the fire happened. They asked me about our insurance policy," she said. "They asked for proof of where I was the day the fire broke out. They asked if I was having an affair. They even asked about you and me and our past. They dug that up."

"That could make me a suspect too," JC surmised. It hadn't occurred to him until that point.

"I told him that I was skiing on that day," Shara said. "Then, I visited an old friend nearby in McHenry. That's in Illinois."

"You don't have to explain yourself to me," JC told her.

"I know," she said quietly. She looked at him like she had looked at him years ago. He always made her feel safe.

She leaned in to press against JC's chest and began to weep.

"What am I going to do?" she cried. "What do I do tomorrow? My husband is dead, someone broke into my home."

"How did they get in?" JC asked. "I don't see any damage to the door and you're on the second floor."

"I didn't even think about that," she said, leaving his embrace and looking around her condo. She wiped her eyes with a tissue.

"They might have Quip's key," JC told her. "I'll help you change the locks before I go."

"Thank you," she said, starting again to weep.

But JC worried that it might be worse than that.

"Shara," he said. "Do you have somewhere you can go? Can you go visit your parents or your sister in California?"

"Why?" Shara asked as she searched for an answer on his face. "I have a lot to do here. I've got to get this place cleaned up and I have to collect Quip's remains. I have to decide where I go from here."

"I know," JC said with compassion. "But could you leave for a little while? It might make you feel better. And when you come back, everything might be settled."

"What settled?" she asked, exploring his eyes. "What needs to be settled that requires me to be in California?"

JC said nothing as he looked at her. They were close enough for him to stroke her face. But he didn't.

Shara's eyes grew wide. She opened her mouth to speak but it took a moment.

"You think they were looking for me!" she said. "You think that poor girl was murdered because they thought she was me!"

"It's possible," he said gently. "They're looking for something. There's not a scratch on your door. Whoever broke in here is good at it. They think you've got something they would do anything to get. Unfortunately, they may decide the only way to protect themselves is to silence you."

"Quip always took measures to protect me," she said.

"But he put a scare into a lot of people," JC replied. "And when you announced that you were turning Quip's papers over to the University of Wisconsin journalism school, including his unfinished business, that may have been more than they could ignore. They may be desperate to stop you before you can do that."

"My God," she whispered. "They want to kill me? That's why they killed that woman in Lake Geneva? They thought she was me?"

"Possibly."

Shara rose and walked over to a table. She reached into the box that was mailed to her from Florida.

"Alright," she said. "I'll go hide in California. But you take these," she said as she handed him an overstuffed folder. It held Quip's papers. "Finish Quip's work. If they're so certain that he was going to catch them, then you do it. *You* catch them, JC."

Shara was named by her parents after a war god, actually a male god who was worshipped in Mesopotamia almost three thousand years before Christ. And Shara still had some fight in her.

25

"Small fractures found around the face and jawbone. Orbital bones are fractured," the medical examiner told a collection of law officers and firefighters. "That's around the eye."

"Is it possible he was rendered unconscious before the fire started?" the sheriff asked.

"It's possible," the medical examiner said. "I believe Quip Kelly was beaten, perhaps savagely. Some evidence of abrasions and edema was lost in the fire, but not all of it. Yes, it is quite possible that his injuries allowed the fire to consume him."

The sheriff, the state Division of Criminal Investigation, the state fire marshal's office and chiefs from a handful of local fire departments were back inside a conference room provided at no cost by the Grand Geneva Resort. This time, the district attorney joined them.

"Doctor, did you find evidence that Mr. Kelly had consumed cigarettes or marijuana?" Agent Nelson inquired.

"None," the doctor replied. "There wasn't much left of his lungs. But I saw no effects of smoking on the remains. There was nothing in his blood. Nor did his fingers show telltale signs of holding a cigarette or a rolled marijuana cigarette."

Many of the men and women shifted in their seats at this revelation. Heads turned toward Deputy State Fire Marshal Jakub Williams, who was handling the investigation of the fire.

"That one-foot square piece of the floor we lifted and brought back to the lab proved to be revealing," the deputy fire marshal told them. "The linoleum had worn through over the years in that old home. There was a hole in the linoleum, slightly less than a square foot, exposing the wooden floor. We found that the wood had absorbed liquid from the foam padding in the couch, which melted. That is to be expected. But we also found significant traces of rubbing alcohol. Rubbing alcohol is a highly flammable substance and not easy to detect. It burns clean and doesn't leave much residue."

"It is likely that the rubbing alcohol was sprayed or dripped from the couch Quip Kelly was sitting on," the fire investigator continued. "We have been in contact with Mrs. Kelly. She tells us that Quip was not complaining about muscle soreness and she did not see him in the presence of rubbing alcohol."

"Could that rubbing alcohol be applied as an accelerant to fuel the type of fire we have here?" the district attorney asked.

"Most certainly," the deputy fire marshal answered.

"May I add," Agent Nelson injected, "the ashtray and the roach, or stub end of the marijuana cigarette found in the ashtray, did not provide a fingerprint of Mr. Kelly's. Not complete and not partial. No other fingerprints were found either. That is rather antiseptic for someone relaxing with a joint."

"Did you find evidence of a cigarette or marijuana cigarette in the couch?" the district attorney asked the fire marshal.

"No," the fire expert replied. "And that's not a surprise. The soft material of the couch was largely incinerated by the fire. As I told Agent Nelson, on some occasions we might find a piece of plastic from the filter of a cigarette. But a joint consists of thin paper and the cannabis itself. Both are expected to be consumed by fire."

"The butane lighter?" the district attorney inquired.

"It may have been dropped by Mr. Kelly, if he was indeed smoking on the couch," the DCI agent theorized. "Or, it may have been dropped by someone else who started the fire, if a second party was involved."

"I'll give you a hypothetical," the deputy fire marshal stated to the group. "We have seen cases where an arsonist poured a flammable onto something and then lit it with a lighter. But, not expecting the burst of fire that resulted when the flame hit the flammable, the fire burned the arsonist's hand and maybe singed his eyebrows. And he dropped the lighter into the fire itself."

"An arsonist," the DA repeated.

"We seem to be heading in that direction," Agent Nelson acknowledged.

"Do we have a hypothesis on who may have started the fire, if that's the case?" the DA inquired.

"We have a list that we are proceeding through," the sheriff informed the room. "Mrs. Kelly is on that list. She tells us that she was skiing nearby after visiting her husband at the home that later caught fire. We have verified through a credit card charge that she purchased a lift ticket at Wilmot. Then, we have confirmed her story that she drove to McHenry, Illinois, to visit a female friend.

"This does not rule out, of course, the possibility that Mrs. Kelly purchased the ski ticket, took a few runs, went to the house and killed her husband and then returned to the ski area to be seen there again. She did purchase a tee shirt at the gift store at Wilmot in the afternoon. But again, that could be viewed as a deliberate effort to mark her presence at the ski area. It does not rule out the chance that she left and came back."

"Are you looking at anyone else?" the district attorney asked.

"The TV newsman from Colorado had a romantic relationship with Mrs. Kelly before she was married," Agent Nelson reported. "We're looking at that, but it doesn't look promising."

"Quite a coincidence, though," the district attorney observed. "That they both turned up here at the same time."

"Yes, it is," the agent agreed. "And we have another avenue that we're investigating. I think we are all aware of Mr. Kelly's brand of journalism. He was bound to make enemies. We do not, however, have any strong suspicions regarding a particular person."

"Does Mrs. Kelly think her husband was a target?" The question came from a local police chief.

"She told us that she believes her husband was a potential target," Nelson responded. "She says he took safeguards to protect the two of them. However, whatever his current project was, Mrs. Kelly believes all of that work by her husband was removed from the house that caught fire. She says that she saw a collection of papers and photographs on the table of the house that morning. We found no trace of them."

"So, we have a couple of motives and evidence that the fire was an arson," the district attorney pronounced. "Is that our understanding? This is an arson?" He turned his eyes to the deputy fire marshal.

"That is my recommendation," Jakub Williams said. "This has all the marks of an arson fire."

Participants of the meeting began to stir. Their duties in the coming days had been stated and assigned. And for public consumption, the fire killing Quip Kelly would be labeled an arson.

The meeting adjourned, DCI Agent Nelson filed out of the room with the others.

"Agent Nelson?"

The law officer turned and saw JC rising from a chair by the door to the conference room.

"Were you at the door listening?" the agent asked.

"No," JC said. "That's not a bad idea, but I'm handcuffed by my own dignity."

"Yes, you'd look pretty stupid," Nelson agreed.

"Am I a suspect in this fire?" JC asked.

"Not much of one," the DCI agent told him. "You were a person of interest in the beginning. We know that you had a relationship with Quip Kelly's wife. And it's quite a coincidence that you both showed up here at the same time."

"I won't argue that. But the romance was a long time ago," JC told him.

"Have you two been in contact more recently?" Nelson asked.

"No, not until we bumped into each other here a few days ago," JC told him. "But I have something that might interest you."

"Such as?" the agent asked without enthusiasm.

JC told him about the conversation with a bartender at the Wilmot Riverside Bar and Grill. The bartender, Walter Schroeder, had served a beer to a man with an injury to his hand at about the time of the fire.

"What kind of injury?" the agent asked.

"It almost sounded like a burn," JC said. "Like if someone was holding a lighter and his hand got singed."

"Holding a lighter, huh?" the agent mused. "I thought you had too much dignity to listen at the door."

"If I'm sitting on a chair and you talk loud enough to be heard through a door," JC told him. "I'm dignified, not deaf."

26

"So, what are we going to do tonight?"

"We?" JC asked Milt.

They were wrapping up their gear after their last live shot before the weekend began.

"Well, I am about to leave for Milwaukee, where I will pick up my girlfriend at the airport," JC said. "Then we, and I mean Robin and I, are going to have a quiet late dinner and probably take a bottle of wine up to our room."

"Can I come?" Milt asked.

"Which inappropriate request am I presently fielding?" JC asked. "Are you asking if you can be present at our quiet romantic dinner, or are you asking to come up to our room afterwards and watch?"

"Don't be silly. I am asking to come with you to..." Milt stopped. JC wondered if he was really considering his options.

"Dinner," Milt finally answered. "I'd like to have dinner with the two of you." And Milt attempted to look at JC with sad puppy dog eyes.

"You realize," JC pointed out. "Your sad puppy dog eyes just look like your eyes any other time."

"I've missed her too, you know," Milt said as he continued to give JC the look.

"Fine, you can have dinner with us," JC told him. Milt's face lit up.

"But after dinner," JC warned. "You are on your own. You cannot sleep at the end of our bed."

"Agreed!" Milt declared with enthusiasm.

"And when you are turned loose on society," JC added. "Do not try to sleep with some murder victim."

"JC, I already told you," Milt responded. "That would be disgusting."

"I mean before they're dead," JC deadpanned.

"Come on," Milt said, dismissing the notion. "That's only happened, like, well, three times now."

"You have got your hands full," Agent Aurek Nelson commiserated with the sheriff, dropping by his office in Kenosha.

"Since you're in town," the sheriff said, nodding in agreement, "do you want to give us a hand?"

"That's what I'm here for," Agent Nelson said. "To serve and protect."

"I'll tell you what we've got," the sheriff said. "We have a new report from our medical examiner. The deceased, Elizabeth Johnson, was found in a field unclothed. Her underwear was found nearby.

"But examination of the body finds there was no sexual assault. Nor is there evidence of sexual activity attached to the underwear. There is no evidence that anyone handled that underwear other than her."

"What do you think that means?" the agent asked.

"Why go to the trouble to undress someone you just killed?" the sheriff asked. "Unless the killer was trying to point us in the wrong direction, disguise it as a sexual assault."

The agent's head nodded in agreement.

"Could the clothing itself have contained incriminating evidence, so it was removed?" Agent Nelson asked. "For example, if the killer bled on the garment, then the garment would have to be removed."

"That's interesting," the sheriff stated. "We also asked the medical examiner if he found fabric in the victim's wound, from her dress or blouse. But he tells me that the position of the wound is such that if she was wearing a low-cut dress or open blouse, the weapon might not have gone through any fabric."

"The fork is from her restaurant, Rainbows?" the agent asked.

"Yes, we think the fork is from there," the sheriff confirmed. "That puts the girlfriend, Cyndi Larsen, in play. They both worked there, so it goes without saying, Ms. Larsen's fingerprints are all over the place."

"Was the restaurant robbed?"

"No," the sheriff replied. "And it was not broken into."

"Do you think she was killed at the restaurant?"

"No," the sheriff said. "There's no evidence of that."

"What about that boot print in the field?" Nelson inquired.

"The boot size is the very most common size," the sheriff told him. "And the boot itself is the most common boot in all of Wisconsin."

"A common boot for a man or for a woman?" the agent queried.

"A man," the sheriff told him. "But that means most women could fit into it."

"Are you bringing in Cyndi Larsen for questioning?" the agent asked.

"Yes," the sheriff responded. "We are looking for her now."

"You've got your hands full," Agent Nelson said again.

JC and Robin entered the restaurant holding hands. They barely arrived in time for their reservation at the Chop House after rushing from the airport in Milwaukee. The Chop House offered fine dining on the grounds of their resort. It was Friday night, and it was crowded.

Milt was waiting for them at their table. He was wearing a sweater and a tie.

"You look nice," Robin said, like she was complimenting a teenager.

Milt stood up and waited for Robin to be seated. He was displaying old-world manners. Robin was impressed.

"Why can't you be more like Milt," Robin said, wearing a broad smile and looking at JC.

"Yeah, JC," Milt said. "Be more like me."

JC cringed.

"How was your date?" Robin asked Milt. "With Branch, right?"

"It was very nice, thank you," Milt told her. "I am living a dream. We're going out again. She is neither obnoxious nor desperate. And she actually seems to enjoy my company."

"I haven't seen her today," JC said. "Is she still alive?"

"Hi!" the perky voice resonated. Her timing was perfect. It was Branch.

"I switched with another server," she said, half-singing. "So, I'll be your server tonight!"

"Hi, JC," Branch said. She had noticed him staring at her. "Is everything alright?"

"I'm looking for strangle marks on your neck," JC said. "Or a bandage over a wound."

"Oh, Milt told me all about that," Branch giggled. "Misunderstandings like that happen all the time."

"See! I told you!" Milt said, as though he'd just won the debate.

"Did you tell them how romantic you are?" Branch asked Milt. Then, she headed for the kitchen.

"You're romantic?" Robin said, egging him on.

"Okay, this is what happened," Milt began. "We had a really good time. We were at a club in Lake Geneva. At the end of the night, she said she was going to stay with a friend in town. I took that to mean that she didn't want to give me a goodnight kiss."

Robin gave JC a stern look before he could make a snarky remark.

"But she insisted that she had a great time," Milt continued. "So, I said, 'Then would you meet me here tomorrow night and we'll do it again?' She said that she would, but I wasn't sure. So, I unzipped my jacket and took off my shirt. For a minute, I wasn't wearing anything above my belt. I was freezing!"

"She saw your body and she still wants to go out with you again?" JC cringed.

"Funny," Milt responded. "So, I'd taken off my shirt, right? And I said, 'This is my favorite shirt. I'm going to give it to you. If you want to see me tomorrow night, take my shirt. You can give it back to me then.'"

"Oh, my goodness," Robin said. "That *is* romantic."

"Wait, it gets better," Milt told her. "So, she starts wiggling around in her jacket. She pulls her arms inside and she's wiggling like a worm. Then, she sticks her arms back out the arms of the jacket and pulls out the blouse she was wearing that night! She says, 'Here's *my* shirt. If you want to see me tomorrow night, you can give it back to me then.'"

Robin was holding her hand on her chest, her mouth open, gasping.

"JC," she said as she hit his arm. "Why can't you be romantic like Milt!"

"Has this world gone crazy?" JC mumbled.

Milt was beaming.

Branch came back to the table with their drinks. She saw Robin, still gasping.

"I know, right?" Branch sang with a big smile.

"Oh my," JC blurted.

"What," Robin asked, looking at him.

"That's not your shirt," JC asked Branch. "Is it?"

Branch just smiled at him, and then at Milt.

"It's mine," Milt said, beaming.

"That is so romantic!" Robin gushed.

"I know, right?" Branch sang to her.

Milt smiled with his new shiny teeth.

The next morning was cold. Children at the base of Big Horizon were blowing steam through their lips like they were blowing smoke rings. It was cold, but it was sunny.

"Hello, TV people!" Linda Smith said happily as she walked by in her racing team vest.

"That's the vice president of the ski racing program for the kids," JC told Robin. "She's usually not that happy."

It was Saturday. JC and Robin decided to go skiing. Robin had left her skis behind in Wisconsin when she flew back to Denver, hoping to return and get more runs in.

Riding the lift to the top, they skied above the racecourse. JC hadn't been in racing gates since a crash last spring. The end result was surgery followed by rehab.

The father of a young racer was on his hands and knees, rubbing short candles on several skis.

"It's candle wax," the man said to them over his shoulder. "I'm impressing on the kids that when it gets this cold, candle wax will work as well as the expensive stuff we buy them."

"Really?" Robin asked JC.

"That's what the old-timers say," JC said, then looking at the man on his knees with his candles, added, "No offense."

"None taken," the man said. "I'm one of the coaches. We emphasize skiers taking responsibility for their technique, rather than blaming their equipment or wax. Bad race runs are not usually the fault of wax or equipment."

"That's good parenting," JC said.

"And we emphasize making crisp turns here. We call them small turns," he said. "If you carve perfect small turns, really perfect ones, the big turns will come easily."

"I need a coach like you," JC told him.

"Do you want to hop in the gates?" the coach asked. "The kids will be coming up the lift. But right now, the course is open, if you want to."

"It's been a while," JC said. "I'd love to."

Robin's goggles hid the anguish in her eyes. She felt a nervous pang. She had only just nursed JC back to health.

JC slid over to the top gate. It would act as the start. He could see about five gates before the hill plunged out of sight.

"Which way does it go?" JC asked the coach.

"After it drops over the top?" the coach asked. "A hard left. It's a transition."

JC pushed off. He relished the feeling, for the first time in many months. He wasn't perfect, he was late on the second and third gate. But he got back where he belonged before he plunged out of sight.

Robin, nervous, hurriedly skied to the edge where she could see the bottom of the run. She was reliving the end of his last race, when she watched him go at high speed into the trees.

Instead, she saw JC standing at the base of Big Horizon, smiling up at her.

On the ride back up the lift, JC listened happily to the metallic pings made by the chair lift.

"Are you going to do it again?" Robin asked. "It's okay if you do."

"Nope," he said. "That was fun. And they told me that I can come back and train. But I'm here with you, and we don't have much time. Sheepy's wake is this afternoon. I'd like to go to it."

They took another run and noticed a woman carving serious arcs on her snowboard. They caught up with her at the bottom of the lift.

"Hi, Cyndi," JC said. It was Sheepy Johnson's girlfriend.

"Hi," responded Cyndi Larsen, sounding exhausted. The lovely Black woman with dreadlocks popped open her bindings and climbed off her snowboard.

"I know this looks weird," she told them. "I'm supposed to be grieving. Lying in bed or sitting on a couch in a room with the lights out, crying. But I've been doing that for days."

"No two people grieve the same way," JC told her. "I've seen enough grieving to learn that."

"*This* makes me feel better," Cyndi told them. "I always go snowboarding when I'm bothered by something. It's time to go to the funeral home, though. Sheepy's parents are handling all the arrangements. There's really nothing for me to do there, except cry more."

"I do the exact same thing when I'm troubled," JC told her. "Skiing always makes me feel better."

"Yeah, maybe not this time," she said as she picked up her board and began to walk to her car. "Will I see you there?"

"Yes," Robin said. "I hope this worked, a little."

27

Music performed by the Grateful Dead played over speakers in the funeral home. Pictures mounted on corkboards showed Sheepy Johnson at Grateful Dead concerts, snowboarding, at high school dances, posing with Cyndi, and on the farm with sheep. There were lots of pictures of her with sheep.

"Are you her sister?" asked a woman as Robin looked at the pictures.

"No, I'm not," Robin said with kindness.

"I'm sorry," the woman said. "It's the red hair."

"Yes," Robin laughed a little laugh, understanding. She gave her long red hair a little flip.

Sheepy's snowboard stood upright by her casket. A mountain bike was nearby. There must have been fifty balloons with rainbows floating overhead.

Cyndi Larsen had left the receiving line to take a seat. She was crying.

Robin looked across the room. She saw a man wearing a trench coat with his large hands crossed in front of him. His dark hair was thick and neatly combed skyward on top of his head. She asked JC who it was.

"That's a state Division of Criminal Investigation agent. His name is Nelson, Aurek Nelson," he told her. "DCI was asked to come in and help with the investigation. I think that's how they do it here in Wisconsin."

Nelson was standing alone in the back of the room. He looked like he had deliberately separated himself from the crowd. His eyes were on Cyndi Larsen.

"I don't think it's her," Robin said when she walked over to him.

"We never want to think it's her," the agent told Robin as he nodded his head in the direction of the crowd. "Or him, or him, or her or anyone else you've met. But someone did this."

Robin didn't respond. But she was thinking that he made a good point.

"You're Robin Smith, the reporter," Nelson said. He had deep smile lines, but she never saw him smile.

"I guess you've got your eye on everyone," Robin said.

"That's why they pay us the big bucks," Nelson replied with a straight face.

"Talk to you later," Robin smiled as she walked away. Agent Nelson watched her.

"Do you think it could have been a case of mistaken identity?"

Nelson took his eyes off of Robin and looked in the direction of the inquiring voice. It was JC.

"Is it possible?" JC asked. "That the killer mistook Sheepy for Shara?"

"It's possible," the agent said, then exhaled. "I've thought about it."

"Shara might know Quip's secrets," JC suggested.

"Yes," Agent Nelson agreed. "And that may have put her in danger. Do you know where she is, by the way?"

"Yes," JC said. "She's somewhere safe."

"The time may come when you will have to tell us," the agent said after giving that some thought.

"I know," JC acknowledged, without offering to tell at that moment. "What about Congressman Bellows?"

"We are looking at suspects," the DCI man said.

"Are you looking at Congressman Bellows?" JC repeated. "Sheepy embarrassed him in front of a lot of people."

"We are looking at suspects," the agent repeated. He wouldn't even make eye contact with JC.

JC's scanned the crowd. So did Agent Nelson's.

"Your girlfriend might be in danger too," Agent Nelson added. "You two come here poking around. That can make people nervous. Quip Kelly was one of *your* people, a newsman. You said yourself, he wanted to share his secrets with you."

"Yep," JC acknowledged. "But he didn't get a chance to."

"As a professional courtesy," the agent said. "Your girlfriend looks a lot like Shara too. You should keep an eye on your girlfriend."

"Duly noted," JC said. "Duly noted."

Robin was now circling the center of the funeral home. She was locked in on the number of jackets with wickets hanging from them, lift tickets adhered to them.

"Excuse me," she finally had to say to one of those wearing a ski jacket. "Is there somewhere I can get a discount on lift tickets around here?"

The woman she approached looked her up and down. Her answer was short but came with a smile, "No, honey. I'm sorry."

A man she asked gave a similar answer, "I don't think so."

"I'm talking about lift tickets that aren't entirely real," Robin clarified. "I'm willing to pay a fair price."

"No, sorry," the man said.

She approached another man, only because no one was standing near him. He might be unafraid to tell her a town secret.

The man looked Robin over. He studied her long red hair that curled at the bottom, and her athletic build squeezed into a dress that complimented her figure.

"I don't care if they're real," she said, expanding her story. "I just want to pay a fair price, you know?"

"Just Big Horizon," he said. "I don't know about the other mountains. But there's a way to get cheap tickets to Big Horizon. You just have to find the right person."

"And how do I find the right person?" she pursued.

"You here alone?" the man asked, leering.

"No," she said, though smiling. "My boyfriend is here." She didn't point out JC because he was becoming known locally. Someone breaking the law would not want to be known to a TV journalist.

The man sized her up. He decided that he wasn't going to get anywhere with the redhead, but he could be nice, just for the sake of it.

"It's pretty easy," he said. "People sell them around town, walking up the aisle of the grocery store. As a last resort, just stand in the parking lot of Big Horizon. You won't have to wait long before you see a lady with a green ski jacket and her hand stuffed in her pocket. She clings to a pile of them in that pocket."

"Are they real or are they fake?" she asked.

"Does it matter?" he said to her.

Leaving the funeral home, JC and Robin saw Milt across the street shooting video. He had come along, just in case Sheepy's murder somehow later worked into the two stories they were covering for their Colorado viewers. That would be the killings of Ronny Schwartz and Quip Kelly.

JC drove the car across the road and pulled into a bank parking lot. Milt met them there, just to avoid adding a circus atmosphere in the funeral home's parking lot.

"How much money could you make," Robin asked. "If you were counterfeiting chairlift tickets at a ski area?"

JC looked at her.

"Which ski area?" he asked. "Aspen? Park City? Minnie's Gap?"

"Big Horizon," she said.

"Only Big Horizon? Not the other ones around Lake Geneva?"

"Just Big Horizon, I think," she told him.

"Not enough to retire on," he guessed. "But enough to go out to some nice dinners or save up for a nice vacation. I remember there were two nurses accused of selling phony cards verifying that unvaccinated people had been vaccinated. It was during the Covid crisis. Selling one card at a time, police say the nurses ended up making over a million dollars before they were caught."

"Wow," said Robin. "So, selling counterfeit lift tickets, day after day, could add up."

"I guess it could," he agreed. "Why?"

"Because I think someone is counterfeiting Big Horizon's tickets," she told him. "And I wonder if Ronny Schwartz was on to them."

"Wow." Now it was JC's turn to say it.

"So, it's true," Landover Scott said, giving Robin a wink. JC was sitting next to her. They had found Scotty at a corner table that they were beginning to think of as their own personal spot in the Igloo Lounge.

"It first happened in the 1990s," Landover Scott told them. "All those new sophisticated printers were coming out. Anyone could buy them at a big-box store and faithfully reproduce almost anything. Some guys actually counterfeited American currency on their printer. It was almost perfect. They got away with it, for a while."

"But in the 1990s," JC steered the conversation back to their question. "Someone was counterfeiting lift tickets at ski areas?"

"Not somebody," Scotty corrected him. "Lots of people. Printers could clone those lift tickets that were sticky on one side and had red stripes or green circles on the other side. It was child's play."

"Was anybody caught?" Robin asked.

"I did a story on it," Scotty told them. "I don't recall anyone getting caught. I don't think it was an organized crime ring or anything. I think it was just college students or anyone with a new printer and a talent for duplication. I think most of them just wanted to ski for free and earn a little pocket money."

"And what happened?" JC asked. "How were they stopped?"

"I spoke with the big ski resorts," Scotty recalled. "I asked them about the problem and most denied it. One or two said something was happening but they had no idea if they were losing significant money."

Scotty shook his finger in the air, like he was about to drive home a point.

"But they weren't being honest with me," he told them. "Because all of the sudden, the wealthiest ski resorts came up with new lift tickets. The tickets had reflective tape on them, impossible to counterfeit on those printers. And they did it in the middle of the season! Can you imagine how expensive and inconvenient it was to do an 'about face' on their lift tickets in the middle of the season? Whatever problem they were trying to address, it must have been significant."

"And now we all get lift tickets with bar codes," JC added.

"Yes," Scotty agreed. "I don't know if that is added protection or just an inventory thing or all of the above. But bar codes aren't easy to counterfeit."

"When is the last time you skied at Big Horizon?" Robin asked.

"It's been years since I skied," Scotty laughed. "On days when my knees feel alright, my hips feel awful. And on days my hips feel good, my knees feel like a truck ran over them."

"They still use the old-fashioned lift tickets at Big Horizon," she told him. "With the blue polka dots and red stripes and whatever."

"Well," Scotty said with a surprised look. "Then they might have a problem, mightn't they?"

28

"It could have been me?"

"That DCI agent thinks so," JC told Robin. "I'm not saying this to frighten you. I just want you to stay close to me or Milt, okay? It's not the time to go for a long walk alone."

"Then, it could have been me," she repeated. "If it's possible that they mistook Sheepy for Shara and killed her, then they could have stumbled across me and thought I was Shara."

The killer also may have mistaken Sheepy for Robin, JC thought. There was an outside chance that Robin was the target. But he didn't need to say it.

"Just stay close," he told her. His voice was firm but caring.

"Hang onto her," Landover Scott said. "You two love each other. Don't let anything happen to her."

Robin looked at JC. They did love each other.

Night had fallen. JC and Robin were still seated with Scotty in a corner of the Igloo Lounge.

"Is there something going on with you and Bunny?" Robin asked Scotty.

"Just like a woman," Scotty said with a smile. "Your antenna is always up."

"Don't avoid the subject," Robin told him.

"Just like a journalist," he replied with a smile. "You won't mind your own business."

"Nope," Robin said in a playful deep voice, trying to imitate JC's frequent 'Nopes' and 'Yeps.'" JC laughed.

"What makes this your business?" Scotty asked with a playful smile.

"It's alright," Robin said. "It's a good thing. Your wife died over a year ago? You're not obligated to be unhappy. She wouldn't want that."

Robin invoking the wants of his own wife made Scotty lower his head and think. Robin was intuitive and, while not the same as having his wife back at his side, it was comforting to have someone like Robin doing her thinking for her.

"No, I suppose not," Scotty said, raising his eyes to meet Robin's.

JC was drinking a Glenfarclas, Robin a red wine. Scotty was drinking a locally brewed Mello Rillo beer.

"I saw you drinking it the other day," Scotty said, holding up the beer. "I thought I'd try it. It's good."

"How come we never see you except if we're in the bar?" Robin asked.

"I never leave," he said smiling at her.

"Don't let him fool you," Bunny said, suddenly appearing at their table. "He's usually in his room writing another book."

They greeted the woman and ordered a red wine for her after she joined them at their table.

"Another book?" Robin asked. "What are you writing about?"

"The same nonsense," Scotty said with humility. "It's titled *Down the Dumb Path*. It's about the dumbing down in America that's going on. The problem is: only smart people will read it. The dumb ones don't read, either."

"It's a good topic, though," JC told him. "You've had some bestsellers, haven't you?"

"I have, in the past. But I'm at a point in my life when I try to invoke the lessons I've learned over time," he said. "My latest books have been me telling everyone else that they're getting dumber."

"Well, are your books selling?" Robin asked.

"These books lately? They're rolling donuts," he replied.

Robin gave him a confused look.

"Zero book sales," he explained. "Or close to it. No one wants to buy a book that tells them they're dumb."

They ordered a bottle of wine, deciding this was good company and a good place to spend the evening.

"Have you solved the crime yet?" Scotty asked JC.

"Nope," he said. "Starting to feel dumb."

"It's an odd threesome, if the murders are connected," Scotty said. "A drowning, a fire and a fork. Not the mark of one killer, is it?"

"Nope," JC agreed. "But the murder rate in this rolling prairie is pretty much rolling donuts. So, it makes you wonder if one particular person has come to town to do some damage."

"And if there's a connection between the three of them, it's not obvious," Robin added. "It's possible that Sheepy's murder was a mistaken identity. I have been informed that the attacker may have thought they were killing Shara, or me."

"That would link Sheepy's killing to Quip, perhaps," JC stated. "But where does Ronny Schwartz fit into this?"

"Well, you told me about the counterfeit lift tickets," Scotty said. "That was probably in Ronny Schwartz's bailiwick, before he disappeared like Houdini."

"Another fine Wisconsin resident," Bunny inserted.

She received curious looks from the others.

"Harry Houdini," she said. "He emigrated from Hungary to Appleton, Wisconsin."

"And bailiwick?" Robin asked. "You know, you lapse in and out of English when you speak." Scotty laughed at this.

"It's a sphere of someone's influence or operation," he said. "My choice of words do seem to be slipping into ancient languages."

JC wanted to get back on the subject. He liked Scotty's input.

"Yes, Ronny Schwartz would have been interested in counterfeit lift tickets," JC said. "But how does that connect him to Quip? He was a government watchdog. And at Shara's apartment, I looked through the things Quip was working on. Lift tickets wasn't one of them."

"And the assortment of murder weapons," Scotty added. "One killer normally sticks to similar methods. He refines his art to his liking."

"A drowning, a fire and a fork," JC said. "I don't see the connection."

"No, not like just using a heater," Scotty said.

"Here we go again," Robin said. "English, please."

"A convincer, a Roscoe," Scotty said, now teasing her.

"Use English like you'd speak since the invention of TikTok," she smiled.

"A Chicago typewriter," Scotty said. "That's my favorite. That's what they used to call a Tommy Gun."

"Oh, we're talking about guns?" Robin laughed. "Why didn't the killer just shoot them?"

"Yes," Scotty grinned. "My apologies."

"Good old-fashioned lead poisoning," Robin suggested with a smile.

"Oh, you're doing your homework," Scotty said in an approving tone. "Yes, lead poisoning, getting shot."

"The killer didn't even try to make Quip's death look like an accident," JC said. "Schwartz didn't mistakenly take a swim in December wearing ski boots. And Sheepy didn't accidentally fall on a fork in a field and then take her clothing off."

They fell silent, thinking about the confusing clues they had to work with.

"And how is the skiing?" Scotty asked, taking another sip from his beer.

"I have acquired a great deal of respect for skiing in the Midwest," JC said. "I love skiing smaller hills. That's how we grew up. That's where our parents took us."

"Do you miss it?" Robin asked Scotty.

"Miss what?" he asked her. "Skiing?"

"No, not skiing," she said. "I wondered if you miss being a reporter. The excitement that comes with journalism. Or even being famous."

"The problem with fame is that so many people tell you that you're wonderful, you think you don't need to fix anything about yourself," he told her. "I left television a decade ago, and I'm still trying to fix what's broken in me."

"You seem alright to me," Robin said with a comforting look.

"I'm glad that I have you fooled," he grinned.

"It's not easy to be normal," JC said.

"Practically no one knows how to do it," Scotty agreed.

For some time, JC had been eyeing a woman at the end of the bar. He recognized her as Gretta Miller, the senator's betrayed wife. She was minding her own business. She had gone unrecognized, though it was possible that people were just afraid of the stern woman. She hadn't spoken to anyone except the bartender.

Another ruined politician walked into the Igloo Lounge, Congressman Bat Bellows. In recent days, he had emailed followers saying that he would not be running for re-election. Like Gretta Miller's husband, he had been caught by Quip.

Now, on top of being despised by many of his own constituents, he was a murder suspect.

It was Saturday night. Bellows figured drinking alone in a bar was better than drinking alone in his room.

His eyes met Gretta Miller's. It was not a meeting he relished. They sat on opposite sides of the political aisle, even if they presently sat in a similar dumpster.

"Oh, for Christ's sake," Gretta Miller said to him in a voice that sounded like she was a Marine master sergeant. "Buy me a drink and sit down."

Bellows obediently slid onto the stool next to the older woman. He looked surprised and terrified. He twisted at a ring on his finger. It had a red stone.

"I'm a little taken aback," he said to her. "Aren't you mad at me?"

"Why?" she asked. "Did you sleep with my husband too?"

"Gosh, no!" he sputtered.

"Well then," she deadpanned. "Why would I be mad at you?"

29

"**S**on of a bitch!"

Tillison Tucker threw the newspaper down on his desk and stood up. He was back in his office at Snow Hat in Colorado.

But he had just seen the headline on the *Kenosha News*. It said, "Back on Top of the Mountain!"

"That back-stabbing hillbilly!" bellowed Tucker. "I made him a millionaire! And this is how he repays me?"

"Is everything alright, Mr. Tucker?" Tina Hernandez, his administrative assistant, poked her head around the door.

Tucker looked at her, hands on his hips. It was her gentle reminder that his outburst would be heard throughout the second floor, down the hall from his office.

"Yes, Tina," he said, composing himself. "Thank you."

She backed away and pulled the door closed behind her.

"Son of a bitch!" he said again, this time using his indoor voice.

The Kenosha, Wisconsin, newspaper story featured Tipper Jones, the sixty-two-year-old former owner of the small ski mountain, Fox River Runs. The article explained that Jones was going into a new business, using the money he made by selling his ski area to Snow Hat.

The paper reported that Tipper Jones had acquired property and the permits to build the first indoor ski area in Chicago.

Strikingly similar plans sat on Tillison Tucker's mahogany desk.

"Son of a bitch," Tucker repeated to himself. "Chicago doesn't need *two* indoor ski areas. I *thought* this was taken care of."

Normally, this was when he'd call Ronny Schwartz to his office and they'd come up with a plan, a way to rescue their fat from the fire.

But Schwartz was dead. And what was supposed to have been taken care of, wasn't.

"The son of a bitch."

"We are going to be rich, honey," Tipper Jones giggled to his wife as he danced around their kitchen in Spring Lakes. "I am going to buy you a mink coat!"

A copy of the same *Kenosha News* sat on the table in the Jones residence, next to a *Chicago Tribune* with a similar story about his announcement.

"Tipper," his wife laughed. "We don't wear mink anymore, goodness. I'm just glad to see you so happy."

"He thought he was dealing with a bunch of woodchucks!" Tipper laughed. "Hard work, honey. It's still all about hard work. But Tillison Tucker has been wearing those fancy suits too long. He forgot how to reach his hands into the grease and get dirty."

The phone was ringing. Well-wishers were calling.

"I hope he won't be mad," Tipper's wife said with a worried look on her face.

"I didn't think it would really happen," Tipper told her, ignoring her fears. He had a big grin stretched over his unshaven chin. "We hit a bump in the road, but in the end, everything was taken care of."

"Son of a bitch!"

Wisconsin Senator Raff Swensen wasn't as much yelling as he was blubbering. He was blindsided.

"Everything was supposed to be taken care of," the senator said to himself as he fell into the seat behind the desk at his Senate office in Madison. In front of him sat a copy of the Madison newspaper.

On the front page was a picture of the senator's car with a bent fender. The headline said, "Senator Focus of Fatal Hit & Run as He Fondles Follower."

On the second page of the story, he is pictured with a topless sunbather whose face and breasts are purposely blurred.

The office phones for Senator Swensen were all ringing.

"Senator, there's a call for you," a voice said, coming from the outer office. Swensen recognized the voice as belonging to his top aide.

"I'm not taking any calls!" the senator shouted.

"It's someone with the state Division of Criminal Investigation," the voice told him.

It was barely nine a.m. on a Monday morning, but the message was clear. His career was over, and he might be going to prison.

His top aide peered into the office.

"Get out!" screamed Swensen. Then, the senator picked up the ringing phone on his desk and threw it across the room, tearing the cord out of the wall.

"That son of a bitch!" he screamed.

After Shara had given JC the papers that Quip had hidden on a boat in Florida, it hadn't taken long for JC to make sense of them. He neatly pieced Quip's puzzle together. He admired Quip's work. The story was bulletproof.

The newspaper in Madison offered to share the byline with him. But JC believed that the credit belonged to Quip Kelly alone. It was his work, part of his legacy.

"Thank you, JC," Shara said in a telephone call from California. "Quip knew that he could trust you. You would have become such good friends."

Swensen went home. The state political party chairman had told him there was no alternative but to resign. Friendships that Swensen had cultivated over two decades wilted within hours. And the DCI still wanted to speak with him.

At his house, in the most fashionable neighborhood in his senate district, he found his wife weeping uncontrollably. Her mascara ran down her cheeks. Her beautifully preserved face was a mud puddle. She was broken.

The senator collapsed into a chair behind the desk in his study. He pulled out the top drawer to his left. There was a small handgun.

"Everything was supposed to be taken care of," he mumbled and began to cry.

JC, Milt and Robin parked at the Big Horizon Ski Resort and headed for The Farmhouse. Word had surfaced that Snow Hat had been competing to build that indoor ski area in Chicago. They wanted to hear the reaction to Tipper Jones's triumph.

To TV viewers in Colorado, the story was about Snow Hat. Their wealth of resources had been outfoxed by "The Fox River Rascal," as a newspaper columnist described Tipper Jones. It was a story about David beating Goliath.

Robin was still in Wisconsin, on a Monday, after scheduling more vacation time when she was back in Denver. It was a hard sell.

"We're at full staff," she had pleaded with their news director, Pat Perilla, before flying to Milwaukee. "Everyone is back from their holiday vacation. JC is giving you material every day. I'm the only one who will be off. And you know I'm working for you, even if my schedule says I'm on vacation."

Outweighing even the strength of her argument, their news director had a soft spot for Robin that he tried not to display. She had, after all, decided to stay with them in Denver instead of taking a job offered by the network. In the end, he let her return to Wisconsin.

"I know you're a great asset to them," Perilla had said. "But do me a favor, get this business finished so you can all come home."

Perilla was rewarded with an unsolicited kiss on the cheek. Perhaps that wasn't professional behavior in the new world of office etiquette, rules he was still learning. But it was still a currency that he appreciated.

So, Robin was back in Wisconsin with JC. They had started their day by shooting an interview with Tipper Jones. His wife gave them cookies and coffee.

Many employees of Big Horizon, who used to work for Tipper at Fox River Runs, and wished they still did, were celebrating the defeat of their new employer. But not one of them dared say so on camera.

Had Snow Hat Ski Enterprises grown too big? Was this a sign of change in the ski industry? These were all questions that would be addressed.

Walking from the parking lot, Robin eyed the rows of vehicles being formed as cars pulled in for the weekday opening of the ski resort, at noon.

Following behind JC and Milt, Robin suddenly grabbed JC's arm.

"Hey, wait a minute," Robin said. "That's the woman selling fake tickets. The guy at the funeral hall said I could get counterfeit tickets from a lady that wore a green jacket."

JC looked down an aisle of parked cars. He saw Linda Smith, the vice president of the ski racing team, collecting money from three men and handing them three lift tickets.

"Come on, before she sees us," JC said. They moved to the next aisle and watched her. They hid between large SUVs and pickup trucks. In less than five minutes, Smith repeated the process with another group of skiers and snowboarders.

"Why?" Robin asked quietly.

"You should hear her talk about this place," JC said. "I can't say this comes as a complete surprise."

"Why sell counterfeit tickets?" Robin asked. "Just to get even? I doubt she's getting rich."

"Revenge is a dish best served cold," JC said. "What better place than the parking lot of a ski area."

Milt now had the camera on his shoulder, using his long lens to capture images of Linda Smith's misdeeds.

She turned, and in the instant that it took Milt to conceal himself behind a Ford Explorer, she saw the camera.

"Son of a bitch," she whispered.

30

"They're staring at you," Robin told JC.

"Maybe they're staring at me," Milt said. "I've reinvented myself."

"No, hon," Robin said. "They're staring at JC."

JC didn't glance up from the beer cheese soup he was enjoying in the Silo Bar at Big Horizon. They were taking a break for lunch after being told at The Farmhouse that there would be no official comment on Tipper Jones's plans to build an indoor ski resort in Chicago. Milt's camera and tripod were tucked under the table.

Others eating lunch in the bar *were* staring at JC. It wasn't something that he was used to in Wisconsin. He was recognized plenty by viewers in Colorado, but not in Wisconsin.

However, by turning over Quip's exposé on Senator Swensen to the newspaper, he had been given permission to use the material in a story for television news. He still attributed the findings to Quip, but television stations in Chicago and across Wisconsin lined up to interview JC about Quip's story.

And the network news was eating it up. JC's report went nationwide, in part because of the scandalous doings of a state senator, and in part because it was Quip Kelly's last scoop.

To JC's viewers in Colorado, the story was very interesting but had little or no impact on their day-to-day life on the Front Range. Still, JC's news director was delighted with the latest report by JC Snow. It put them in the national spotlight. And now, the network and their affiliates in Chicago and Wisconsin would all owe them one.

"JC," the news director said. "You hit another one out of the ballpark."

Robin, JC and Milt stared out the window of the bar. They watched the skiers and snowboarders on the hill. They added an order of brats to their beer cheese soup.

"Do you know who that is?" Robin said, pointing out the window. "On the chairlift. The snowboarders on the third lift from the bottom?"

"I can't tell," JC said. "I can only see their backs."

"But I saw them in line," Robin said smiling. "The one on the left is Cyndi Larsen and the one on the right is a very good-looking woman we haven't seen before."

"Cyndi likes girly girls," JC said.

"Oops," Robin exclaimed. "Cyndi just put her arm around the girly girl."

"How many days has it been since Sheepy's funeral?" Milt asked.

"Two," Robin answered.

"Wow," Milt said.

"Holy shit," Robin said.

"That's jumping to conclusions," JC told her. "Maybe that's her rabbi or something, consoling her."

"No, not 'Holy shit' that," Robin said. "Look at those men by the ski racks, looking up the hill."

"That's Agent Nelson," JC stated. "The DCI guy, right?"

"And I recognize that deputy with him," Milt added. "He was one of the guys who took me in for questioning. He drove the car. He's a terrible driver."

"Why don't you take your camera out on the porch and roll on them," JC suggested to Milt. "Who knows what might unfold before your trained eye."

Milt smiled and headed for the porch with his camera. Some customers in the bar noticed him and looked out the window to see what caught the attention of a television photographer.

JC and Robin watched as the law officers approached Cyndi Larsen when she arrived back at the bottom of the hill. Without being able to hear them, they watched Cyndi's animated response to the cops' side of the conversation.

"Are they going to arrest Cyndi?" Robin asked JC.

Then, the DCI agent and deputy walked past Larsen, their interest in her seemingly over.

They approached another woman, sliding to a stop on her skis by the chairlift.

"That's Linda Smith, the lady selling counterfeit lift tickets!" Robin exclaimed.

They watched as Smith stepped out of her skis and walked them over to a ski rack. She locked them up and then placed her hands behind her back. Agent Nelson slipped handcuffs onto her wrists.

JC scrambled away from the table and out of the Silo Bar.

"We'll be right back," Robin said when she stopped at the bar just long enough to tell them they weren't running on their check.

JC pushed the door open and ran onto the snow, looking for the law officers and their detainee. He saw them rounding the corner of the ski lodge and disappearing from sight.

"We have nothing to say right now," Agent Nelson said when JC caught up with them.

The agent and the deputy arrived at a marked county sheriff's vehicle and opened a backseat door to place Smith inside the cage.

"Linda," JC quickly asked. "What do they say you did?"

Linda Smith only looked up at JC through the bangs of her carefully styled hair. She looked frightened.

"Counterfeit lift tickets?" JC asked Agent Nelson as the law officer pushed past to climb into the front seat of the car. "Killing Ronny Schwartz?"

Nelson locked eyes with JC but said nothing, and the patrol car pulled away.

Milt joined JC and Robin at the curb. He was panting.

"I got here as quickly as I could," Milt said, gasping for air after running from his position on the porch. "I got pictures of her in handcuffs. Sorry I didn't get here in time to do an interview."

"That's alright," JC told him. "They weren't going to say anything anyway."

"That was Linda Smith, right?" Milt asked. "The mean queen of the ski racing program for kids?"

"Yep," JC told him.

"Well, what about Cyndi Larsen?" Milt asked, still trying to catch his breath.

"Maybe she had the right answers to their questions," JC said. "At least for now."

JC gave Robin money for their lunch bill, asking her to go back upstairs and settle things. JC and Milt headed for the chairlift being used by the junior ski racing team.

He wouldn't interview the children unless he had their parent's permission. Really, JC just wanted to learn what the parents knew about Linda Smith's arrest.

"Good riddance," one parent said. "Want to be our new vice president?"

"She was pretty entitled," another parent said. "She wasn't that pleasant to be around. Even the Snow Hat parent company had to step in because she wasn't being fair to the kids."

"She thought she got to pick which kids got on the top team instead of the coaches," another parent added. "And she would do it according to which parents were her friends. Now, maybe the fastest kids can be on the fastest team."

"Did you hear her ever talk about Ronny Schwartz?" JC asked. "The Snow Hat executive who disappeared after coming here?"

"She does not like Snow Hat," a parent said. "So, that probably includes Mr. Schwartz. It's a shame about him."

"What about counterfeit tickets?" JC asked. "Did she ever talk about counterfeit tickets?"

The talkative parents suddenly lost their tongue. They looked elsewhere and mumbled things like "I don't know anything about that."

In quick order, they excused themselves and walked away in different directions.

"Murder?" Linda Smith shouted. "I didn't murder anybody!"

DCI Agent Aurek Nelson sat in a small room with her. His face was emotionless. The deep lines on his face looked deeper in the poor lighting.

"I didn't kill anybody," Smith pleaded. She was sweating. To start with, she was too warm, wearing her turtleneck sweater beneath a fleece vest that said, "Big Horizon Racing Team."

"Then how do you explain the emails you exchanged with Tipper Jones?" the agent asked. He was so lacking in emotion, he almost seemed disinterested.

But that made Linda Smith nervous.

Aurek's name in Polish translated into something like "Bold and Blond." His hair was dark brown, almost black. His parents were certain that he'd be blond.

But he was bold. He knew he had all the advantages over this woman, and he was using them.

His thick hands pulled a rubber band off a file stuffed with papers. He began to twirl the rubber band in his fingers. It gave Linda Smith the impression that he was in no hurry to go anywhere else.

"Look," Linda Smith blurted. "All I did was sell counterfeit lift tickets. That's what Tipper and I were talking about in those emails. He printed the tickets and then I sold them."

Agent Nelson looked at her but said nothing, like he still had to be convinced that she wasn't responsible for worse.

"We just wanted to get a little payback," Smith then told him. "That Snow Hat group is ruining our small mountain. It's *our* mountain! We just wanted to…I don't know. I guess it got a little out of control."

Agent Nelson ran his tongue along his gums inside his mouth, like something was stuck in his teeth.

"You'll have to do better than that," he said, before standing up and walking out of the room.

Leaving Linda Smith alone with her thoughts.

31

"Murder at a Mom and Pop Mountain!"

The headline screamed off a particular New York City newspaper whose headlines often screamed. Agent Nelson tossed the paper in front of Linda Smith, when he returned to the uncomfortable interrogation room where Smith had been sitting alone for quite some time.

"I didn't murder anyone," she whimpered. Her shoulders shook as she started to cry.

Agent Nelson watched. He didn't say a word.

Finally convinced that she wasn't going to incriminate herself, Nelson told Linda Smith that she was being arrested and charged for manufacturing and selling counterfeit lift tickets.

"We know that your proceeds exceeded well over one thousand dollars, so that's a felony," he told the frightened suspect. "That means prison time."

Linda Smith was faint. She was confused.

"And we've just gotten started," the DCI agent told her.

She felt sick.

Tipper Jones was also brought in for questioning. Agent Nelson found him more difficult to scare. Tipper Jones never cracked.

"You got me," Jones quickly told the agent in the interview room. "I guess the counterfeiting was a stupid thing to do. I'll pay my fine. Tell me how much I owe. Sorry for your trouble. But kill Ronny Schwartz? Don't be ridiculous."

When Nelson had exhausted his line of interrogation, Jones was also charged with counterfeiting. Then, he was allowed to go free on an appearance ticket.

"I thought you were going to bring Cyndi Larsen in for questioning," the sheriff said to Agent Nelson over the phone.

"We had one car and two suspects," Nelson replied. "Linda Smith is going to make our case against Tipper Jones. He's tough, but she's weak. She'll give us Tipper. Cyndi won't be hard to find when we want to talk to her."

"Is it enough to kill over?" JC asked. "I mean, if Ronny Schwartz caught them selling counterfeit tickets, would it really be worth killing him?"

"I wouldn't think so," Scotty said, sipping a Scotch at the Igloo at the end of the day.

JC had reported, during his live shot to Denver that evening, what the sheriff had told him. Linda Smith and Tipper Jones had been taken into custody and released on appearance tickets. More charges could follow, the sheriff said. But the sheriff stopped just short of connecting them to Ronny Schwartz's murder.

"They're putting a scare into Linda Smith," JC speculated. "They're hoping she knows more than she's telling them and will roll over on Tipper Jones."

"What about this indoor ski resort business?" Scotty asked.

"Now, that's worth killing over," JC nodded. "That's worth millions."

Robin and Milt entered the bar and joined them in their corner, Milt with an Old Style and Robin with a glass of red wine.

"What kind of ski boots was he wearing?" Robin asked.

"Who?" JC said, looking at her.

"Ronny Schwartz," she answered. "He was pulled out of the water wearing ski boots. What kind?"

JC quietly contemplated the question. Scotty, who hadn't pulled on ski boots in years, just shook his head. He admired the question.

"I do not know why you hang out with a dumb guy like me," JC finally said to Robin, and he pulled out his phone.

"Everyone asks the same question," Milt added. "What do you see in him?"

"At the time," Robin teased Milt. "You were already taken."

"That explains it," Milt said, maybe believing it.

JC pulled a slip of paper from his wallet.

"A deputy gave me Agent Nelson's business card when he wanted me to call him," JC smiled. "That means I have his number even when he *doesn't* want me to call him."

JC listened as his call was put through.

"DCI Agent Aurek Nelson," the voice said. JC identified himself and heard a sigh on the other end.

"What kind of ski boots was Ronny Schwartz wearing when he was pulled from the water?" JC asked.

"Are you doing a fashion segment?" the agent asked.

"Ski boots all come from somewhere," JC explained. "There's not a ski boot fairy. Someone bought the ski boots and someone sold the ski boots. It might lead you to the killer."

Agent Nelson was quiet on the other line. He was digesting the information.

"That detective in Colorado said you could be useful," Nelson finally said. "Once in a while."

"I think we made him smile," JC said when he determined that the agent had terminated the call.

Nelson returned to a conference room where he was interviewing another suspect in another crime.

"Sorry for the interruption, Congressman Bellows," the agent said as he returned to his seat at the table. "Where were we?"

Disgraced or not, Agent Nelson knew not to fool with a congressman from his own state unless he had the goods. Nelson did not have the goods, yet.

So, Nelson was handling Bat Bellows with kid gloves. He questioned the suspect in a conference room with comfortable chairs and a coffee maker, rather than the stark solitary interrogation room.

"Are you waiting for me to tell you how awful the murder of Quip Kelly was?" Bellows asked. "Did you expect me to shed a tear?"

"What he did to you," the agent said, seizing on the moment. "He ruined you. No one would blame you if you evened the score. A man defends his honor."

"Oh please," Bellows said with an amount of snark. "Don't treat me like I'm a compulsive idiot. Look, because of Quip Kelly, I'm a leper now. I'm not even welcome in my own house! My son is gay! He used to be proud of me."

"Quip Kelly took all of that away from you," Agent Nelson said. "The hero-worship, the stature in the community, the perks, the pension, your *family*. All gone because of Quip Kelly."

Bellows didn't put up an argument.

"What are you doing here?" the agent asked. "Why, of all the places to go into hiding, did you pick virtually the same spot where Quip Kelly was murdered?"

Congressman Bellows looked at the DCI agent. There was realization in his eyes. He twirled his ring with the red stone.

"Okay, look," Bellows said. "Maybe I wanted to bump into him. Maybe I wanted to give him a piece of my mind. Wouldn't you? But I didn't kill him."

The congressman was allowed to leave without being charged for Quip Kelly's murder. But neither, Agent Nelson thought to himself, had he exonerated himself.

Walking back to a desk that was temporarily assigned to him in the sheriff's office, a deputy handed Nelson a two-page report.

"Alright," the agent told the deputy. "Go pick him up."

"Back in Sturgis," Landover Scott told his friends as they sat on their soft chairs in their darkened corner at the Igloo Lounge, "a girl would get gussied up before coming out for an evening at a nice establishment like this."

"Are you saying that I'm not gussied up?" Robin asked, laughing.

"You're spectacular," Scotty told her. "I'm talking about back in the 1960s, anyway. In Sturgis, the girls would put big rollers in their hair on the afternoon before a big date. Back in that day, the best big rollers were empty cylinders that frozen orange juice was packaged in at the grocery store. My sister used to do it. I think that made bigger curls."

"You don't think my hair looks nice?" Robin asked.

"You're really putting me on the spot," Scotty laughed. "Anyway, I haven't finished describing the ritual. So, after securing those cardboard orange juice cylinders in their hair, with bobby pins, I guess. The girls would climb into a car and drive downtown. They'd think of any excuse to go downtown wearing those big curlers in their hair. Because that was the way, without being conceited about it, they could let everyone know that they had a big date that night."

"If I roll my hair in big orange juice cans," Robin summarized, "I'll be popular. Got it."

"Good," Scotty laughed.

Scotty stood up and excused himself, saying he wanted to go out on the porch and enjoy a cigarette.

Robin moved closer to JC on the seat they shared, taking his arm affectionately.

"He's like you, thirty years from now," she said.

"Scotty? You think so?" JC said with a smile. "I'll be bald?"

"He's still sexy," she told him. "And you'll still be sexy."

JC was still smiling when he saw two uniformed deputies walk into the Igloo. The law officers stopped at the bar and the bartender pointed toward JC's table.

"Mr. Lemon," one deputy said. "We'd like you to come with us."

"Why, pray tell?" Milt said, still holding his Old Style beer.

"Agent Nelson would like a word with you," the deputy told him.

Milt looked at JC. He killed his beer and stood up.

"Can we stop at the grocery store on the way over," Milt asked. "I just ran out of beer."

JC and Robin watched as Milt was walked out of the bar and down the hallway toward the lobby. Scotty came back to the table.

"I couldn't help but witnessing that," Scotty said. "Your friend is in a spot of trouble."

"Somehow, I don't think so," JC said. "I think they just can't figure him out. Maybe they want to do a science experiment on him."

32

"You lied, Mr. Lemon."

DCI Agent Aurek Nelson was seated on one side of the table in the dirty interrogation room and Milt Lemon sat on the other side.

"I was nervous," Milt told the agent. "You guys want to arrest me for murder!"

"We don't arrest innocent people," the agent told him. "But innocent people don't lie."

"Okay, I did see her later. I admit it," Milt said to the DCI agent.

"I know you did," Nelson told him with an emotionless face. "We've watched it over and over again, on a security camera that you didn't know about."

"I wasn't looking for security cameras," Milt said, exasperated.

"No, or you would have seen them," the agent stated. "And then what would you have done?"

"The same thing?" Milt responded meekly.

"And what is that?" Nelson asked. "What would you have done the same? Followed her somewhere there weren't security cameras and taken one last stab at having sex with her? Doesn't it piss you off, when they won't have sex with you?"

"Yes," Milt said. "I mean, no. No."

"You were pissed off with Sheepy, though, weren't you?" the agent pressed.

"No," Milt insisted. "I really wasn't. I wanted to apologize."

"You made her feel uncomfortable, so you followed her?" Nelson asked.

"No, I didn't follow her," Milt told him. "I bumped into her. But that gave me the chance to apologize again."

"You told me that you apologized the first time," the law officer reminded Milt.

"I did," Milt said in a voice that was squeezed higher because he was nervous. "I did apologize before. But when we bumped into each other again, I apologized again."

"And you moved in," Nelson said.

"What?" Milt asked, not following.

"I've watched the security camera video!" the agent said, raising his voice. "You grabbed her! I saw you grab her!"

"I didn't grab her," Milt argued. "I gave her a hug. I was sorry for making a pass at her. I gave her a hug."

Agent Nelson was silent. He just stared at Milt. The agent's face looked like it could break into a grimace or a grin. It was balanced right in between.

"And she hugged me back," Milt whimpered. He was emotionally spent.

"What?" Nelson barked. "I couldn't hear you."

"She hugged me back," Milt repeated, a little louder. "She was really nice."

"She was really nice and so you lied about it," the agent said.

"Yeah," Milt mumbled. "Yeah, I lied."

Agent Nelson left the room without another word. In about thirty minutes, without anything else for law officers to work with, Milt was allowed to leave. In the hallway, he passed two deputies leading Cyndi Larsen to the room he had just exited.

"The Mona Lisa Murder!" a newspaper screamed the next morning. JC and Robin were sitting at a table, waiting for Milt to join them for breakfast.

There was a picture in the newspaper, taken from the back, of a man leaving the sheriff's office. The man's face wasn't shown, but JC recognized the back. It was Milt's back.

"Try this!"

JC and Robin were startled by the enthusiastic voice. They dropped the newspaper to the table top.

Branch was there, urging them to try a plate of food she pushed in front of them. She filled their coffee cups and walked away, leaving behind a plate of baked items that resembled donuts.

"How do we play this?" Robin asked. "What do we say to Milt when he comes down to breakfast?"

"About the fact that Milt spent half the night being accused of murdering Sheepy?" JC asked.

"I was hoping we could put it more gently than that," Robin told him.

"The fact that his picture is in the newspaper below the headline 'Mona Lisa Murderer?'" JC added.

"It didn't say 'Murderer,' it said 'Murder,'" she corrected him. "It wasn't saying that he was the murderer. It was saying that there was a murder and his picture was under it."

"Much better," JC agreed with sarcasm. "I think my mom would be okay if my picture was just *under* the headline about a murder."

"JC," Robin said with a bit of edge. "Do you think he murdered Sheepy?"

"No," JC said. "I'm just mad at him."

"Well, you're one of the few friends he has," Robin scolded him. "Start behaving like it."

"He's your friend too," JC reminded her.

"Oh, brother. That's right," she said, her head collapsing into her hands. "I've got to find new friends."

"Good morning!" Milt chimed as he took a seat with them. He had a broad smile with white teeth. "Wow, what are these?"

Milt dove into the dish that Branch left behind. JC and Robin, more concerned with how to console Milt, had forgotten the food.

"They're paczki!" Branch told them as she returned to the table. "They're Polish donuts, sort of. They're one of Wisconsin's favorite foods!"

Milt was happily chewing.

"How are you doing, friend?" JC asked Milt, as sensitively as he could.

"These are great!" Milt said, holding up the remains of his paczki.

"That's it!" JC exclaimed. "I can't be sensitive any longer!" he announced to Robin. "This is the third time, in my short employment as a co-worker of Milt Lemon, that *in my presence*, he has been accused of murder! What kind of person attracts that kind of attention?"

"JC," Robin said in a calming voice. "Now is not the time."

"Milt," Robin said, turning to the photographer. "My grandmother used to ask me a question at times like these. She'd say, 'What is wedged inside that thick skull of yours, goose feathers?'"

Milt stopped chewing his second Polish donut. He looked at Robin. His eyes began to water.

"I didn't kill her," he said somberly to the two of them.

"I know you didn't kill her," JC barked back. "You're like a six-year-old. The only thing you could kill is a beer keg. But why do you go across the country convincing police officers that you murder people?"

Milt just looked at them with sad eyes, searching for an answer.

"I make a lot of friends," he said, thinking that might explain it.

JC began to laugh. Then Robin did. Then Milt did.

"You are not allowed to laugh," JC growled at him, pointing. Milt stopped laughing and snapped to attention. JC slowly reached for a paczki. He smiled a little.

"It's good, isn't it?" Milt said.

"He's like a dog that just peed on the carpet," JC said to Robin. "You can't put him to sleep for that. You'd just like to."

At the end of their breakfast, Milt pushed away from the table.

"I am fuller than a two-day-old pimple!" Milt announced. Branch laughed as she left the check.

"I will be resurrected," Senator Raff Swensen told his top two aides as they sat in his office in Madison. "I don't mean in the holy sense. I'm not being blasphemous. I just mean, I am going to prove that I am rehabilitated, and I am going to win re-election!"

Senator Swensen had a triumphant smile on his face. Only days ago, his life had been in ruins. He had been caught by Quip. He had done everything but murder a nun and show up at a sorority house with his pants off.

But his moment of ultimate humiliation was followed by days of silence. His attorneys were working on lowering his guilty plea in the hit-and-run to a misdemeanor.

"Our client thought that he hit a deer," they would suggest to the district attorney behind closed doors. At first, they had formed their explanation to say that the senator thought he hit a dog. But, they reasoned, people liked dogs. It would be despicable to hit a dog and not stop to help the suffering animal.

But a deer, they reasoned, was an animal that was subjected to a hunting season each year. A lot of people killed deer. So, from that moment on, the senator would explain that he thought he hit a deer.

And no one had much more to say about his sexual escapades. They had publicly announced how horrified and disgusted they were by the senator's behavior, and then there was nothing more to say.

Of course, everyone expected Swensen to do the honorable thing and announce his resignation, as Senator Miller had done. And Congressman Bellows declared that he would leave Washington at the end of the year.

But Senator Swensen knew he had a few cards he could play. The first one was the voters' short memory and shorter attention span.

"Okay, guys," Swensen told his aides. "That's it for the day. I'm heading home."

Swensen thought about his strategy as he climbed into his car. If he could lay low and stick with the story about the deer, he might be forgiven. Or even better, forgotten.

And he could claim that Amanda Taylor was driving the car. Who could prove that she wasn't? It would be his word against hers.

Then he would accuse Quip of lying, of being funded by Swensen's political opponents. Swensen couldn't prove a lick of it. But heck, who demanded proof anymore? Just tell them what they want to hear.

Swensen represented a district dominated by his political party. It wouldn't be hard to convince his fellow senators, at least those on his side of the aisle, that he could still deliver the vote on important issues.

Maybe his dream of being governor was over, but being a senator was a pretty great job, he thought. Everyone wanted to buy him dinner, and drinks. And he wasn't getting any poorer while he was at the capitol.

First, he had to convince his single most important constituent.

"Honey, I'm home," Swensen announced as he came through the front door of their nice home in a nice neighborhood.

He found his wife, sitting on the couch doing what she had been doing since Quip's story had come out. She was weeping.

She was dressed in clothing that she would wear to a campaign rally. Respectable apparel that would offend no one.

But she had nowhere to go. There were no invitations.

"Honey," the senator said, laboring to sound sincere. "Let's talk."

In his hand, he held the newspaper with a picture of his car with the crumpled fender.

"I guess I must have hit him," the senator told her, contrite. "Honestly? I thought I hit a deer. If I knew that I'd hit a human being, of course I would have stopped. I thought I hit a deer. It was dark as heck on that road. And what was he doing in that road? Anyway, our attorney is talking with the district attorney's office. It's all being ironed out."

Then, he opened the paper to the picture of him on a boat with his arm around two topless interns.

"And this picture, honey. I'm afraid it's the truth," he told her. "I need to use better judgment. I was invited to go on that boat out onto Lake Mendota. Now, did I know there would be women on board who would later take their clothes off?" He laughed a little laugh. His wife's red eyes rose to look at him.

"No," the senator said. "I didn't know who would be on that boat at all! You know those knuckleheads. You don't know what they're going to do from one moment to the next." He laughed another little laugh.

"Anyway," the senator continued. "I was enjoying being out on the water and having a conversation with another senator, who I shall not name because I don't want him to find himself in the position I am sorry to find myself in. But these charming sunbathers approach me and tell me how much they admire my positions at the capitol. They tell me that they admire my strength to stand up for my beliefs. And then they ask if I would take a picture with them. What was I going to say to them? A vote is a vote is a vote. Isn't that what we always say, sweetie?"

"Honey," the senator said, preparing for his big finish. "The rest of the pictures are garbage. Why do you suppose the faces are covered with black squares? Because they're fakes! Different people posed for those pictures and then they superimposed my face on the guy."

His wife sniffed and wiped her nose with a tissue. Then she rose from the couch and picked up the newspapers, examining the pictures.

"But honey," the senator said with humility. "This picture, of me posing with the girls, is authentic. I wasn't thinking. I mean, nothing happened." He laughed a slightly larger laugh. "What would pretty young women like that want with an old fart like me!"

She stood before him and looked into his eyes.

"But honey," Swensen said, "I should have had more sense than that. I'm never going to go anywhere without you at my side. You would have stopped me from doing that. I'm sorry, honey. I apologize."

Swensen then held the newspaper in front of him, looking at himself with a topless woman under each arm.

"Honey," he said with a sheepish grin. "Without you at my side, boys will be boys." He smiled at her. "Right? Boys will be boys."

His wife moved toward him and tucked herself in his arms.

"You naughty boy," she purred. "You're my naughty boy."

"I'm *your* naughty boy," he said, holding her close.

Now, the senator thought, if it's only that easy to convince voters.

33

Walter Schroeder wasn't going to make a dime off the two men sitting in front of him. They had each ordered a glass of water.

The bartender at the Wilmot Riverside Bar and Grill was fielding questions from the DCI agent for a second time. A uniformed sheriff's deputy sat silently next to the agent. The deputy was wearing a regulation knit cap with "Sheriff" stitched on it. It was cold outside.

The lunchtime crowd was coming in, some of them taking a break from skiing at Wilmot, just down the road. Other customers were on their allotted half hour for lunch before returning to work. They were in a hurry.

It was the busiest time of day for the bar until dinner. But the bartender couldn't ignore the law officers. That was never a good plan.

"We thought that we'd come in at about the same time you said that man with the injured hand came in," Agent Nelson told the bartender. "Do you see him here?"

"No," said Schroeder. "I haven't seen him since the day of the fire."

Agent Nelson again asked Schroeder to describe the man who sat at the bar on the day of the fire that killed Quip Kelly.

He asked Walter, again, to recall the entire encounter with the mysterious man.

Agent Nelson believed that the man *was* there at the fire. He set it. Then, he drove down the road to the bar and took a seat long enough to confirm he had done his job properly.

The DCI agent pictured it as though he were there. The arsonist, staying at the bar long enough to hear the sirens of the fire engine, and hear someone come into the tavern and say, "Wow, there's a big fire down the road."

Then, the mystery man stood. He paid for his beer, left a tip, and walked out the door like he had never been there.

The agent could see it, but he couldn't see the man's face. It told the DCI agent that they were chasing a contract killer. A very good one.

"Was Quip Kelly in your bar on the day of the fire?" the agent asked the bartender.

Schroeder excused himself so that he could take an order from customers at a table who had been waiting patiently.

"Before the fire?" Schroeder asked when he came back and put a food order into the kitchen.

"If Quip Kelly came into the bar *after* the fire, now is the time to tell me," the agent responded.

"Oh, yeah, right," Schroeder said. "I see your point." The bartender gave that some thought while he poured a beer for another man at the bar.

"No," Schroeder finally said. "No, I can't say that Quip came into the bar that day. He did come in on other days before that."

Agent Nelson had been told by Shara that Quip didn't smoke pot or cigarettes. But she said he did like to have a drink.

If he was drunk, Nelson thought to himself, he'd be a lot easier for the arsonist to subdue. But Schroeder said that Quip didn't come in that day.

Agent Nelson had wondered if the arsonist used a woman to get Quip Kelly to drop his guard. It was a successful technique used by killers who knew what they were doing.

"Women?" Nelson then asked the bartender. "Did Quip ever bring a woman with him to the bar, or maybe meet one here and leave with her?"

"He brought his wife a couple of times," Schroeder to the DCI man. "That's the only woman I ever saw him with."

Nelson patted a few of his pockets before pulling out a photograph of Shara Adams Kelly.

"Have you ever seen this woman?" the agent asked, showing the picture of Shara to the bartender.

"Yes," Walter Schroeder said. "That's Mrs. Kelly. At least, that's how Quip introduced her. Is she someone else?"

"No, no," assured the agent. "That's Mrs. Kelly. I was just wondering if he might have been fooling around."

"It's nice to know someone is faithful to their wife," Schroeder told him. "The way our politicians are gallivanting around. At least, that's what I read."

Schroeder excused himself again and picked up a food order in the kitchen and walked it out to a table. Then, he refilled the beer of another man at the bar.

"What else can I help you with?" the bartender asked when he returned.

"Nothing else," Nelson said. "Thanks."

Agent Nelson pushed away from the bar, placed ten dollars down and departed. The deputy followed him in silence.

Aurek Nelson sat alone in his own car, provided by DCI. Behind him, the silent deputy sat behind the steering wheel of his patrol unit, waiting for an order. He was essentially a tour guide assigned to the DCI agent.

Something struck Nelson as odd. He was investigating three different murders in the area and none of them involved drugs. That was something of a rarity.

The Quip Kelly fire investigation had hit a wall. He was looking for an arsonist who had the ability to turn invisible.

Nelson opened a file on Linda Smith and Tipper Jones and the Ronny Schwartz murder.

There was a statement made in an email that kept nagging at him. Jones had told Smith, "We hit a bump in the road, but in the end, everything was taken care of."

What did Jones mean by that? What was the bump? And how was it taken care of?

He also wondered if Tipper Jones and Linda Smith were having an affair. Jones could have needed a mole at Big Horizon. Linda Smith seemed like mole material.

Nelson's phone rang. He looked at the readout and saw that it was the sheriff calling.

"You asked about the ski boots Ronny Schwartz was wearing?" the sheriff asked. "That was a good hunch."

"You sent some men over to look in Tipper Jones's garage?" Agent Nelson asked.

"We did," the sheriff confirmed. "They just got back. Jones has about a dozen pairs of ski boots in his garage. They all look identical, except they're different sizes. The report calls them rear-entry and gray in color. The markings on them say they were rental boots left over from when Jones owned the Big Horizon ski area, then known as Fox River Runs."

"And the ski boots found on Ronny Schwartz when he was fished from the water?" Agent Nelson asked the sheriff.

"Gray, rear-entry," the sheriff told him. "They're virtually identical."

"Do you think we have enough to bring Tipper Jones back in for questioning?" the agent asked.

"Don't you?" the sheriff said.

"Why don't we bring Linda Smith in too," Agent Nelson suggested. "Let's put them in separate rooms and pit them against each other. That's always amusing."

The wind howled in the night. The temperature outside was below zero. A frost halo wrapped itself around the moon.

JC, Robin and Milt joined Scotty and Bunny for dinner in one of the plastic igloos on the porch of the Grand Geneva, overlooking the lake. While the wind buffeted the plastic siding, they were warmed inside by a space heater and ate hot tapas while drinking hot beverages.

There were tempura vegetables, pot stickers, wings and egg rolls. There was Baileys mixed with hot chocolate and whipped cream, and hot buttered rum.

At the end of the night, JC and Robin huddled under a blanket while they sat together in their room. They had pulled the couch around again, to stare out of the sliding glass door into the night sky.

They each had a book to read and a glass of red wine. The bright moon cast a dark shadow of the wineglass on the page JC's book was opened to.

But he was staring at the legs of the wine, created as he absent-mindedly tipped the glass. He was lost in thought.

"We should go to Evanston," he said.

34

"I f The Cold Doesn't Get You, The Killer Will!"

The headline splattered on a weekly magazine was probably giving chills to local tourism officials. The only thing worse for tourism than freezing temperatures was the chance of getting murdered there.

Tipper Jones's attorney had already prepared his client for his imminent arrest on murder charges. The matching ski boots proved to be too much for investigators to overlook.

During intense questioning, Jones continued to deny he killed Ronny Schwartz. But he kept admitting how much he hated Snow Hat Ski Enterprises. Aurek Nelson believed that to Tipper Jones, Ronny Schwartz was as much a face of the company as Tillison Tucker.

Agent Nelson knew that Ronny Schwartz was the man in the trenches for Snow Hat while they negotiated the acquisition of Fox River Runs a few short years ago. Schwartz was the man across the table from Jones. And it had to be a memory that Tipper Jones had come to despise.

What better symbolism was there, Nelson believed, than to place that emissary of Snow Hat Ski Enterprises into a pair of ski boots and send him on a Wisconsin winter swim?

But Tipper Jones argued that he offered Ronny Schwartz a job. Jones was close to being the first one to nail down the permits and paperwork to build that indoor ski area in Chicago. Jones claimed that he wanted Schwartz to run it, and then open indoor ski areas elsewhere in the country.

"Schwartz was even going to do it," Jones pleaded. "I thought we had a deal. But then he backed out."

"Did he sign a contract with you?" Nelson asked.

"No," Tipper admitted.

It was bullshit, the DCI man thought. He even checked with Tillison Tucker to see if Schwartz had submitted his resignation. If he had even brought it up.

"That is preposterous," Tucker told the investigator.

Tipper Jones had been caught in his own lie.

Now, all they needed was a confession. Nelson agreed with the district attorney who said that too much of the case was still circumstantial.

Linda Smith was, so far, proving useless to Nelson. She confessed to selling counterfeit lift tickets every time she opened her mouth. Luckily, Nelson thought, she was dumb enough to believe she could almost get the death penalty for that. She was terrified.

The DCI agent knew he had her primed and loaded. She was on the edge of exploding. But she hadn't said anything to incriminate Tipper Jones in the murder of Schwartz.

Maybe he was right about them having an affair, Nelson thought. Maybe she was willing to fall on her sword for the man she loved.

Nelson had already tried to convince Jones that they were going to throw the book at Linda Smith if Jones didn't come clean about the murder. But Jones didn't budge. In the same sentence, he would tell them that he hated Snow Hat, but he didn't kill anyone.

"Maybe it's time to let a little something leak," Agent Nelson suggested to the sheriff. "Maybe if we leak just a little bit, someone will come forward with what they know. Maybe it will jog their memory. Or maybe Jones's attorney will tell his client that it's time to bargain. Confess to something and see what they can get in return."

Evanston, Illinois, was less than a two-hour drive south from Lake Geneva. The trip was flat and mostly highway. But, turning off the Kennedy Expressway and heading toward Lake Michigan, they passed through old Midwestern towns with tree-lined streets and diverse residential neighborhoods.

They drove through the village of Skokie. After World War Two, Skokie claimed to have the largest number of Nazi Holocaust survivors in the world, outside of Israel.

The village of Winnetka was the face of teen angst movies like *Sixteen Candles*, two *Home Alone* movies and *Ferris Bueller's Day Off.*

The city of Evanston sat on Lake Michigan. Parks and beaches lined the lake. Big houses loomed across the street.

JC, Robin and Milt pulled up to a home on Forest Avenue, about three blocks from the lake and a mile from Northwestern University. This was where Ronny Schwartz grew up.

The house where his parents still lived had three stories and was made of red stone. During the summer, vines crawling up the house turned green and leafy.

In front, there was a large open porch. In the back, there was an old carriage house turned into a garage.

"He loved working at Snow Hat," the mother of Ronny Schwartz said. "For years."

They sat in a large living room that overlooked the front porch. There was plenty of light shining in. They were surrounded by art and knickknacks picked up during trips around the world. Flames snapped in a fireplace.

"Ronny was raised to respect hard work," his mother said. "He was also taught that good work should be rewarded. If they didn't appreciate you where you were, there would always be somewhere else to go. Every employer is looking for people who work hard."

"Did he not feel appreciated?" JC asked. Milt stood behind his camera, rolling on the interview.

"He did at first," she said. "He loved it there, and really gave his life to the company. He was married once, but he couldn't find time for a family. He was always working."

"What did he think of Tillison Tucker?" JC inquired.

"Mr. Tucker was almost like a father figure to Ronny," she answered. "Aside from Ronny's own father, of course."

JC nodded his understanding.

"But after some time," Mrs. Schwartz continued. "Ronny told us how successful they were. He worked hard to create the big ski pass and acquire ski areas to join their company. Ronny said he spent a piece of every week traveling, trying to bring in another big deal."

"And he didn't like that?" JC asked.

"Oh, he didn't mind the travel, or any of the hard work," she said. "Then the money from those deals began to come in, and it was a lot of money, mind you. Ronny didn't think he was getting his fair share. He said Tillison Tucker was being rewarded generously by the board, but Ronny felt forgotten."

"So, his attitude about Snow Hat changed?" JC asked her.

"I suppose," Ronny's mother reflected. "I think he just felt that it was time to move on. He knew he was ready to run his own company."

"Did he have any feelers out?" asked JC. "Was he talking to anyone about actually leaving?"

"He told me that he was," she said. "He expected something to happen in a very short time. He told me so when he stopped by, on the start of this trip to Wisconsin."

"He said that it was going to happen soon?" JC asked.

"Yes, he did," the woman confirmed. "He said he expected something to happen very soon, and it might bring him back here, closer to home."

"Did he tell you exactly what it was?" JC asked, hopefully.

"No," she said. "But it doesn't matter. He called me. It was the last time I ever spoke with him. And he said he'd decided to turn down that job offer. In the end, he was very loyal to Mr. Tucker. He didn't want to leave him that way, he said."

The aging woman looked into her lap, where her hands were grasped. JC and Robin could see the sorrow washing over her.

"Do you know what happened to Ronny?" the woman asked in a weakened voice, her eyes starting to tear.

"I only know what you know, Mrs. Schwartz. But we're going to get to the bottom of this."

They departed and walked to their car, parked on Forest Avenue.

"Let's go get something to eat," JC said. It was cold outside and they climbed into the car as quickly as possible.

Robin's GPS directed them to Bob's Pizza. It was across the street from the Northwestern University campus. Most of the room inside was filled by a large horseshoe-shaped bar. JC supposed that Bob's Pizza did a good business, being the first bar college students could reach when they left campus.

A cold wind whipped at pedestrians walking outside past the big windows. Lake Michigan was only a few blocks away.

"I thought *Chicago* was 'The Windy City,'" Robin said, still warming up.

"Chicago is only about two miles south," JC said, pointing in that direction. "This is Suburban Windy City."

They each ordered a couple of slices of pizza from the bartender. He looked to be about forty years old.

"Do you know Ronny Schwartz?" Robin asked the man.

He gave her a neutral look.

"Seriously? Ronny Schwartz?" the bartender then asked. "We went to high school together."

Robin laughed.

"How does she know this stuff?" JC asked Milt.

"He's out in Colorado now, isn't he?" the bartender asked. "He's with some big ski company?"

"That's right," Robin replied.

"I always knew he'd make it," the man told her. "He worked his ass off. He was going to do whatever he wanted to do."

"Did he have any enemies?" JC asked.

The bartender looked at JC like he had just ruined the party.

"No, man. Everyone respected him. He was friendly, worked hard. He was elected class president. And he was loyal. If you were his friend, you would remain his friend, no matter what."

JC thanked the bartender and paid the bill.

"Let's go for a walk," JC said to his companions.

They fastened their coats and stepped outside onto Davis Street. Robin had a scarf wrapped around her neck and pulled a soft wool hat out of her coat pocket to pull over her head.

"You're a lot smarter than we are," JC said after sizing up her armament against the cold wind and then taking a look at Milt. The ears on both men were already turning red.

"Girls rule," she said. "Boys drool."

JC motioned them down the block and onto Northwestern campus. The architecture was a mix of modern and European Gothic.

Milt ran ahead with his camera, devouring the photogenic setting.

"There are a lot of beautiful homes here," Robin told JC.

"People work hard for the privilege of living in Evanston," JC told her.

"Maybe Ronny Schwartz was spoiled after growing up here," she suggested, squinting into the breeze. Her nose was red and sometimes she had to wipe tears from her eyes.

They were walking below the towering structure of Deering Library. It looked like a medieval cathedral.

"Milt!" JC shouted ahead of them. "Do you want to duck inside the library and warm up?"

Milt had a look of gratitude as he dropped the camera off his shoulder, carried it like a suitcase, and bounded up the steps and inside the building. Above the entrance, words were carved in granite saying, "The Fountain of Wisdom Flows Through Books."

Inside, they climbed up a set of stone stairs. Their hands and faces almost ached as they thawed out.

In every direction, there were large reading rooms, carved wood, and sculptures. There were stained-glass windows with images of the world's greatest thinkers.

"No single moment in time determines its circumstances," JC said.

"Where does it say that?" Robin asked.

"Nowhere. It's just something I read, once. Just walking in here, I felt my IQ go up about ten points," JC said with a smile.

"Does it apply to Ronny Schwartz?"

"I have a feeling that it does. Ronny Schwartz had been barreling toward that final instant of his life for years. He just didn't know it," JC said. "Look around at this amazing campus where he went to school and the neighborhood he lived in. As a little boy growing up here, he was already a marked man."

"Is this some argument that man doesn't determine his own destiny?" she asked. "Is this a fatalist thing?"

"Maybe it's just looking backwards. He grew up among big, beautiful homes and parks, the beach and Lake Michigan. It's a charmed existence. Whoever Ronny Schwartz was, and whatever became of him, began when he was a child living here. It sounds like he was a good guy and he was taught to have a strong work ethic. He also knew what success felt like."

"He expected it to look and feel like this?" Robin offered, envisioning everything she had seen in Evanston.

"Yep," JC said. "And if he wasn't getting this, he probably felt he wasn't getting enough."

"It sounds like police are about to charge Tipper Jones with murder," Robin said. "What's all this got to do with Tipper Jones?"

"Exactly," JC said. "Tipper Jones was a snowmobile mechanic. He expected nothing out of life that he didn't build with his own two hands. How does anything we've seen or heard today connect to Tipper Jones?"

"If you're so smart," Milt piped in, "figure out how to get us back to our car without freezing our asses off."

35

"It's going to take a little longer to finish up what we came to do," JC told Branch.

She was working behind the check-in desk in the lobby. JC extended the room reservations for himself and Robin and for Milt.

"We are full!" Branch said. "You're lucky. We had a two-week reservation that would have carried into the next few days. It was for Snow Hat. But Mr. Tucker's administrative assistant called on Christmas Eve and cancelled it. I remember, I was on the desk and took the call myself. Otherwise, we would have been completely booked tonight."

"And we'd be sleeping in our car," JC said with a smile.

"We would have found something for you," Branch smiled back. "I'm not sure what that would have been, but we would have found something for you."

"Mr. Tucker was planning to fly here from Colorado on Christmas Eve?" JC asked.

"No," Branch said, after flipping to a previous screen on her computer. "The reservation was for Mr. Schwartz. But he was a Snow Hat employee, right? He'd already been staying here for a couple of weeks."

"Yep, he worked for Snow Hat," JC confirmed. "And Mr. Tucker cancelled Ronny's reservation on Christmas Eve?"

"Yes, he did," Branch said with a smile and a song.

He thanked Branch and walked away from the check-in desk. He wasn't walking anywhere in particular. He was lost in thought.

Robin emerged from a shop off the hotel lobby, where she was waiting for JC.

"Tillison Tucker cancelled Ronny Schwartz's room reservation on Christmas Eve, the day Schwartz's car was found in Gills Rock," JC told her. "But Schwartz's body wasn't found for another day, not until Christmas Day. Does that strike you as odd?"

"Like Tucker knew that Ronny was going to be found dead?" Robin said.

"Yep. You want lunch?" JC asked. "Call Milt and ask him to join us."

They had more beer soup and cheese curds. JC had come to like the local dishes. They sat in a living room off the Igloo Lounge.

"It's odd," JC said. "I don't know how to explain Tucker cancelling Ronny Schwartz's room reservation before his body had been found."

Robin and Milt shook their heads. They couldn't come up with a plausible explanation either.

"There is something that I saw, a while ago," JC said. "I didn't give it much thought. But now I think it may be pretty significant."

"What's that?" Milt asked.

"Do you remember when we visited Tipper Jones at his house? He took us into his den and flashed the paperwork and drawings for his indoor ski resort plan," JC reminded them. "It was the paperwork. I only got a glance at it before Tipper pulled it away. But there were two permits from the city of Chicago, the planning department. There was a signature on the bottom, but it wasn't Tipper's signature. I thought that was odd."

"Whose signature was it?" Robin asked.

"I didn't recognize it at the time," JC said. "But I haven't forgotten it. I can picture it. I think it was Ronny Schwartz's signature."

"On papers moving ahead Tipper Jones's plans?" Robin asked.

"Yep," JC said. "If he signed those papers, he *had* switched teams. He may have become Tipper's partner on the indoor ski area and just hadn't told Tucker yet."

"Remember what Ronny's mother said?" Robin asked them. "She said that Ronny was going to take another job. But he changed his mind at the last minute. His loyalty to Tucker wouldn't let him leave, in good conscience."

"I remember," JC said. "But the change of heart may have come after he did a little paperwork for Tipper Jones."

"Tucker was competing with Tipper to be the first to land that indoor ski area in Chicago," Robin said. "If those permits were on file with the city planning department, Tucker could have seen them. He would have thought Ronny had betrayed him."

"And if Tucker thought that a loyal soldier was trying to betray him," JC wondered. "What would he have done to prevent that from succeeding? He might have questioned whether Tipper could really pull off that indoor ski area. But he knew that Ronny could."

JC wanted to take a ride out to the Big Horizon Ski Resort.

They drove out Fox River Road, turned into the parking lot of Big Horizon and parked near the building where guests picked up their rental skis and snowboards.

The manager of the rental department was a holdover from the days of Fox River Runs. He wore an apron to keep the grease and ski wax off of his clothing.

"Did Tillison Tucker request a pair of rental ski boots?" JC inquired. "It would have been a month or so ago."

"Not that I'm aware of," the manager replied. "And I'd know. If Mr. Tucker wanted a pair of boots shipped to him, I would have handled it. The rest of my employees are seasonal, mostly kids. I would have personally handled a shipment to Mr. Tucker."

"What does it require to rent a set of skis and boots and poles?" JC asked.

"Leave an imprint of your credit card and go have fun," the employee said.

The building where customers rented ski equipment was cold, dark and dirty. It could have been the oldest building on the ski resort's property. It was one large room, divided in two by a pair of long counters.

"So, you'd have a credit card imprint if someone rented skis and boots and did not return them," JC pursued. "Do you have a credit card imprint for something like that?"

"Let me look," the rental manager answered. "You said it would be in the last month or so?"

"I think so," JC told him.

The manager walked to the other counter, where customers returned their rental equipment at the end of the day. He opened a beaten wooden box. It looked like it also predated the days of Big Horizon. It may have gone back to the days of Cob Hill.

"I did find one," the manager said "That doesn't happen very often. If they don't return their rental equipment, we charge them as though the stuff was new. It's not cheap."

"So, the credit card imprint. There's a name?" JC asked.

"Yessir," the manager replied with a smile. "It says, let's see. It says Vladimir Putin. We get a lot of Slavs and Eastern Europeans here."

"Vladimir Putin rented skis and boots and poles here?" JC asked.

"That's the name on the credit card," the manager confirmed.

"You think the authoritarian leader of Russia comes here to ski and rents equipment?" JC asked.

"If this is his credit card, he does," the manager answered before the name rang a bell with him.

They looked at each other.

"Maybe it's a fake credit card, huh?" the man said.

"That's just a guess on my part," JC responded. "Does that mean he didn't return his skis, boots and poles?"

"I can check," the rental manager said, still embarrassed by his oversight. "Everything has a number on it. Except the poles. They're just poles. No one steals our poles."

The manager tucked the credit card slip into a pocket on his apron and walked to the back of the room behind the counters. Rental skis and snowboards hung from racks in long rows.

"Huh," the manager said. "Here are the skis. He returned them. Let me check on the boots."

He walked to another side of the room, where at least two hundred gray rear-entry boots of all sizes were lined up.

He pulled the rental slip back out of his pocket and looked it over. He walked to a collection of boots and checked the numbers. Then, he walked to the box containing that day's rental slips.

"No, those boots are definitely missing," the manager said.

"I found those skis, if that's what you're talking about," said a young woman who was hurrying to the other counter to match a customer with ski equipment. She was probably high school-age. Her dark hair was pulled back to keep it out of her face.

"You did?" the manager said.

"I found them leaning against a ski rack at the end of the day," the young woman said. "The poles were there too. They weren't locked and the night skiing had ended. So, I brought them back here and put them back into circulation. I figured that whoever had left them would come in and settle things."

"But the boots are still gone?" JC asked the manager.

"Well, they're not here," the man answered.

"Do you remember what Mr. Putin looked like?" JC asked.

"Have you seen this place when everyone is trying to get their rental equipment?" the manager asked. "The line is out the door, everyone is wearing helmets and scarves and jackets. They are hot and impatient, especially impatient. We just try to size them up for their equipment and get them out the door."

"Anyone rent skis with a Russian accent?" Milt asked.

"I told you," the manager responded. "We have a lot of Russians, Eastern Europeans, Slavs. They come up from Chicago. Listen, I've got to get back to work. Are we through?"

"Yep," JC said. "But tell me this. What number was the pair of ski boots. You said they all had numbers."

"Yeah," the man said, and looked at the slip of paper. "One forty-seven."

"So," Milt said as they emerged outside the rental shop. "We're ruling out Putin as the murderer?"

36

"It's his superpower," Robin whispered to Milt. "He sees stuff."

JC was out of earshot. He was sitting at a table in the café at the Grand Geneva, alone with DCI Agent Aurek Nelson. They both had a cup of coffee in front of them.

The reporter had telephoned the agent, who said he was driving near the Grand Geneva and would stop by. When he arrived, he asked Robin and Milt to allow him to have a private word with JC.

Nelson was willing to listen to the reporter, but he didn't want an audience. He didn't forget that he was dealing with members of the news media. He didn't trust most members of the news media. And he didn't feel like being outnumbered at the table.

"Tillison Tucker thought that Ronny Schwartz had stabbed him in the back," JC explained. "They were close. Tucker was even a kind of father figure to Schwartz. Betrayal could have provoked an extreme emotional response from Tucker. Remember, millions of dollars were on the line."

"And the motive?" Nelson asked.

"Maybe it was just rage," JC said. "Tucker thought he had seen proof of Ronny's traitorous behavior with his own eyes. He saw two permits that Tipper Jones had obtained from the city of Chicago, paving the way to build an indoor ski area in the city and beating Tucker and Snow Hat, who were trying to do the same thing."

"If Ronny Schwartz's signature was on the permits," the agent said. "Then Tucker was right. Schwartz was a double agent, taking steps to betray him."

"And I think he was," JC agreed. "But he had a change of heart. He called his mother in Evanston. He told her that he decided not to take a job offer. He said he would remain loyal to Tucker. I think Tipper Jones offered him that partnership. It's the only way Ronny Schwartz's signature would have shown up on those permits."

"But Schwartz changed his mind and turned down Jones after those permits were issued," Agent Nelson said. "And Tucker never knew that Schwartz had decided to stay with Snow Hat, in the end."

"Yep," JC said. "I think I can explain the ski boots too. You found a dozen old rental ski boots in Tipper Jones's garage. But when Tucker purchased Big Horizon, he purchased Fox River Runs' entire inventory.

"He bought the coffee cups and tee shirts in the souvenir store. He bought beef patties that were still in the freezer in the cafeteria. And he had access to about two hundred ski boots in the rental shop. I actually think I can identify the pair that were found on Schwartz's body."

"Oh yeah?" the agent asked, still skeptical. "How would you do that?"

"I think there will be a number one forty-seven on them," JC answered.

"How the hell did you know that?" Agent Nelson asked.

JC informed the DCI man of his understanding of how ski rentals work, and their visit to the rental shop at Big Horizon.

"Did the guy at the rental shop say Tucker came in and asked for a pair of rental boots?" Nelson inquired.

"No," JC said. "I know you'll talk to the rental shop manager yourself. But he told me that he had no idea what the guy looked like. I'm beginning to wonder if this wasn't a professional killing. When is the last time you got this far along in an investigation, and no one said that they saw something?"

Agent Nelson rubbed his chin. He didn't answer the question. But he'd been thinking the same thing, they were dealing with a hit man who was very good at his craft. One hit man who committed two murders, maybe three.

"Anything else?" the agent asked.

"Tucker cancelled Ronny Schwartz's hotel room reservation when the car was found. The body hadn't been found yet," JC told him. "Did Tucker already know that the body would soon be found?"

Snow was coming down in bunches at the Snow Hat Ski Resort in Colorado.

It was quiet when it snowed that hard. The snow fell silently, and most people stayed inside until it let up. The scent of smoke filled the valley. Fireplaces were burning. The chairlifts wouldn't open for a couple of hours.

Drivers had been warned to stay off the roads until plows had a chance to come by. Interstate 70, west of the Eisenhower Tunnel, had only just reopened after being buried under the snowfall.

Tillison Tucker was already in his office, despite it being a Saturday. His hands were shoved into his pockets. He stared out the window.

Tina Hernandez made sure that she was in the office whenever her boss was, even on a Saturday. She made him some coffee, but he didn't drink it. The cup sat on his desk. His stomach was troubling him.

There was a knock at his door.

JC Snow stood on the porch of the hotel room he shared with Robin in Wisconsin. His hands were shoved in his pockets to keep them warm.

He listened to the ice pop on the lake shaped like a bunny.

His phone rang. He put it to his ear and heard the voice of Agent Aurek Nelson.

"My counterparts with the Colorado Bureau of Investigation just picked up Tillison Tucker. He'll be flown to Wisconsin and charged with murder."

"Congratulations," JC said. It would be a significant addition to the agent's portfolio.

I don't think he killed Ronny Schwartz with his own hands," the agent said, ignoring the compliment. "I think he hired a hit. We'll look for the contract killer, but so far, he's been hard to track."

"Do you think Tucker tried to frame Tipper Jones?" JC asked.

"Maybe. There was a lot of circumstantial evidence pointing at Mr. Jones," Nelson said. "The counterfeiting thing was real. He'll have to face charges on that. The venom he has for Snow Hat and the ski boots, none of that made him look innocent."

"And Linda Smith?" JC asked.

"Counterfeiting, that's all," the agent said. "They weren't even having an affair."

"Tucker killed Ronny Schwartz when Schwartz actually had already chosen not to betray his boss," JC said. "He stayed loyal."

"You know, I told Tucker that," the agent disclosed. "He didn't say anything, but he looked sick. Really sick."

JC joined Robin and Milt after the call ended. Robin had gone to Milt's room to do some editing. She found him reading *To Kill a Mockingbird*.

"We have a new story to tell," JC informed them. "Tucker just got arrested for the murder of Ronny Schwartz."

They went about planning the story they would broadcast live to Denver that evening. Even though it was a Saturday, they'd be working.

Next, JC made a phone call to his news director, Pat Perilla. That required making a call to Perilla's home. As was normal, Perilla's wife didn't want to let JC disturb her husband on his day off. She was a good sentinel for their home front.

"He'll want to hear this," JC said. "Sorry."

JC informed his boss of Tucker's arrest for the murder of Ronny Schwartz, the story they had been sent to Wisconsin to cover.

"I never thought this was the way it would end," Perilla said. "Well, good job. Thanks for working on a Saturday to deliver the news tonight to viewers here. Then, you can come home. I'll get you on a flight for Monday."

"I don't think it's time to come home," JC told his superior. "Give us a couple of days to see where the investigation into Quip Kelly's murder is going."

"JC," the news director said. "You drink more than your share from our company money fountain. You do a great job whenever we send you across the country to cover a story. But generally, when you come home, our travel budget for the year is bankrupt. It's time to come home."

"I hear you're having a big snowstorm," JC said. "We are too. We might not be able to fly out until Tuesday."

There was an audible sigh on the other end of the phone line, then silence.

"JC, my wife is giving me a look that you don't ever want to be on the receiving end of. I promised her that we would not be disturbed today. Alright, Tuesday. But we're booking flights for the three of you on Tuesday. And if you cancel those, you will walk home."

"Thanks, Pat," JC answered. "You are a journalist's journalist."

"I told you," Robin said to Milt when JC put the phone back in his pocket. "It's his superpower. He can see things that other people just can't see."

"Don't go all tinfoil on me," Milt told her.

"You've seen it too," Robin insisted. Milt looked at her.

"Hey, JC," Milt said. "When you heard that Tipper Jones was going to be charged with murder, did it pass the smell test?"

"Nope," JC said, smiling.

"That's just old-school," Milt said.

37

"You must be very proud of yourself." The speaker didn't make it sound like a compliment.

State Representative Vic Brown berated JC in the lobby of the Grand Geneva. The politician was there having lunch with Gretta Miller, soon to be the ex-wife of the disgraced *Senator* Stansfield Miller.

JC recognized Vic Brown's name. He had read a few pages of material Quip had accumulated regarding the politician, something about bribes. JC had the impression that Brown would have been Quip's next target.

"I suppose you're eager to take Quip Kelly's place, now?" Representative Brown sneered. "I know you're the one who finished Kelly's story about Senator Swensen. Do you feel like a big man, after ruining someone's marriage and breaking his wife's heart? Do you know how many days in a row she cried? That's on you, mister."

Robin and Milt stood aside as they watched Brown shake his finger at JC. The state lawmaker chose to wear his ring on his index finger, the one with the red stone.

"You must be mistaking me for someone who forced Senator Swensen to take off when he killed that pedestrian with his car," JC responded. "Or maybe you think I forced him to cheat on his wife."

"I just hope you're proud of yourself," Brown said tersely and turned to leave.

"I am," JC told him. "And good luck with your search."

"What do I have to search for?" the state legislator turned and asked.

"Your moral compass," JC told him.

He has no idea how lucky he is, JC thought, as he watched the politician storm off.

JC joined Robin and Milt and they went for lunch at the Igloo Lounge.

"Where did old-fashioned shame disappear to?" JC asked. "Remember the old days when a politician would say, 'I've been caught. I am ashamed and I am resigning because I am not worthy of this responsibility you have bestowed on me?'"

"They took voters seriously then," Robin added. "Many of them don't anymore."

"The last time I heard a politician admit his guilt," Milt said, "was the same day I saw a fish climbing a waterfall with a dog in its mouth."

"You have a phone call from Chicago, Agent Nelson."

"DCI Agent Aurek Nelson," he said into the phone when the call was transferred.

The law officer listened and jotted down some notes.

"I think we can be there in two hours," the agent said.

"Okay, see you then. Thank you, Doctor."

Wisconsin DCI Agent Nelson and Deputy Krueger took Route 12 south and then hopped onto I-94 to Chicago and the Ohio Street exit. It was sixty-five miles.

They crossed a bridge over the Chicago River, turned down Michigan Avenue, the Magnificent Mile, and then turned toward Lake Michigan.

Northwestern Memorial Hospital was a short walk from Lake Shore Drive. He found parking in a garage across the street and was accompanied by the deputy into the building.

"I remember coming to Chicago and going to Lincoln Park Zoo when I was a kid," Agent Nelson told the deputy. "I loved going to zoos, and my parents had taken me to the Milwaukee Zoo about a hundred times. They thought I was going to become a zoologist or something."

They waited for an elevator.

"Anyway," the agent went on. "I fell off a pile of rocks or something and they brought me to this hospital. It was different then. I think it was called Wesley, then."

They arrived at a nurses' station and asked for Dr. Peter Lattanzio.

"Agent Nelson?" asked a mustached man in scrubs who emerged from an office.

"Thanks for calling, Doctor," the agent said and introduced the deputy.

"I'm sorry you can't talk to him," Dr. Lattanzio said. "But he wasn't with us very long. He should have sought medical attention days ago."

"Then he died when?" Nelson asked.

"About four hours ago?" the doctor said while looking at his wrist watch. "We were informed that you were looking for a man with a burned hand."

"What is that smell?" the DCI man asked, grimacing.

"Our first clue," the doctor said with a smile. "The gentleman happens to be on the other side of the curtain next to you. Let me show you."

They pulled open the curtain just enough for the three of them to enter and then pulled the curtain closed behind them.

"The stench is an obvious sign of serious infection," Dr. Lattanzio told them. "It is probably what finally caused him to seek medical attention. Like I said, he should have come in earlier."

The doctor pulled back a sheet that covered the deceased. The dead man's hand and arm were exposed. The skin was purple in color. There were open sores.

"It was covered in purulent drainage when he came in," the doctor told them. "A thick, milky brown liquid."

Deputy Krueger cringed. The smell and the sight of the putrefied wound nearly gagged him.

"And this all started with a burn?" the state agent asked.

"To the hand, yes," the doctor replied. "I doubt he ever had it treated. He had rather classic symptoms. He had a fever. And then blood poisoning killed him. Sepsis."

Agent Nelson stared at the man lying on the bed. The law officer pulled out his phone and snapped a few pictures of the corpse. Then he walked out past the curtain, the doctor and the deputy following him.

"Do you have his belongings?" the agent asked.

"Yes," the doctor said. He asked a nurse for the bag where they had placed everything.

Nelson looked around him for a table to pour the bag's contents onto. But the ward was busy and there weren't any empty spaces. He turned and walked back into the curtained room where they had just been.

The agent overturned the bag and poured out its contents on the legs of the dead man, still covered by the sheet.

The doctor raised his eyebrows at the agent's decision but said nothing.

Agent Nelson made fast work of his search. He checked in the pants and jacket pockets. He came up with a burner phone. Nelson shoved the phone in his pocket, put everything back into the bag and handed the bag to the deputy.

"We'll be in touch about the body," Nelson said, preparing to leave. "We're going to talk to the coroner here in Chicago about working with us. We'll want fingerprints, DNA, the whole works. Thanks, Doc."

They shook hands and Agent Nelson was gone, Deputy Krueger in pursuit.

"We never would have caught him," the agent told the deputy as they drove north, "if he hadn't burned his hand. We never would have seen him again."

"He fits the description you got from the bartender at the Bar in Wilmot, doesn't he?" noted the deputy.

"He sure does," Nelson answered. "I think we've got our man."

"What now?" Deputy Krueger asked.

"We've got to get into this burner phone," Nelson replied. "Dead men tell no tales. But their phones do."

38

"Fingerprints, DNA, photo identification. We even have him on a few security cameras on his drive through Door County," Agent Nelson said.

"Too bad he's dead," the sheriff told him. "We could have nailed him to the wall."

"Yeah," the agent agreed. "I won't miss him, though. I suspect we'll be following his tracks for a while. He lived in a nice condo in Chicago. He was making a good living."

"So, who is he?" the sheriff asked.

"Feliks Papierski," the agent responded. He was reading the dead contract killer's name off a fresh profile of their hitman. "Polish, like me."

The agent got on his phone, hoping to hear there was progress cracking the security code on Papierski's burner phone. It wasn't easy when a burner phone was used for clandestine purposes.

But IT nerds with the Wisconsin Department of Justice liked a good challenge. And while not finished, they provided some good news. They could supply the investigator with two telephone numbers Papierski called on multiple occasions.

Armed with the phone numbers, one with a Madison area code and one with an area code in Colorado, Nelson did some cross-checking on his own computer. He came up with two names.

"The office of Tillison Tucker at Snow Hat Ski Enterprises, and the office of Wisconsin state Senator Raff Swensen," Nelson informed the head of DCI.

"Well, let's visit Mr. Tucker first," Nelson was ordered. "He's arrived in Wisconsin, and we are eager to give him reason to stay, perhaps for life."

Tillison Tucker was being held in custody after his extradition from Colorado. When confronted with the contract killer's phone number, he offered no denial.

Tucker had quit, Nelson thought. He was going to carry the guilt for the rest of his life, for killing a man who remained loyal to him.

Things were not going to move as swiftly with Senator Raff Swensen. The politician's attorney accused the DCI of going on a fishing expedition and resisted even making the senator available for questioning.

"The senator informs me that the phone number you have is an office number at the state capitol," the lawyer said. "Multiple people answer that phone, for a multiple number of reasons. Whoever answered that call may not even have worked in the senator's office."

"What else have we got linking Swensen to Quip's murder?" the DCI agent asked the sheriff. "We need more than a phone number."

"We don't have much," the sheriff admitted. "The bartender from Wilmot looked at the photo and thinks Papierski is the guy with the burned hand who stopped in the bar. But that convicts Papierski, not the senator."

Agent Nelson's phone rang. Putting it to his ear, he gestured that it was something the sheriff would be interested in.

"Guess who crossed paths?" Nelson said to the sheriff when he got off the phone. "That was one of my DCI guys. He does good work, and he's been checking out Papierski's comings and goings. It turns out that he ate at a restaurant in Madison called 'The Statehouse' on the same date and the same time as Quip Kelly and his wife."

"So, they may have even encountered each other," the sheriff said.

"The agent wanted to see how far he could take this," Nelson reported. "The restaurant tracked a code on the checks that Kelly and Papierski paid that night. Their tables were right next to each other."

"Could they have known each other?" the sheriff wondered aloud.

"They weren't sitting at the same table," the agent said. "If they were acquainted, they might have shared a table. But their tables were *next* to each other. And then, they both spent the night at the Edgewater Hotel, which is right there."

"Did they all share a room?" the sheriff asked. "Or have adjoining rooms?"

"No," Nelson told him. "In fact, their rooms were almost as far from each other as they could be. Opposite ends of the building and different floors. Papierski checked into his room using an alias."

"Where is she?"

"Where is who?" JC asked.

"You know who," Agent Nelson said tersely. "Shara Kelly, your ex-girlfriend."

"Aren't we grumpy," JC responded. "Why do you need Shara?"

"None of your business," the agent said back.

"Shara and I have a lot of history," JC said with a smug tone. "I still look out for her, as any friend would."

"Cut the crap, Snow!" the agent barked.

Nelson wanted to discuss that dinner and the night Shara spent at the Edgewater Hotel with Quip. He wanted to know if the name Feliks Papierski rang a bell. He wanted to know if she and her husband shared a conversation with a man sitting at the next table.

"I am sitting in my hotel room with my girlfriend," JC told the agent. "We've spent an awful lot of time together and we've run out of items to talk about. Maybe you could freshen things up. Is there anything you can tell me?"

Robin, sitting at a chair near the sliding glass window, was both amused and alarmed by the conversation she was hearing. Milt was also there. He was just amused.

The DCI man felt his blood pressure elevate. He did not like being played. But he wanted to speak to Shara Kelly.

And JC Snow, in all his arrogance, seemed to be her gatekeeper at the moment.

"Fine," the agent spit. "But then you tell me where she is, or so help me I will arrest you for obstruction of justice!"

"Feliks Papierski?" JC repeated into the phone. "Tucker *and* the senator?"

Then, living up to his end of the bargain, and satisfied with the product of his leverage, JC gave the agent a phone number where Shara could be reached, as she herself had advised him to do.

JC listened to Agent Nelson terminate the call and turned to tell his colleagues what he had learned.

"The hitman was having a two-for-one sale," JC told them.

"Bargains, bargains, bargains," Milt exclaimed.

"Is it possible that Papierski was already here to kill Ronny Schwartz when he came across Quip and the story he was writing about the senator?" JC asked them. "DCI is *convinced* that the same hitman killed Ronny Schwartz, Quip Kelly and Sheepy Johnson."

"And Sheepy could have been mistaken for me?" Robin asked.

"No," JC said sympathetically. "He was definitely after Shara. She was at dinner with Quip when Papierski saw them. He knew that Quip shared his secrets with his wife. Heck, if he was sitting at the next table, he may have eavesdropped on their conversation."

"And they only caught this guy because he was dead?" Milt asked.

"Probably. He didn't leave any other evidence behind," JC responded. "Tucker has admitted that he hired the contract killer. Senator Swensen is denying it and fighting this all the way. All the DCI has on Swensen, so far, is the phone. And that doesn't prove what was discussed during the call."

"But how else can he explain being on the burner phone of a contract killer?" Robin asked.

"Exactly," JC said. "Swensen hired this guy to prevent the story about him getting out. He thought Quip's death accomplished that. Papierski took all the original paperwork and photos from the house before starting the fire. And it was probably him looking for duplicates in Madison, rifling through Quip and Shara's condo. When he didn't' find any, he had reason to believe that he wiped the board clean."

"What about the money?" Milt asked. "Swensen must have paid him. That would prove something."

"It would," JC agreed. "So far, DCI can't find the money. It may have been cryptocurrency. That can be difficult to track."

JC's live shot that evening reported the discovery by law officers that a contract killer from Chicago named Feliks Papierski was the man hired by Tillison Tucker to kill Ronny Schwartz, a Colorado resident and employee of Snow Hat Ski Enterprises. Papierski was also considered to be the killer of Quip Kelly and Sheepy Johnson.

JC did not mention Senator Raff Swensen among those arrested, because he wasn't. Swensen wasn't even mentioned in the press briefing by the sheriff and DCI. Both were certain that Swensen put the hit out on Quip Kelly, but they didn't have the evidence.

Even Tillison Tucker said he didn't know the true identity of the man he hired to kill Ronny Schwartz. He admitted in a sworn statement that he paid a man in cryptocurrency through a blind box.

"You're amazing, JC," his news director told him over the phone, following the broadcast. "Just when I doubt my sanity for sending you out there, you solve all the world's problems and make me look like a genius."

"Thanks, Pat," JC said. "Milt and Robin deserve a lot of the credit. This was a team win."

"Of course, it was," the news director gushed. "You are scheduled to fly out of Chicago on Tuesday. Take a day off and go skiing or something. Nice job, JC."

"It's Sunday, the sun has set and it's wine o'clock," Robin declared when they packed up Milt's camera and gear after the live shot. "I think we deserve to celebrate."

39

The wind clawed at his ski goggles. JC had underestimated the racecourse. It plunged and quickly rolled into a blind turn, challenging the racer to stay on his skis.

It was JC's first race since his high-speed collision with several trees. But he was enthused to pull on a racing bib again.

Wilmot Mountain called itself the "Matterhorn of the Midwest." Rope tows, then T-bars and now seven chairlifts had been bringing Midwest skiers to the top of the hill since the Depression.

The small mountain was a big bump in an otherwise flat landscape. The racecourse snaked to the left and then back to the right, following a cranker of a hairpin. It lengthened the giant slalom course on a small mountain.

JC thought it was a fun layout and there were some quality racers. Many of his competitors exhibited that gracious nature of the people of the Great Prairie.

"I hope you win," said a racer lined up behind JC. The man wore a form-fitting racing suit with "Chill Ski Club" written down the leg.

"Does it make me a bad person if I hope you finish second?" JC responded with a smile.

"Behind you?" the skier racer answered and laughed. "No, it just makes you an honest person. I hope you finish second too."

The age of the racers stretched from their twenties to their eighties.

"They call this a 'Masters Race,' huh?" a racer from Ladysmith remarked. "If I had mastered this thing, I would have given it up years ago!"

JC had never competed against this particular group of Midwestern racers. But they cordially extended their congratulations after the newcomer won the first of two runs. The second and last run would happen as soon as they could get back to the top of the mountain.

He rode up the chairlift with the racer from Ladysmith.

"You know what our claim to fame is in Ladysmith?" the man asked. "About a hundred years ago, two loggers were splitting trees when they claimed to find a petrified man inside one of them. They had their moment in the sun and then they were exposed for faking the whole thing. But for that short time, Ladysmith made headlines across the world."

Back at the peak of the Matterhorn of the Midwest, JC took time to scan his surroundings. He had come to admire the Midwest ski scene. The skiers and snowboarders were passionate, and the resorts were accommodating.

He listened to a group of older racers talk with each other. They spoke in an Eastern European language. They probably grew up skiing in the Carpathians or Caucasus Mountains. Whatever brought them to the Midwest, they found their way to Wilmot, Alpine Valley, Mountain Top and Big Horizon.

The smallest ski hills lacked the amenities to compete with more famous slopes on bigger mountains. But they lacked nothing in the fervor for their sport.

"Racer ready!" the starter at the top of the racecourse shouted.

JC felt more confident at the start of his second run. He thought the cranker, reversing the direction of the course, was a key to being the fastest. When he reached that combination, he set an edge and enjoyed the power generated by the bend in his ski.

He nailed a left-footed turn, steering him toward the finish line, and crouched into a tuck until he tripped the electronic timer at the bottom. He looked up, trying to hold his head steady while his heart throbbed and his breathing was more of a pant.

His eyes found Robin, cheering him in a silly fashion. Maybe that was why his heart was throbbing. He skied to her and received a victory kiss.

"Are you going to take any runs today?" he asked, still panting a little.

"I'm ready!" she said. "Let me get my skis, I'll ride up the lift with you."

JC rode up the chairlift with Robin after receiving congratulations from his fellow racers. He'd won by a narrow margin over a man with an Austrian accent.

"Aren't you freezing?" Robin asked. JC was still only covered by his tight micro-polyester racing suit. He'd discarded his warmer jacket and pants before he left the starting gate.

"I'm still pretty heated up," he said. "But it won't last long."

JC pulled his warm jacket and pants back on at the top of the racecourse and they skied away. He led Robin to a spot near three trees, where they could be alone.

The low winter sun sparkled when it hit snowflakes lying on the ground.

"They look like diamonds," Robin said.

"Yes, ma'am," JC told her as he picked up one diamond in particular.

Robin turned to examine his discovery. She found that he had clicked out of his skis and was kneeling in front of her. He brushed the snow off the diamond he held in his hand.

She covered her mouth as she gasped.

"Marry me, Robin," he said, holding out the diamond ring.

"Where did that come from?" she asked, tears clouding her vision as she pulled up her goggles.

"I was carrying it in my glove during the race," he said. "You brought me luck. You always bring me luck."

She dropped to her knees so she could look at him.

"Of course, I will," she said. "What made you think that you even had to ask?"

40

"If it's a boy, will you name him Milt?" he asked. "After me?"

"We're getting married, Milt," JC told him. "We're not having a baby."

"Oh," Milt responded. "I just assumed you were getting married because..."

"Milt," Robin said sharply. "Just because you think it doesn't mean you have to say it."

"Oh, right," Milt said apologetically.

New logs placed in the fireplace popped as they burned. They were real logs, a real fire, not a gas-fueled substitute. The room was filled with the aroma of burning wood. It was a warm smell, an old smell.

"Do you know," Scotty said. "Logs don't actually burn? A fire investigator told me a long time ago, it's actually the vapor that burns as the logs decompose. Something like that."

Robin rested her head on JC's shoulder. It was late and she was tired. They all sat in the living room attached to the Igloo Lounge.

"It's about time for me to go upstairs," Robin said. "I want to slip into a fresh pair of skivvies and go to bed." She smiled at Scotty.

"I'm glad that I could teach you something," Scotty said, returning the smile. "And I hope you two will be as happy as my wife and I were."

"Would you come to Colorado and see us?" Robin asked. "In addition to coming to the wedding, I mean."

"I'd love to," Landover Scott responded. "I enjoy watching you two do your sleuthing."

"What time to we have to leave here tomorrow?" JC asked, sipping the last of his Glenfarclas.

"Should we leave around noon?" Robin asked. "That gives us two hours to Chicago and another couple of hours to return our rental car, check our baggage and stand in line at security."

"Good," JC said. "I want to run into Lake Geneva in the morning."

The scream startled them as they sat at their breakfast table.

Branch was their server. She had just noticed Robin's engagement ring.

"We're going to celebrate with a Kringle," the ever-perky waitress told them. "It's Wisconsin's official pastry! There's icing all over the top. And it will be on the house!"

"You had me at icing," Robin laughed, and Branch brought two circular Kringles to their table, one raspberry and one pecan.

After finishing off the sweet desert, JC and Robin left Milt behind to say his goodbyes to Branch.

"Lucky woman," JC told Robin. "Milt lives in Colorado and Branch lives in Wisconsin."

"Did you give Branch a few sawbucks for a tip?" Robin asked with a smile. "I'm trying to use up the new words Scotty taught me before we leave, in case they don't work in Colorado."

Robin wanted to stay at the resort and finish packing, so JC climbed into the rental car alone and headed for Lake Geneva.

Pulling into a parking place on Wrigley Drive, he was careful to park between the lines.

The sun was shining but the air was cold as he walked toward the lake house. JC saw ice fishers standing outside their shanties.

"Mr. Snow!"

JC looked across the street where there was a line of bars and restaurants, including Sheepy Johnson's restaurant.

Tipper Jones was walking out the door of Rainbows.

"Just finished breakfast," he said with a smile. He jerked a thumb behind him, at Rainbows. "It's a shame what happened to that girl. I remember her growing up, bringing her snowboard to our ski area."

JC looked at the restaurant, but in his mind, he saw Sheepy. In the end, she was collateral damage to a corrupted politician.

"I'm grateful to you," Tipper told JC. "That's why I came out to talk to you. I don't think the police believed me. Maybe I was too honest, admitting how much I hated Snow Hat and Ronny Schwartz. But I'm not the kind of man to take a human life. That's not how I solve my problems. Anyway, you led them to the real killer. I owe you one."

"Do you still face charges for counterfeiting those lift tickets?" JC asked him. He knew the charges would never rise to more than a misdemeanor.

"Yeah. How stupid can I be?" Jones responded. "My lawyer is trying to whittle down the size of the fine."

"Are you going ahead with plans to build that indoor ski area in Chicago?" JC asked.

"You bet I am," Tipper said enthusiastically. "I think I'll call it 'The Blizzard.'"

"That's a great name," JC smiled.

"It's a shame though," Tipper told him. "There won't be any old trees with car wheels fastened overhead. You know, where the old rope tows used to go. It will be another small mountain, but it won't have the same sense of history."

"You could always put up a few trees along the wall," JC said. "And put some car wheels up there."

"That is a fine idea," Tipper said. "That is a fine idea of yours. I just may do that." Tipper began to walk back to the restaurant but stopped.

"You know, if I built this indoor contraption in Wisconsin, that would be the state's thirty-second ski area," he said, smiling. "That would put it one ahead of Colorado."

The wind did a good job of keeping the ice clear on Lake Geneva. A few ice-sailing boats were out on the frozen surface. JC looked at the boats with curiosity.

There were people with cardboard signs collecting near him. They were chatting and drinking hot coffee to try and stay warm.

The signs said, "Welcome, Senator Swensen." The politician had planned a stop in Lake Geneva for a small political pep rally.

He was touring the entire state, to rehabilitate his image. His picture would get in the paper, and if he could escape quickly enough, he might avoid embarrassing questions from the news media.

"I just want to see him in person," JC had told Robin. "For all the trouble he's caused, I've never laid eyes on him."

"Are you going to say anything to him?" she asked.

"He's not worth the trouble. The DCI and the sheriff will keep digging," JC told her. "They might get him yet."

JC looked down the street, trying to see a car coming down the road that might befit a state senator. Politicians usually preferred comfortable Ford Expeditions or GMC Yukons. Those cars were American-built and had plenty of room for their passengers.

Instead, he saw a redhead, her hair blowing in the breeze. She wore sunglasses and had her hands shoved into the big pockets of her sheepskin jacket.

"Hi, Shara," he said. "What brings you back to town?"

"Hi, JC," she said, giving him a kiss on the cheek. "I have some paperwork to sign.

"And you just happened across this?" JC asked her.

"Did he do it?" she asked meekly. JC looked at the ground, thinking about if there was a better answer than the truth. There wasn't.

"Yep," he said softly, reluctantly. "There's no question. There's just not very good evidence."

She let out a breath. Frustration, he supposed.

A GMC Yukon drove down the street toward them and stopped in front of the small crowd. The group holding cardboard signs lifted them above their head and shouted their approval. A local newspaper photographer began taking pictures.

All according to plan.

"Raff Swensen," was the folksy way he introduced himself to the cardboard-sign carriers. He shook each of their hands, making certain that he was facing the camera. Two police officers fulfilled routine duty by standing near the senator. They glanced at the crowd without expectation of trouble.

Senator Swensen looked like a thousand other politicians to JC. He was dressed to look nice, but below his actual pay scale. Stylish, but not offensive to any demographic.

He wore a plain long black coat. It was indistinguishable from a thousand other black coats. But you could bet that it was expensive.

The cost didn't matter. It had been paid for by campaign contributions.

JC noticed a ring on Swensen's finger, with a red stone. It flashed in the cold winter sun.

Someone else emerged from the GMC Yukon. It was Mrs. Swensen.

She wore a wide smile that showed whitened teeth. She slid up to the senator's side and began shaking the same hands he had shaken. The handful of followers seemed genuinely enthused. They were making contact with someone they saw on television.

Sadly, for the senator, the last thing voters saw on television news was a story that was neither confirmed nor denied by law enforcement. The report said that Swensen was under investigation for a fatal hit-and-run.

"I just want you to know," the senator said, deciding to give a little address.

"I just want you to know that I am aware that I stumbled," he said as he projected his voice. "Yes, the press lied about most of it. But I made mistakes too. And I am going to be a better man, and a better senator, from this moment on!"

The people holding carboard cheered.

"When did you get back from California?" JC asked Shara as they watched the little spectacle.

"Yesterday," she said. Her eyes were fixed on Swensen.

"How can people still support him?" Shara asked JC. "Quip caught him killing someone and cheating on his wife. And he killed my husband. How can they still come out and support him?"

"They don't know he killed your husband," JC told her. "He hasn't been arrested yet."

Shara stared in disbelief at the scene that was unfolding in front of her.

"They're close, Shara," JC said. "They'll get him. They just can't get him yet."

"What am I going to do, JC?" Shara asked, sounding like the air was being let out of her balloon.

"I was thinking about that," JC told her. "If you want to stay in Madison, you could open a bar and restaurant. You're good at that. Call it 'Quips.' He's a local legend. People would come in droves. Your restaurant would be a landmark from the moment it opened. And a place to remember all of his good work."

"I watched this happen to you too, JC," Shara said, ignoring his optimistic view of the future. "I learned that sometimes the bad guys get away with it. That ate at you when it happened, and it ate at Quip, too. And it makes me sick that the bad guy who killed Quip is going to get away with it."

"No, Shara," JC said to comfort her, not knowing if it was true. "He won't."

Turning his eyes back toward the political rally, JC noticed that the senator looked directly at Shara Kelly. Swensen had a look on his face as though he was trying to place her.

The senator's wife didn't look at Shara at all. She just smiled for the camera, looking out like she was seeing a far bigger crowd than there was. The camera would shoot pictures of her and her husband, not the little crowd.

JC looked back at Shara, who was pulling an envelope out from beneath her jacket.

Senator Swensen finished his little speech and the people holding the cardboard signs shoved them under their arms so that they could applaud.

When JC looked again at Shara, she wasn't there. She was no longer at his side.

He saw her approaching Mrs. Swensen, the senator's wife. Shara handed the woman the eight-by-ten envelope.

"This is why he killed my husband," Shara said to the woman, whose face melted when she heard Shara's words.

The senator approached his wife to see if there was something he needed to attend to. His eyes seized on Shara's face, making the connection.

The sound of a gunshot exploded over the murmur of the crowd.

A shocked look came over the face of Raff Swensen. His black heavy coat opened at the chest. Bright red blood could be seen spreading across his white dress shirt.

The senator's face went blank as he fell to the ground. He coughed and blood escaped from his mouth.

"Oh my God!" screamed the senator's wife and a couple of the cardboard carriers.

The senator's wife dropped on her knees, next to her husband. The envelope that Shara had given her lay on the sidewalk. Some of the contents had spilled out.

The wind licked at a photograph of the senator groping the naked breasts of the girls he posed with on the boat.

Another photo showed the senator below deck. One of the girls was giving him everything she had to offer.

JC looked at Shara. She held Quip's 1911 A1 Colt .45 World War Two service revolver.

She stared at the senator as his life escaped through the bloody wound. The two police officers grabbed Shara with one arm and grabbed her hands with the other, lowering the gun's aim to the ground so no one else would be hurt. Shara had only pulled the trigger once.

If Shara were a man, the law officers would have thrown her to the ground. But their Midwestern mothers had taught them never to hit a woman.

They held her securely in their grasp and removed the gun from her hand. She didn't resist.

Shara looked over her shoulder at JC, with a look of shock at what she had done and at the terminal outcome of her actions.

Then, she gave him a small smile.

Acknowledgements

The people of the Midwest are as nice as they come. There's even a term for it, "Midwestern Nice."

Thank you to Dawn Kendzior, Katie Nagel, Liz Gilding and John Ray at the Grand Geneva Resort. These talented multi-taskers told me wonderful stories about the past and present in the Lake Geneva Region. They could write a book of their own. Katie is the Mail Jumper. You can actually buy tickets to ride on the boat and watch her jump onto piers to make mail drops.

Pete Lattanzio was the very able Chief of the Town of Colonie, New York, Department of Fire Prevention and Investigation for a long time. He put facts behind the fire.

Jen Yonkers inspects chapters that I submit to her when I need to ask, "Did I cross the line here?"

Anne and Carl Copps are wonderful friends and were "First Readers" this time, though I'm not certain of the privilege in being handed a mess that was only the second draft.

Dean Micheli is our Digital Sorcerer. Sometimes, he laughs at us.

Deirdre Stoelzle is our wonderful nurturing editor, and Debbi Wraga is our talented formatter. They've been with us from the start.

And thank you to my wife, Carolyn. She is always my very First Reader. She also designs the covers, has immeasurable input in the books, and always has my back.

About the Author

Phil Bayly grew up skiing at Wilmot, Alpine Valley and other small mountains in Wisconsin and Michigan.

He got an education in Colorado while being as much of a ski bum as he could. He studied at the University of Denver and graduated from Colorado State University.

He became a journalist on television and radio for over forty years, working in Colorado, Wyoming, Pennsylvania and New York.

And he pursued becoming an accomplished ski racer. He found that while all things going up do come down, they come down at unequal velocity, especially at blind transition gates.

Phil now resides with his wife in Saratoga County, New York.

You can learn more about Phil and his books at murderonskis.com.

Made in the USA
Middletown, DE
20 October 2024